# arianna & finn (royals of valleria #3)

## MARIANNE KNIGHTLY

# *also by marianne knightly*

Sign up for Marianne's newsletter (www.marianneknightly.-com/newsletter) for exclusive news about sales and releases!

## Royals of Valleria Series

Meet the Royals of Valleria, a country as old as the fall of the Roman Empire. The reigning king and patriarch rules with his beloved queen. Nine children, now grown, ranging from the eldest twins to the youngest son, watch over the country they love and care for. Bound by honour, duty, and loyalty, follow their lives as they fall in love, face tragedies, and triumph against the evils facing them.

Book 1: Alexander & Rebecca

Book 2: Marcello & Grace

Book 3: Arianna & Finn

Book 4: Charlotte & Nate

Book 5: A Royal Holiday (Novella)

Book 6: Catharine & Edward

Book 7: Royally Ever After

Book 8: Lorenzo & Lily

Book 9: Sarah & Vittorio

Book 10: Permanently Princess (Novella)

Book 11: Ethan & Anda

Book 12: Crowned

Box Set: Books 1-3

Box Set: Books 4-6

Box Set: Books 7-9

## Royals of Valleria Short Stories

Story 1: **Delusional** (featuring Prince Alex & Rebecca)

Story 2: **Loved** (featuring Prince Alex & Rebecca)

Story 3: **Annoyed** (featuring Prince Alex & Rebecca)

Story 4: **Crush** (featuring Prince Alex & Rebecca)

Story 5: **Wish** (featuring Prince Alex & Rebecca)

Story 6: **Please** (featuring Prince Nate & Charlie)

Story 7: **Goddess** (featuring Prince Marcello & Grace)

Story 8: **Impatient** (featuring Princess Catharine & Edward)

Story 9: **Together** (featuring Princess Sarah & Prince Vittorio)

## Brazenbourg Royals Duet

Welcome to Brazenbourg, a small but mighty country nestled in the heart of Europe. Follow Prince Finn de Bara and his love, Arianna, former princess of Valleria, as they discover family secrets and battle for the future of Brazenbourg and their family.

Book 1: Bastard (*note: this book ends in a cliffhanger!*)

Book 2: Battle

Box Set (Full Duet, Books 1-2)

## Seaside Valleria Series

Welcome to Valleria, a country nestled along the Mediterranean. Whether it's the small towns or larger port cities, you're sure to find a friendly face— or more—along Valleria's seaside shores. Far from the politics of the palace, follow this group of friends as they find love, support each other, and perhaps even meet a royal or two at the local Masillian pub, the Seashell.

Book 1: Rush (Hector & Millie)

Book 2: Ripple (Persy & Sully)

Book 3: Raw (Frannie & Aiden)

Book 4: Ravage (Beth & Everett)

Book 5: Rise (Liz & Luke)

Box Set (Full Series, Books 1-5)

## The Italian Shipping Millionaires Series

Meet four sexy Italian men, brothers in all but blood and business partners. Follow their lives as they overcome past tragedies and pain, and open themselves up to love.

Book 1: Dante

Book 2: Adrian

Book 3: Giovanni

Book 4: Luc

Box Set: Books 1-4

*To everyone who has made a mistake in love.*

# about the book & content warnings

***A Princess engaged to a man she doesn't love.***
Proper Princess Arianna vowed to stay on the straight and
narrow after a disastrous decision years ago embarrassed both her
and her royal family. When a marriage of convenience is proposed
between her and Brazenbourg's ruling prince, she jumps at the
chance for redemption. She doesn't believe in love anymore – at least
she thought she didn't until she met her fiancé's
brother, Prince Finn.

***Drawn to another man she shouldn't want.***
As second in line to the throne of Brazenbourg, bad boy Prince
Finn cares little for his arrogant older brother Henry, but does care
deeply for Brazenbourg. When Henry becomes engaged to Arianna
for convenience and not love, he can't help but be intrigued by a
woman who would give up her future for her country. When the
passionate nature she hides breaks through her prim exterior, Finn
realizes he wants her and not just in bed. He knows his brother may
make a more proper match, but can he convince her, and himself, to
take a chance on each other despite the international fallout?

***For a love that won't be denied.***
When Henry's true motives are revealed and Arianna is placed in danger's path, can Finn act quickly enough to help her? Or will Arianna need to save herself?

This novel features a proposed marriage of convenience with the wrong man and a love that can't be denied with the right man, a royal family that loves one another (even while they annoy each other), and a look behind fictional palace walls.

*\*This is a standalone book in the series with no cliffhanger, and features sexy scenes and swearing.*

*CW: feelings of negative self-worth, betrayal by previous partner, threats of physical harm and SA (not between the main couple), physical injuries (not caused by the main couple)*

Meet the Royals of Valleria, a country as old as the fall of the Roman Empire. The reigning king and patriarch rules with his beloved queen. Nine children, now grown, ranging from the eldest twins to the youngest son, watch over the country they love and care for. Bound by honor, duty, and loyalty, follow their lives as they fall in love, face tragedies, and triumph against the evils facing them.

# VALLERIAN ROYAL FAMILY TREE

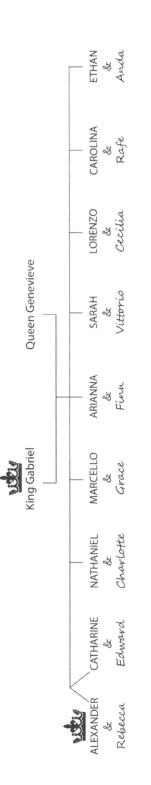

King Gabriel — Queen Genevieve

ALEXANDER
&
Rebecca

CATHARINE
&
Edward

NATHANIEL
&
Charlotte

MARCELLO
&
Grace

ARIANNA
&
Finn

SARAH
&
Vittorio

LORENZO
&
Cecilia

CAROLINA
&
Rafe

ETHAN
&
Anda

This is the royal family tree for the House of Santoro, the current royal family line.

Visit marianneknightly.com/royal-family-tree to download your own copy!

# *one*

## ARIANNA

Princess Arianna delicately patted her upswept hair as she walked down an ornate hallway. Satisfied that nary a lock of her caramel-colored hair was out of place, her hand fell to her side and brushed the lines of her fitted forest green skirt suit. The suit was chosen not because she liked it, though she did; it was chosen for diplomatic reasons above all else. The color was a favorite of the royal family in Brazenbourg, where they currently were for a royal visit.

Her heels clicked softly against the marble floors of the Brazenbourg Royal Palace, echoing against the others walking around her. Her eldest brother and heir to the throne of Valleria, Prince Alexander, was next to her, his confident stride slow and steady, allowing her to keep up with him in her muted nude-colored heels.

Arianna and Alex were on their way to meet Prince Henry de Bara, the reigning monarch of Brazenbourg. It was a whim that had made Arianna volunteer to go with Alex when their father, King Gabriel, had not been able to come. Perhaps it had been fate.

The Vallerian Royal Protection Service agents with them halted in front of a set of ornate wooden doors etched in gold with the Brazenbourg family coat of arms. The Brazenbourg men standing guard nodded and opened the double doors. Arianna stifled a gasp after she walked inside, as her eyes, which were as rich a caramel color as her hair, took in the room around her.

This was clearly the throne room of the palace. Two large ornate chairs sat at the far end of the room, also etched with a golden coat of arms. The white-gray marble floors and columns stood in graceful opulence. The walls, lined with wallpaper a similar shade as her outfit, were also covered with works by well-known Brazenbourg artists. Her eyes drifted upward and she found another work of art, as elegant, diamond-shaped murals crisscrossed the ceiling. From the looks of things, they must have been restored in recent years, as they seemed to glow brightly with colors and not be dull with their age. An astonishing crystal and gold chandelier hung from the center of the ceiling and easily illuminated the entire room.

While the Vallerian Royal Palace certainly had its own share of opulence, it was clear this small country boasted their own palace to intimidate, if necessary.

"I wonder why they showed us to the throne room," Arianna muttered as she glanced at Alex's narrowed eyes. "Henry's not even here."

"He should have met us at the entrance. He wants us to know he holds the upper hand by bringing us to him rather than meeting us," Alex said in a very low voice. "I don't appreciate tactics like these. They're disrespectful."

"We'll have to put up with it, I suppose. We're the ones who need his help, after all."

"But at what price will we get it?" Alex's words struck a sense of foreboding into her.

"This way, Your Highnesses," one of the Brazenbourg guards said, and led them towards a door in the far left corner of the room.

When they entered the next room, it was to find a series of offices. The walls here were covered in rich green and chocolate brown wallpaper, and burnished wood furniture was scattered around the rooms for efficiency.

One of the royal assistants stood waiting for them and bowed twice when they neared, once to each of them. "This way, Your Highnesses," he said in an affected accent and led them into the next room.

"Prince Alexander. Princess Arianna. Welcome to Brazenbourg," Prince Henry said in a very posh accent, from behind a formidable desk clearly meant to intimidate. He bowed to each of them and then walked around his desk to greet them.

Arianna had never met Prince Henry before, though he looked much like the pictures she had seen. His raven hair had one streak of gray slashing across the front. His dark mustache matched the black eyes set in his round face, and hid a pair of thin lips. His body, clad in a dark suit, was slim and his shoulders were square. He held the bearing of a ruler and the arrogance of one compensating for the size of his country or, perhaps, something else.

Alex bowed briefly in return and shook the man's hand. "Prince Henry."

When Henry turned to her, Arianna dipped into a small curtsy and held out her hand. Henry took it and brushed her knuckles with his lips. His mustache tickled against Arianna's hand, but decorum kept her from reacting. When he lingered a few moments too long, Alex impatiently cleared his throat in warning. Henry smiled and let go, then gestured for them to take a seat.

"Thank you for meeting with us," Alex said, sitting comfortably back in his chair with one leg crossed over the other. The difference in the two men struck Arianna. Alex, though he was not the reigning monarch yet, held the regal bearing of a confident ruler. It was echoed in the movement of his broad body, the way his sharp, black eyes took in everything around him, and even in the way he brushed back his dark hair with an easy confidence. Henry, on the other hand, seemed to be trying too hard to look intimidating.

Henry sat down, adjusting his jacket as he did so. "Thank you for agreeing to meet with me in Brazenbourg. I know it has been a hectic time for you in Valleria."

Though Alex appeared relaxed, his eyes flashed. "Indeed. Though I find, as a ruler, it is always pleasantly busy. Seeing to the needs of our citizens, after all, is a twenty-four hour a day duty."

"Indeed," Henry said dryly.

"Where is Prince Finn?" Alex asked. "I believe he was also meant to be in this meeting, was he not?"

Henry's thin lips seemed to become even thinner. "Yes, I must apologize for my brother's absence. He was unavoidably detained."

Alex nodded with a small smile on his face. If the tabloids were telling the truth for once, then even Arianna could have guessed what may have been keeping Finn. The Brazenbourg prince was well known for his late-night antics, which tended to be brimming with both women and alcohol. As the second son, Finn seemed to have all the fun that Henry avoided.

"I'm sure you know how it is, Your Highness. You have some rascals as brothers yourselves, do you not?"

"Do I?" Alex asked, his voice deceptively mild.

"Oh, yes. I've heard all about your terrible brothers. What a handful. It is so hard to keep siblings in line, don't you find?"

Arianna could feel the tension wind tight around Alex; he would never stand for anyone insulting his family, even if the statement were partially true. Sensing the need for some relaxed conversation before Alex's temper got the best of him, she put her hand on Alex's arm and intervened. "Prince Henry, could we trouble you for some tea or something to eat? No doubt our conversations will be much easier after we've had some refreshments, or rested a bit first."

Henry flushed as he realized the faux pas he had made; he should have offered that to them when they had first arrived. "Of course. Certainly. Yes. We'll retire to a sitting room, unless you would prefer to rest first?"

Alex gave Arianna a furtive glance before responding. "We'll rest. Perhaps we can regroup for dinner?"

"Of course. I'll have someone see you to your rooms. We'll dine in three hours."

"Does that suit you, Arianna?" Alex asked and Henry hid a scowl.

"Yes, just fine," she said as she stood. Alex, gentleman that he was, stood immediately, but Henry stood only after a pointed glance from Alex.

"I'm glad it meets with your approval," Henry said in a mildly condescending tone. Alex quirked an eyebrow but did not say anything in response. Alex shook Henry's hand and they left the room.

When they were clear of his offices and were being led towards their rooms, Alex spoke in a low tone. "Why did you interrupt?"

"I thought a break might be best, even though we'd barely sat down. I could see your temper starting to go. That was a very odd meeting, Alex. He didn't follow protocol at all."

Alex scowled. "He didn't follow basic manners, either. He disrespected our family."

"He disrespected *you*, Alex. You're the future king. It doesn't really matter how I'm treated."

Alex took hold of her arm and she turned to face him, halting their progress in the hall. His face was contorted in disbelief. "Do you really think so little of yourself?"

Arianna shook her head; she only spoke the truth. She was nobody next to her accomplished brothers and sisters. She deserved to be nobody after what she'd done in the past. "It doesn't matter. I'm just here as a buffer, anyway."

His hand tightened around her slim arm. "It *does* matter. What's going on with you, little sister?"

She recalled their brother Marcello asking her a similar question a few weeks ago. "This is neither the time nor the place," she said as she looked up into Alex's eyes. Though she was tall, she was not nearly as tall as Alex.

After a few moments, when Alex's gaze threatened to rock her carefully crafted comportment, he nodded and let go of her arm. "Later, then." As they began walking once more, he said, "I don't like seeing you this way."

"What way?"

"Sad."

Apparently, she wasn't as good at hiding her emotions as she thought. "I'm not sad. Not exactly."

"If you think we don't see it, you're blind," he said as they turned a corner and began walking up a long flight of stairs. "It breaks our hearts, Ari."

The use of her nickname had her throat tightening. None of her older brothers and sister could say her full name when she had been born, so 'Ari' had stuck until they were older. Though she was the fifth child, smack dab in the middle of all of them, her older siblings had still been quite young when she had come along. Her younger brothers and sisters had the same issue as they grew up; the nickname stuck with them, too.

Arianna cleared her throat. "Please stop worrying about me. I'll be just fine. You need to focus on diplomacy right now, not your little sister."

Alex's lips curved in a smug expression. "You forget that I'm very adept at multi-tasking. I can do both."

Arianna's lips quirked at that. "It's a shame Rebecca couldn't come along on this trip. I could have been spared some time with my overbearing big brother."

Alex's expression softened at the mention of his fiancée. "There will be other opportunities for Rebecca. We're finalizing some wedding details in the next few days and she needed to stay at home. Besides, if she didn't stay back, there's no telling what Mama may have agreed to on her behalf."

Arianna laughed. Their mother, Queen Genevieve, was thoroughly enjoying wedding planning. "Poor Rebecca."

"Indeed," he said with a smile. "Anyway, we hope to finalize some of the details by the time Mama and Papa's fortieth anniversary celebration comes around in a few days."

Arianna sighed. What must it be like to be married to your true love for forty years? Arianna knew she would never find out; she didn't believe in love anymore, not for her.

"Well, hopefully we can finish up here quickly so we don't miss it."

"We won't miss it," Alex said simply. "Even if Henry and I haven't come to terms by then, we'll take a break and go home. You don't need to stay the whole time."

"Of course I'll stay. You need me. I could tell you wanted to smack Henry across the face, and I very deftly diffused the situation for you."

"Was I that obvious?"

"Only to the little sister who has known you her whole life."

"Well, since I'm sure I'll feel that way again, perhaps it is best that you stay."

"You should relax a little," Arianna said as they reached the landing for the next floor and began a trek down a long corridor filled with rooms. "I'm sure Henry's behavior today was the exception, not the rule. You probably just overwhelmed him. You are quite foreboding at times."

"Am I?"

Arianna chuckled. "Oh, yes. All my brothers are. Except for maybe Ethan," she said, referring to the youngest of them all, who was currently a doctor in the Vallerian Royal Navy. Everybody doted on Ethan.

"Ethan can be plenty scary if he wanted to be, trust me. He just enjoys how we all spoil him."

"Who wouldn't?" she said simply as they stopped outside one of the doors.

"This is your room, Prince Alexander," one of the guards said.

"Thank you," Alex said, then gave Arianna a kiss on each cheek. "You're a good sister."

"You're a good brother."

He smiled. "I'll swing by your room to pick you up for dinner. Don't be late."

"I think you have me confused with Cat," she said, referring to her older sister and Alex's younger twin sister, Catharine. "But I'll be ready," she said with a wave as she continued her trek to the end of the long hall, where her room lay.

Once inside, she sighed, happy to be alone again. As she headed for the bathroom, she realized that it was not being alone that made her happy; it was dropping all the pretense of propriety. It took a considerable amount of work to stay prim and proper.

As her hands delved into her hair and began to pull out the pins resting there, she knew she didn't mind the hard work it took to keep up the persona. She owed it to her family after what she had done all those years ago. She would do whatever it took to keep their respect; it had certainly taken long enough to earn it back after what had happened.

Arianna turned the silver knobs of the bath and let a rush of steaming water begin to fill a large copper tub. As she began to undress, she knew she would do anything to make her family proud. She was older now, wiser. She wouldn't be charmed by a man with ulterior motives again, and put her family and her country at risk.

No, never again.

## *FINN*

Finn de Bara strode down the long halls towards his older brother, Henry's, office. He ran a careless hand through his hair, which was a deep, rich dark brown, bordering on black. His brilliant green eyes, set in a square face he inherited from his mother, were wary and held a hint of his exhaustion. He rubbed his hand down over his face in a feeble attempt to become more alert. He had not bothered to shave today, so his strong chin and talented upper lip were covered with a layer of scruffy hair. Where Henry's mustache made him look older, a day's worth of growth on Finn's face made him look dangerous and sexy.

Finn tucked his shirt into his pants as he walked. He had been woken by Henry's assistant banging on his door not ten minutes ago. Finn supposed it was his own fault for staying out so late again. But what no one, not even his brother, understood was that his late-night partying rarely had anything to do with debauchery and more to do with helping the citizens of his country.

Having a drink with them at the end of a long day was often the best way for him to help his people. As second in line to the throne, he had no real authority in the kingdom. He could only make recommendations to Henry and to their district mayors. Listening to his people talk over a drink helped him to learn what was really going on in their country. Though Brazenbourg was small, it was full of history and life. He loved his homeland. What he didn't always love, was Henry.

It was hard for a man to admit he disliked his older brother. They had never seen eye-to-eye, particularly after their parents died and he ascended the throne. For a long time, Finn wondered if it was jealousy fueling his feelings—as Henry was the ruler, not him—but he knew now that wasn't true. Of course, even Henry's dislike for Finn didn't keep Finn from hoping his brother's feelings would one day change. He still hoped they could reconcile and become true brothers, even if it was a futile hope.

Making matters more complicated was the fact that Henry had a dark side to him that few ever saw. He hoped their guests didn't see it, either.

Finn was sorry that his late arrival would look bad in front of the Vallerian royals, whom he was interested in meeting. By all accounts, King Gabriel and Prince Alexander did an excellent job as rulers. Despite some recent security issues Valleria had since resolved, Finn felt as though he could learn a lot from Alexander.

Just because Finn would not be leading his country, did not mean he couldn't be a leader in his own right. Since Henry seemed to need him less and less, he had wondered about becoming a district mayor in the next election cycle. Working on the ground with the people, now that was something he could do. He just had to convince Henry of the idea, too.

Finn approached the offices with careless confidence. He swung open the door, an apology waiting on his lips. He held back, however, when he realized only Henry was in the room.

"Did you scare off the guests already, Henry?" Finn took a chair in front of his brother's disgustingly large desk. Because he knew it would bother Henry, Finn propped his feet on the edge of the desk and crossed them at the ankles. He leaned back in his chair and gave his brother a devilish smile.

Henry scowled—it happened so often that Finn was sure Henry's face would soon become permanently etched with the expression—and walked around the desk towards Finn. He forcibly pushed Finn's feet off the desk, then took a few moments to rub a handkerchief over the spot where his feet had been, though nary a speck of dirt was there.

"Where the hell have you been?" Henry said as he strode back to his chair.

"You know where I've been."

"Sleeping off another hangover, no doubt," Henry huffed. Finn had stopped correcting Henry's assumptions years ago. Even though Henry had Finn followed wherever he went, Henry still never believed where Finn had really been.

"I hope the whore you were with last night isn't still around. The Vallerian royals are here and they don't need to run into her."

"I wasn't with anybody last night, Hank," Finn said, smiling broader when Henry snarled at the use of his despised nickname. Finn had also given up trying to explain that he was not a womanizing asshole like the tabloids made him out to be. He'd been with a number of women, that was true, but he had never treated them with disrespect. But all that was in the past. If people knew how long it had really been since he'd buried himself in the tight heat of a woman, they probably wouldn't believe him. Henry certainly wouldn't.

"Took a night off, eh?" Henry asked. "Losing your touch?"

"Every guy needs some rest," Finn smiled back. "So, which sister came with Prince Alexander on this visit?"

"Princess Arianna. They're resting before dinner, at her suggestion. The Prince wouldn't even entertain any discussions once she started talking. Why the hell he wanted to bring a woman along, I don't know."

Finn had long known about Henry's dismal view of women and never understood where it came from. Their mother was a strong woman who had always instilled respect for women into her sons, but Henry had never really learned. "Which one is she? Is she Prince Alexander's twin?"

"No, it's one of his other sisters. No family needs that many children."

"Tell them how you really feel," Finn said sarcastically. "I'm sure that will make them very amenable to the diplomacy we're trying to accomplish."

"You mean the diplomacy *I* am trying to accomplish. You're just the royal spare."

Finn absorbed the shock of Henry's words but kept his face a mask of indifference. Sitting across from Finn was the only family he really had left in the world, and Henry hated him. Finn wasn't sure he would ever get over it.

"Spare or not, I'm still useful."

"Well, use your 'talents' to distract the Princess at dinner tonight. Of course, that means you'll have to forego a night of drinking to have a peaceful meal."

Finn did not mention that last night he'd had a peaceful meal at the home of one of their citizens. He had met a farmer yesterday at a local bar, and then had gone to his home to share a drink and dinner with him and his delightful family. The farmer was having trouble irrigating his crops, as the country underwent a low rain season and a drought might be imminent. Finn helped the man however he could, which, unfortunately, was not much.

"I'll be at dinner, Henry," Finn said as he stood. "I'll be there on time, too, don't worry. Which room is she in? I could escort her to dinner and apologize for not being there when she arrived."

"She's in the Yellow Room. The Prince is in the Purple Room."

"I'm shocked you remembered purple is the favored color of Vallerian royalty."

"I didn't assign the rooms."

"Ah. Now, that makes much more sense. I'll have to compliment your assistant on my way out."

"I don't need you distracting him."

"I won't," Finn said as he stopped in the doorway to look at Henry again. "I'm going to give you some advice, dear brother."

Henry huffed a laugh. "This should be amusing. All right, go ahead."

"Don't be such an asshole tonight. If this is how you acted when you met them, it's no wonder they went running to their rooms."

"Get out," Henry said with suppressed rage. Finn gave him a broad smile and walked out the door.

# *two*

## *ARIANNA*

Arianna put the finishing touches on her makeup and took a critical look in the bathroom mirror. Giving herself a nod of approval, she walked back out to the bedroom while patting her hair gently. She had coiled it at the base of her neck, and she was praying it would stay put.

She was clad only in delicate lingerie and stockings as she walked to the closet where her dress hung. She did not wear the decadent lingerie for a man. No, she had not had a lover for a very long time, not since the last man had betrayed her and her family. She wore them for herself, because she liked the way the soft lace and sheer stockings felt against her skin.

Arianna slipped on her sky-high heels next and began to put on her jewelry, a beautiful set of emerald, amethyst, and diamond, woven together seamlessly with delicate gold strands, as though the stones were meant to be together.

Next, she gently removed the dress from a velvet-lined hanger. It was a long line of rich forest green silk, worn again in deference to

Brazenbourg. The strapless dress had a heart-shaped neckline, which displayed the top of her larger than average cleavage. With a fitted waist and straight skirt, it made her appear taller and slimmer than she really was. The dress had a matching cropped jacket covered in bright silver embroidery, so that it appeared to sparkle in the dim light of the room.

She had eased the dress over her hips and was holding it against her chest while she tried to zip it up from the back one-handed. Why hadn't she been provided with a maid to help her? She would need to remember to bring her own the next time she traveled.

When she heard a knock at the door, she paused to check the time. Alex was running a little late today, it seemed, as was she. Hopefully, he could help her with the dress. Not expecting anyone else, she asked, "Could you come in and help me?"

She was busy fussing with the dress, and didn't immediately check to see who had entered. She did turn around a few moments later, her nimble fingers still holding the front of the dress secure.

When she saw a strange man in a tuxedo standing there, and not Alex, she gasped. Her grip on the bodice of the dress slipped and only her wide hips kept the dress from falling farther than her waist. She quickly lifted up the fabric again, but it was too late. Whoever he was, he had now seen her breasts in the lacy strapless bra, along with a great deal of skin.

"What do you want?" she asked, her voice a desperate plea as her hands held the dress in a fierce grip at her cleavage. "How did you get past the guards? It doesn't matter. If you come one step closer, I will scream this bloody palace down."

The man stood in shock for a few moments before he held up both of his hands in front of him in surrender. "Your Highness, please. I didn't mean to upset you. Allow me to introduce myself."

"I don't care who you are," she said as she inched backwards and hoped she didn't trip on the edge of her dress.

"I'm Prince Finn de Bara, Your Highness," he blurted out.

"What? You're who?"

"Prince Finn. I came to apologize for not meeting you when you arrived, and to provide you with an escort to dinner. I certainly didn't mean to intrude," he said as he ran an unsteady hand through his dark brown hair.

"Oh," she said as she sagged against the dresser. "Oh my God. You took ten years off my life."

"Then I apologize for cutting your life short as well."

Calmer, Arianna was finally able to really look at the Prince. The tuxedo he wore seemed molded to his body, and his wide, bright green eyes were alight with remorse and a touch of humour. She could drown in those eyes, she mused fleetingly and shook her head free of the thought.

"I'm sorry as well. I shouldn't have reacted so strongly."

"You were right to do so. A woman can never be too careful in this day and age, even a princess. Who were you expecting?"

"My brother, Alex. He's supposed to escort me to dinner." She tightened her grip on the silky fabric.

"I'll leave and let you finish dressing." She'd expected Finn to take advantage of the situation, given his reputation. Her face must have shown surprise, because he smiled. God, what a mouth he had. She hadn't been intrigued by a man's mouth in ages.

"Did I say the wrong thing, Princess? Would you rather I stay and help you with your dress?"

Sense finally seemed to filter into her consciousness. "Oh, I don't know that it's appropriate for you to help me, Your Highness," Arianna said as she backed up against the wall while he inched closer.

"Please, call me Finn." His voice was an octave lower than before and the tone sent goosebumps jumping across her skin. "I think we've moved past the formal pleasantries, don't you?" His lips were tipped up in a gentle curve and she wondered how they might move against hers.

Propriety told her to throw him out, and she was about to do just that. In the next moment, however, Finn placed his hands—complete with wide palms and long, capable fingers—on her hips and she held her breath. His touch felt too warm, especially through the flimsy layer of silk.

For the first time in several years, a surge of desire coursed through her veins, compelling her to draw him in and feel his hard body against hers. She had not wanted a man in so long; why was she reacting this way now?

She'd forgotten what an addiction physical attraction could be, how it made her pulse race and her body yearn. However, even with her last boyfriend years ago, she'd never felt an instant spark like she seemed to have with Finn. Intrigued, she decided to see where the spark would take her. "All right. If you can remain a gentleman, I would appreciate your assistance."

She was proud of her voice for sounding even, though Finn raised a brow at her comment. "All right. Turn around, Princess," he said as his hands, which still rested on her hips, began to turn her.

The thought of him seeing her back, which was bare but for her bra, kept her still. "You can reach around and pull up the zipper. Your arms are certainly long enough." What was she saying? Had all sense left her? Now, he would essentially be hugging her.

A devious smile spread across his face, even while his gaze remained curious. "Your call, Princess."

"Arianna. You may call me Arianna."

"I find I like calling you 'Princess'," he mumbled as he stepped closer. Too close. Her eyes fell to his lips once more.

His tuxedo jacket brushed her bare arm and she held her breath. His hands shifted from her hips and slid around to her back, grazing the bare skin at the base of her spine and pulling her against him in the process; she let out a gasping breath.

"Steady, Princess," he murmured, his eyes now as dark a green as her dress. She couldn't look away. His arms felt so good and terrible at the same time. Strong and steady, his hands found the zipper. He didn't linger, but instead swiftly zipped her up and clasped the hook at the top. She needed to readjust the front of her dress, but held back.

His voice was thick when he spoke. "God, you're beautiful."

"Thank you," she said, her voice barely a whisper. When was the last time a man she wasn't related to had called her beautiful?

"Was that gentlemanly enough for you?"

"Yes."

"Then am I forgiven?"

"Depends on what you're asking forgiveness for," a menacing voice said to them. Arianna looked past Finn's shoulder to see Alex glaring at them. *Oh, no.*

Finn stepped away from Arianna and she felt a rush of cool air wash over her at the loss of his body heat. It did help clear her mind, however, and she realized what had almost happened. Heat flushed her skin once more as mortification and shame swept through her.

Finn strode over to Alex with a pleasant expression and bowed. "Your Highness," he said and held out his hand. "I'm Prince Finn de Bara. Welcome to Brazenbourg. I apologize for not meeting you earlier."

Alex gave a short bow and reluctantly shook Finn's hand as his narrowed eyes darted between her and Finn, who was charming and unperturbed at being caught with his arms around a visiting princess. Arianna could tell Alex was holding back his anger, whether for her or for political reasons, she didn't know.

"Prince Finn. Would you care to tell me just what you were doing with my sister?"

A contrite expression, which may or may not have been genuine, crossed Finn's face. "I take full responsibility. I wanted to apologize to the Princess for not receiving her earlier, as I have just done to you. When I knocked, however, she must have been expecting you, as she asked me to come in and assist her. She was surprised to see me there, as you can imagine."

Alex gave him a fierce stare, though Finn remained undaunted. A look like that from Alex would fell most men, but apparently not

Finn. Anger laced Alex's words when he spoke. "That still doesn't explain why you were accosting her in her own room."

"Alex, it's not his fault," Arianna said and both men turned towards her. Why had she spoken up when she really wanted to crawl away and hide?

"Really?" Alex asked with disbelief.

"Yes. I was having trouble with my dress and he was helping me."

"Is that what they're calling it these days?" Alex muttered.

"Your Highness, please don't blame the Princess."

Alex crossed his arms over his broad chest. "Do you honestly think I would place any blame for this situation on my sister? Who the hell do you think you are?"

"I'm Finn," he said with a slight smile, still not reacting to Alex's anger. "Listen, it was an honest mistake. I certainly didn't mean to intrude and I meant no harm to the Princess. What say we head down for some pre-dinner drinks and put this behind us?"

Alex considered for a moment and glanced at Arianna who nodded her approval of Finn's suggestion. "All right," Alex said. "We'll put this behind us, but know this: you harm my sister in any form or fashion, you will regret it. I don't care who you are."

Arianna saw Finn's smile slip slightly at Alex's intense words, but he recovered quickly. "I would expect no less, Your Highness."

"Call me Alex. Now, if you'll wait outside for us, we'll need a few more minutes."

"Of course," Finn said with a charming smile and a small bow. "Alex. Princess," he said and walked out, shutting the door behind him.

"Are you all right?" Alex asked as he walked over and placed his hands on her shoulders. His eyes searched hers for any signs of trauma. He had given her the same look years ago when she had made another mistake with a man.

"Yes, I'm fine," she said, giving him a small smile and hoping he would believe the lie. "It was a misunderstanding, that's all."

"Take care, Ari. His reputation with women is deplorable."

"So are Nate's and Lorenzo's," Arianna said, referring to two of their brothers. "But you don't take them to task."

"That's where you're wrong. I frequently scold them, and so do our parents, but don't try to change the subject. Was he telling the truth about what happened?"

"Yes, he was. They didn't supply me with a maid or assistant to help me dress, so there was no one to answer the door. I thought it was you, in any case, but I should have checked first. If anything, it was my fault." *It was always her fault.*

Alex gave her shoulders a squeeze. "Don't say things like that. We're a guest in his palace. If anything, *he* should have known better." He sighed. "Look, if you tell me to drop it, I will, but I'm still going to keep an eye on him."

"Really, Alex, it's fine. Don't make this into something it's not." That was advice she would use herself. "Why were you late tonight anyway?"

He frowned and stepped away, taking a seat in a small sitting area near the window. Arianna took a moment while his back was turned to adjust the front of her dress, then walked over to join him. "I was on the phone."

She put a hand over his. "Is something wrong? Is someone hurt?" Their brother Marcello, who was Valleria's Minister of Security and Defense, had been injured about a month ago while on a top-secret mission.

Alex gave her hand a squeeze. "No, nothing like that. Don't upset yourself."

"Oh. Well, were you too busy talking to Rebecca to remember your dear sister?" she asked with a smile on her face. Alex lifted one corner of his mouth in amusement. "I did speak to Rebecca a little while ago, yes, but I was actually speaking with Marcello. He's concerned."

"Is Grace all right?" Grace was Marcello's lady love and a long-time friend of their sister Catharine. Marcello and Grace were currently in England, where Grace had a home, while they awaited trial of the man who had attacked Grace and Cat over a month ago.

"Yes, he told me they actually won't need to go to trial and are pursuing a plea deal. The sworn statements from Grace, Cat, and others are enough to ensure his guilt. However, since he attacked Cat, a royal of another nation, I doubt he'll ever breathe free air again."

"That's excellent news."

Alex nodded. "What isn't excellent is the fallout from the covert mission Marcello completed."

"Do we need to go back to Valleria?"

Alex shook his head. "Not tonight. Marcello is having his team do some more digging."

"What really happened, Alex? Neither you nor Marcello ever said."

"It was to protect you, all of you. However, since I'm going to be distracted with it, I think you deserve to know. You know as much as the media does, correct?" She nodded.

"Good. Then you know Marcello led a mission into Gardar Rus, one of the largest countries in the world. Their leader, Vlad, who was arrested afterwards by the International Police Force, was threatening to invade three nearby countries. What no one knew, however, was that two of those countries had teamed up with Gardar Rus to ambush Marcello and the others. Fortunately, our brother had the foresight to realize that and had planned accordingly."

Arianna's head was reeling. She shuddered when she thought of what could have happened to her older brother. "Is that all?"

"No. Marcello learned that night that another country, not present during the mission, was also involved in the ambush. Marcello thinks he's close to finding out who it is."

"Oh my God. Are we safe? Would they come after us?"

"We're fine, Ari. Believe me, I never would have left Valleria if I didn't think otherwise. Brazenbourg may be able to help us, and that's why we're actually here. I don't care much for Henry, but if his intelligence forces have picked up on anything, it would help us a great deal."

"Do you think he'll help you?"

"I don't know. I also don't know what he'll want in return. Brazenbourg is a small country, but Henry, from what I've heard, has big ambitions."

"Well, I'll do whatever I can to help. Truly." When the clock chimed, they both glanced up. "I think we'd better go. If we need Brazenbourg's help, we don't want to be too late to dinner."

As they both stood, Alex said, "We'll blame it on Finn."

"Alex," Arianna said in a warning tone.

"Don't worry, I'll be good."

"See that you are, or my first call will be to your fiancée and the next call will be to Mama."

Alex winced. "Arianna, that's not necessary."

Arianna laughed at the worried look on his face. "Come on, big brother. Let's not keep them waiting."

## FINN

FINN PACED LIGHTLY IN THE HALLWAY WHILE HE WAITED FOR the Vallerian royals to come out of the Princess's room. He adjusted his pants yet again at the thought of the Princess and her voluptuous curves dressed in sinful lace, and wondered if the rest of her lingerie matched her bra. He had wanted to bury his hands in her rich caramel-colored hair that had eyes to match, and kiss away the color on her full, painted lips.

He ran a frustrated hand through his hair. It was his fault for intruding on her privacy—he may never forgive himself for that—but, Jesus, she was one of the sexiest women he'd ever met.

When his arms had gone around her, pushing her full breasts

against his chest, he'd felt more than a punch of desire. He'd wanted to hold her and kiss away the surprise that still lingered in her eyes. She'd felt desire for him, too; he was experienced enough to recognize that.

With a sister like that, it was no wonder that Alex wanted to rip his head off. Finn, who was used to even worse tirades from Henry, hadn't batted an eye at Alex's anger, at least for the most part.

The sound of her sultry laughter carried into the hallway. Jesus, she even had a sexy laugh, and the palace seemed brighter as a result of it. When she and Alex exited a few moments later, her bare shoulders were covered in a sparkling jacket. Pity. Even if he couldn't touch her soft skin again, he'd love to see it, and imagine what it would taste like.

Her eyes were bright and both she and Alex were smiling. He wondered what it would be like to have a woman like her smile at him. He'd had women grin and flirt with him before, but she was different and he wasn't sure why. Even the dress she wore was in Brazenbourg colors, the jewelry a symbolic mix of their two countries. She could easily be a Brazenbourg bride dressed as she was, and the thought unnerved him.

"All set?" Finn asked, his voice a little gruffer than expected.

"Yes, thank you," Alex replied as they began walking down the hall, security following in their wake. Arianna slipped her hand under Alex's arm for support; Finn wished her arm was resting on his.

Finn cleared his throat. "Allow me to apologize again. I certainly didn't mean to intrude or offend either of you, and I hope you'll not think poorly of Brazenbourg because of it."

"Think nothing of it," Arianna said and gave him a small smile, which sent a burst of warmth scattering inside him. He nodded in return even while an ache seemed to settle in his chest. Try as he might, he had a sinking feeling he could never think 'nothing' about what had happened.

As they walked, Finn began gesturing to various points of interest around the palace, things he loved or that had a bit of interesting history attached to them, anything to keep his mind off the woman a few feet away from him and the soft click of her heels.

When they finally reached the sitting room, Henry was waiting. Finn could already tell he was in a surly mood. Henry's moods turned faster than a breath these days, so Finn hoped he became more pleasant soon.

Before Henry could berate them for being tardy, which Finn knew he would do, Finn spoke first. "Sorry for the lateness, Henry. You can blame it on me."

"We share equal blame, I'm sure," Alex said as he led Arianna to a couch near the fire.

"Prince Henry, I'm afraid they're both just covering for me. I did take a little extra time getting ready this evening," Arianna said with a demure smile.

"Nonsense," Henry said and returned her smile. It seemed Henry's mood had changed just in time. "Of course you should take as long as you need, and I can see that the effort was well worth the wait." Arianna thanked Henry while Finn wondered why Henry was trying to flirt with the Princess.

"My sister was not supplied with a maid or anyone to help her. Had I known that would be the case, we could have easily brought one of our own from Valleria."

Henry stiffened and Finn did, too, while he waited to see which way Henry would swing this time. Fortunately, Henry relaxed. "I do apologize. You see, since our mother passed, there has not been anyone to advise us about such things. We are sorry for any inconvenience."

"It was no inconvenience, I assure you," Arianna said and shot a quick glance to Finn. Were his eyes deceiving him or had her skin become flushed? No doubt it was due to the fire beside her. Yes, that was it.

"May I get everyone a drink?" Finn asked, hoping to keep his hands busy and his mind distracted for a moment. As everyone stated their drinks, Finn walked across the room to make them. A few moments later, he walked over with two glasses of white wine in his hand and handed one to Arianna first.

"Thank you," she said in her soft, sultry voice as she took the glass. Her hand brushed against his and she gasped lightly; was she feeling the spark between them, too? Maybe she was just as affected by him as he was by her.

"You are quite welcome, Princess." Her eyes, which seemed to glow against the firelight, grew wider.

"Alex," Finn said as he handed him the other glass. Alex glared at him but said nothing.

"Really, Finn," Henry scowled. "You should at least address our guests properly. I do apologize, Your Highnesses."

"There's no need to scold him," Alex said easily as he relaxed in the seat beside Arianna. "I asked him to call me 'Alex' and you are welcome to do the same."

"And you are free to call me 'Arianna' as well, if you prefer."

"Ah," Henry said flustered; Finn knew Henry hated to be off his game, even for a moment. "Of course, you may also call me 'Henry', if you choose."

"Thank you," Alex said as his eyes darted between the two brothers. As Finn handed Henry a glass of scotch and kept a glass of wine for himself, Finn wondered what Alex saw. "I find that formal titles can be quite tedious at times, don't you?" Alex asked before he took a sip.

"Do you?" Henry asked with disbelief. "I find them quite appropriate. Though, with other royalty, perhaps you are correct." Alex gave Henry an even smile, as a butler came in to announce dinner.

As they made their way down the hall, Henry held out his arm for Arianna, who graciously accepted, leaving Finn and Alex to walk a little ways behind them.

"You and your brother are very different, aren't you?" Alex asked as they slowly made their way down the hall.

"As different as night on one planet and day on another. Aren't you and the Princess different from each of your siblings, as well as each other?"

"Yes, I suppose that's true. May I be blunt?"

"Blunt I can appreciate. Insults, however, I do not take kindly to."

"Understood. Henry does not seem to be very consistent. His emotions swing faster than a pendulum."

"You're very astute, Alex. I won't say you're wrong, because I'll speak the truth as I know it, and what you said is true."

"Not insulted, then?"

"No. Not yet, anyway."

"Then I hope you'll not be offended by my next statement, either. There doesn't seem to be any love lost between you and your brother."

"I'm not offended. No, you're right. However, most people don't pick up on it. We've never been fond of each other, but we are still brothers," Finn warned him.

Alex smiled. "I understand. I'd like to talk more with you, Finn. Will you join Henry and me in our conversations tomorrow?"

"I'm not involved in matters of the state," Finn said simply. He knew the Vallerian royal children all worked in some fashion for their crown and country. Henry had always opposed such an idea when it came to Finn.

"Well, perhaps it's time you started," Alex said as they entered the dining room.

Henry sat Arianna near him at the head of the table, with Finn beside her and Alex across from her. Finn's leg gently brushed hers after he sat down, and she tensed. Even through the clothes they wore, the briefest touch felt like fire against him.

As she laid her napkin over her lap, he noticed how graceful she was. Her arms and hands moved fluidly as she reached for her wine or her meal; he couldn't help but wonder how those elegant hands would feel as they grazed and marked his body in pleasure.

Though her smile was easy—with darkened lips sliding comfortably over impeccable teeth, and her movements even—her demeanor seemed at odds with the woman who had almost fallen apart in his arms. She had been incredibly responsive in her room but, looking at the proper woman beside him, no one would guess it.

Throughout dinner, every chance he got, he brushed his arm or hand against hers. He kept bumping her leg underneath the table or sliding his foot against hers. At first, she seemed to shift away, keeping her body tense, but eventually she either gave up or gave in, and he wondered which it was.

Topics at dinner were kept to general subjects, neither country willing to mar the fine meal with political discourse. Arianna, he learned, was also incredibly intelligent—far smarter than him, he realized—as she could talk expertly on any subject they discussed. Besides wanting to hear her voice, he realized he truly yearned to know more about her opinions.

In a twisted stroke of fate, Finn seemed to be lacking his natural charm, whereas Henry seemed to have an abundance of it. Finn, who wanted to interject and tease his brother, was off his game all of a sudden, as his usual careless style seemed to have left him. He hoped some of it returned before dinner was over; otherwise, he may never find a moment to speak to Arianna again, and he very much wanted to.

As a steady stream of polite conversation continued throughout the meal, Finn continued to innocently brush against the enchanting woman beside him. Despite the brushes and casual caresses, Arianna took great pains to avoid looking at him, rarely glancing at him at all unless he spoke to her directly. In his experience, women avoided a man's gaze either because they weren't interested at all, or they were too interested and weren't sure what to do about it. Before the night was over, Finn would find out which his proper Princess was.

Not that she was his, of course.

He wouldn't mind if that changed, he realized. Perhaps it was due to his growing urge to touch her, taste her, and feel her hot skin underneath his hands. Lust had struck him like a lightning bolt, and his cock grew painful just imagining the tight heat of her body. Even watching her eat had been an experience. He'd barely tasted anything while he'd examined each tasty morsel pass her lips and heard the sounds of pleasure she'd made.

"The meal was delicious," Arianna said as she put down her dessert fork. "This damson fruit tart was particularly decadent. Damson ripens in September, is that correct?"

Henry smiled. "You are quite right, Arianna. This tart is a specialty dessert of Brazenbourg."

"Well, it is one I could happily eat the rest of my days, though my waistline may not agree with me." Everyone chuckled. Finn, however, wasn't put off by the thought of her curves filling out even more. Based on what he'd seen of her, she was plenty ripe and bountiful herself.

"Well, I am happy you were pleased with it. Tomorrow, we'll have another traditional dessert; it's our version of a cheesecake."

"Mmmm. Sounds delicious."

After a lingering smile at Arianna, Henry turned to Alex. "I'm sure you'd like to go straight to your room, but I hope you'll spare a few minutes for me. Perhaps we can have a quick nightcap."

"Of course," Alex said smoothly. "I'll just escort my sister to her room first."

"Nonsense. One of the guards can show her."

"I'd prefer to take her myself."

"I can take her," Finn said and all eyes swung towards him, even Arianna's. "It would be my pleasure if the Princess does not mind." Finn was acutely aware of Alex growing tenser across the table.

Arianna's smile seemed forced when she spoke. "No, of course I don't mind."

"Well, then, it's settled." Henry gave a pointed glare to Finn before turning to Alex. "Please follow me, Alex."

Alex stood and helped Arianna from her chair. He whispered quickly to her and she nodded. Alex gave Finn one last look of warning before he followed Henry out the door.

"Well, Princess," Finn said as he walked towards her, "looks like it's just the two of us again."

# three

## ARIANNA

Arianna swallowed as Finn stopped in front of her. Her eyes fell to his lips, which were quirked in a half smile.

"Shall we?" he asked as he held out an arm for her.

"Thank you," she said as lightly as she could. Her slim hand slipped into the crook of his firm arm and rested on his soft jacket. His warm hand came over hers and pulled her more snugly against him. Even through his jacket, she could tell he was fit and toned. Though he was not as broad as Henry or as muscled as Alex, there was an undeniable strength to him.

As much as she should push away, she didn't. She liked the feel of him. She'd even liked the way he'd 'accidentally' found ways to touch her throughout the meal. She had felt a spark of electricity with each one, then a rush of anticipation waiting for the next. Her nerves were frazzled, to say the least.

"Shouldn't you be in the meeting with our brothers?" she asked, hoping to fill the silence with something, anything but the heat that seemed to flash between them.

"I'd much rather be here with you," he said with a smile, and she sighed internally; the man was impossibly charming. While his charm seemed to disappear during dinner in front of Henry, it was back in full force now.

"Well, have you traveled much out of Brazenbourg?"

"Here and there. To me, however, Brazenbourg is home. This is where I was born, and this is where I plan to live until I die."

She tilted her face to his. "You really love your homeland."

"Is there any reason I shouldn't? Do you not feel the same for Valleria?"

Arianna answered a little too quickly. "Yes, of course I love Valleria."

"But do you love it with the same passion as Alex does?"

Arianna bristled at the question. "Alex will lead the country one day. I won't."

"You didn't answer my question."

"And I don't intend to," she said as they reached the long set of stairs. She loved Valleria, and she loved her family. However, since the 'incident' years ago, all she had wanted to do was run away from everyone and everything. She had forced herself to stay and earn back the respect of her family.

"I didn't mean to intrude or upset you," Finn said quietly, and she paused on the stairs to face him. "It seems to be all I do when I'm near you."

"You didn't upset me," she lied.

Finn stepped towards her and she stepped back, halting only when the banister bumped against her. His knuckles lifted to brush her cheek and she felt a spark of heat where he touched. "You don't need to lie to me, Princess." *How had he known she was?* "You can trust me."

The memory of another man saying those same words rushed back and broke the link between them. She slid away from his touch and the heat of his body, and then began walking up the rest of the stairs.

"Have I upset you again?" he asked as he caught up beside her. Despite herself, she was disappointed he didn't take her arm and help her up the stairs.

"No. I am perfectly fine," she said, using the most even voice she could.

"Damn it," he said as he grabbed her arm and forced her to face him. "Stop acting so damn polite."

"This is how I act. This is who I am. If it's offensive to you, you needn't escort me. I can find my own way."

"I'm taking you to your door," he said through gritted teeth and led her up the stairs and around the corner.

"Why are you so angry?"

"I'm not angry. I'm frustrated."

"Why are you frustrated?"

"Because I want to push you against the wall and kiss you senseless, and I can't tell if you'd like it if I did."

She gasped. "What?"

He ran an impatient hand through his hair. "I'm sorry if I've made you uncomfortable, but you're one of the sexiest women I've ever met. God, Princess. Do you work at being that sexy or does it come naturally to you?"

"Me?" *Sexy?* "Me?" she said again in disbelief. Sexy wasn't something she ever tried to be in public, not anymore. "I'm sorry if I gave you the wrong impression."

He pinned her with an intense stare. "Are you telling me you don't feel this connection between us, too? Am I alone in this? I know you feel something. You react to my touch every time. Every damn time. Do you have any idea how arousing that is?"

She swallowed and backed away from his advancing steps. Then she turned and began walking down the hall again. Her shoes made it easy for him to catch up with her, which he did moments later.

"Do you deny it? Remember, I know when you're lying, Princess."

"I-I just want to go to my room." She continued walking, mindful of the guards nearby. It didn't matter what she felt; she would never succumb to those feelings. Not again.

With a low growl of frustration, he continued to walk beside her. When they reached her door a minute later, he blocked her way inside.

"Let me pass, please."

Unlike a few moments ago, he seemed to have some semblance of control. "Answer a question first, Arianna."

She had never thought much about her name, but on his lips it sounded like a lover's caress. "What?"

"Are you truly all right?"

She sighed. "I'm fine, Finn. Really."

"Did I upset you earlier? I didn't mean to. Despite what you may have heard, I'm not the sort of man who upsets women just for kicks."

"No. No, I suppose you're not."

"So, you believe me? Why?"

She spoke without thinking first. "Your eyes. They look kind."

"Thank you for the compliment, Princess, though I have to say they're nothing next to yours."

"You like my eyes?"

"God, yes. They're a rich caramel that a man could drown in; I must have drowned myself a few times already."

"You have?"

His hand reached up to cup her face, his thumbs brushing her temples. "Oh, yes." She swallowed, unsure of what to do or say next.

"But I don't just like your eyes, Arianna."

"Oh?"

"I like your mouth—graceful and intelligent. I like your hands—small and elegant. I like the way your body felt when I brushed against you at dinner, and the sharp way your mind works. I have to admit, I could barely form a coherent thought with you and your soft scent next to me."

Such lovely words, compliments she hadn't heard in a very long time, even from family. Lust was easy, wasn't it? Two bodies with an explosive chemistry that knew just what they wanted. Liking someone for their own sake, well, that was harder.

She swallowed again. "It sounds like you like me."

Finn smiled broadly. "I think you'll find few people in the world who wouldn't like someone as lovely as you."

"Thank you."

"You're welcome, Princess. I'll leave you then." His hands dropped away.

"Wait." She knew she should let him go. If she were honest with herself, however, she knew she didn't want him to go. She wanted him. He had called her sexy and beautiful and wanted to kiss her senseless; no one had in a very long time. She hadn't wanted passion and desire with anyone, and had told herself she didn't need it. If she took some time with Finn now, what did that say about her? What would it mean?

Would one night even make a difference? Could she just let go and just live for once? Memories swirled but she pushed them away. Hadn't she paid enough for her crimes? Hadn't she been the perfect daughter and sister since that fateful time?

She took his hand in hers. So strong and capable. Warm. His fingers wrapped around hers as though they'd been together for years. As she glanced down at their joined hands, she caught sight of the ring she wore. The amethyst sparkled in the dim lights of the hall, and the weight of her duties fell heavy upon her once more.

Maybe they could have a few stolen moments together, ones that she could remember during cold nights alone.

"I still need help with my dress."

His breath caught. "Are you sure, Princess?"

In response, she opened the door and pulled him inside.

∾

∾

## FINN

Finn let Arianna lead the way into her room. Once inside, he shut the door and flipped the lock, which made a very definitive click.

He turned to face her as he leaned back against the door. She stood several feet away, facing him. Her body was stiff with tension and her eyes had a shadow of nerves in them.

"Don't be nervous, Princess," he said in a soft voice as he began to walk towards her. "You have all the control here. You want me to leave, I will."

"No," she said quickly then licked her lips. "No, I don't want that. This is a delicate situation, that's all."

"That's the first time I've heard it called that."

"No, I mean, we're here on for diplomatic reasons. I don't want to make a mess of things."

"You won't. You couldn't." He reached up and tucked a loose strand of hair behind her ear. "Do you trust me?"

"I want to, but I don't know. We only met each other a few hours ago. Oh, what am I doing?" She turned around and put a hand to her forehead.

"You're not doing anything except churning yourself up. I can walk out right now if you want me to. There's no pressure here, except for what you're putting on yourself." He paused to let his words sink in before he asked his question again. "Do you feel something for me? Anything?"

She turned around, and her hands now gripped the sides of her dress. Tension? Fear? Lust? He would finally find out. "Yes," she breathed.

"Are you afraid of the attraction between us?"

She looked away. "Yes."

"Do you want me to leave?"

"No, but I also don't want to, you know."

"Kiss? You don't want to kiss?" he asked, teasing her lightly. She shook her head. "So, you don't want to kiss me?"

She met his gaze once more. "No. I mean, yes. I do want to kiss you. I just don't want to do anything else."

He could tell she still didn't trust him. He'd have to work harder to earn it, then. "All right. Just kissing. Go stand against the wall." Finn gestured to a space of wall between her bed and a sitting area with two chairs that was situated by shuttered windows.

She looked at him curiously but did as he asked, carefully lifting the hem of her dress to walk over in her sky-high heels. When she positioned herself, he spoke again. "Take off your jacket." She widened her eyes and her hands gripped the sparkling silk. "You don't have to if you don't want to, but I think you'll be more comfortable if you do."

She looked uncertain for a moment, but then shook off the fitted jacket, her lush breasts tipping slightly forward as she did so. Finn bit his lip to hold back a groan.

Arianna tossed the jacket on a chair nearby, over which her robe also lay. Her soft, tanned skin was calling to him, but he resisted. He was used to holding back his pleasure while his lover found hers first. Arianna would be an excellent lover, he could already tell. Tonight, however, was about trust, as well as seduction and foreplay. It was not about the endgame that accompanied them.

Finn walked over to her and placed his hands on either side of her head, his palms flat against the wall. He held his body away from her and she didn't reach for him. He knew she would want to, though, eventually.

"Just a kiss then. I won't even touch you unless you tell me to." As he leaned forward, he watched as her eyes fluttered shut. Her body was tense and tight in anticipation. He wanted to lick each inch of her exposed skin. Instead, he waited a few moments, then brushed his lips lightly against hers.

She gasped and her breath, sweet from dessert and wine, washed over him. He pressed his lips firmly against hers and she sagged against the wall. The urge to gather her in his arms, hold her up, and keep her safe was strong, but he held back. It had to be her choice.

When she took a breath for air, his tongue joined the action. He took and took, then gave back even more. His teeth nipped lightly at her lips, then soothed with his tongue. She was heady and addictive, and he used no more than his mouth to take what he wanted.

"Finn," she gasped as she pulled her head to the side. Finn was gasping as well, his hands now fisted against the wall in a battle for control.

"Yes, Princess?"

He saw her struggling with the words, struggling with whatever inner demons were haunting her and pulling her in different directions.

"Shall I leave?" Every molecule in his body rebelled at the thought.

"No." Her hands fisted in his jacket, holding him still. "Don't leave."

"What do you want, Princess?"

"You, it seems," she said with a sigh. Why did she seem so sad about it?

"We don't do anything you don't want to do, Arianna. I think I proved to you that I meant that. You told me you only wanted a kiss, and that's all I did."

"Finn?"

"Yes?"

"Kiss me somewhere else."

Finn swallowed as his cock twitched. He did not think four words had ever held such meaning or such promise.

"Please?"

That did it.

*four*

## ARIANNA

Arianna was not sure what had possessed her tonight. She had never felt this instant chemistry with anyone, not even Huck, the man who'd betrayed her and her family years ago. Perhaps it was just Finn, with his darkening green eyes and complete control. Even though he had not touched her with anything but his lips, she was still shifting uncomfortably against the wall as her body ached for more. Just the heat of his gaze was enough to send her nipples peaking. She felt desired and consumed, and without even a single touch. How did he do that?

"Where should I kiss you?" he asked, his voice husky.

"Anywhere you want to. Just kissing though," she reminded him, though she knew his lips could be even more tantalizing than his touch.

He smiled lightly. "Take off your dress."

She gasped. God, what would his lips do if she were standing there only in her lingerie and high heels?

"Do you want some help?" he asked with a quirked eyebrow.

She nodded her head. Some of her hair fell loose and framed her face. Getting a vixen-like idea, she pulled the pins from her hair, letting them all drop to the floor. She pushed away from the wall and Finn stepped back, keeping his promise not to touch her. In that moment, she realized she trusted him.

She knew of his reputation: dark, dangerous, and passionate. Despite all that, or perhaps because of it, she felt safe with him. Maybe she trusted him because she had been all that, too, at one time. Maybe she still was.

Arianna turned and pushed her hair aside, giving him access to her back. She barely felt his fingers as he unhooked the dress and drew down the zipper.

When she turned again, the tops of her breasts were on display and Finn's eyes fell to her larger than average curves. His possessive gaze alone had her body trembling.

Finn's nostrils flared as the bodice of the dress fell away. Her broad hips once again kept the dress from falling to her feet, and for once she wished she was built less curvy, as some of her sisters were. She shifted her hips from side-to-side as she eased the dress over them, letting it finally fall to the floor with a soft swish.

For a minute, all Finn did was stare at every exposed inch of her. He followed her heels up her stocking-clad legs to her garter and lace panties. She shifted uncomfortably on her feet, unused to feeling so exposed. Yet, she also felt incredibly aroused from him simply consuming her with his eyes.

"Step out of the dress," he said gruffly. "I don't want you to trip and fall."

She stepped out and then began to reach down and pick it up when he stopped her. "I'll do that. Damn, woman, are you trying to kill me by kneeling over in that getup?" Arianna bit her lip to hold back a giggle. She honestly hadn't even thought about it.

He picked up the dress and held it to his face, inhaling her scent before groaning. "I can smell your arousal, did you know that?"

Her eyes widened. "No," she breathed.

"And I don't just mean in your dress," he said as he laid it across the chair with her jacket. She blushed with mortification.

"You shouldn't be embarrassed by that," he said firmly. "Be proud of your sensuality, your passion." She'd spent too long suppressing it to be proud of it, but she could try.

"Lean back against the wall again," he murmured as he stepped towards her, and she stepped back. "Where should I start? You're like a goddamn buffet I'll never get enough of."

Just as she was about to respond, his hands flattened against the wall on either side of her. "Keep your hands behind you or above your head. If I can't touch you, you can't touch me either." She felt her panties getting wetter, but did as he asked and rested her hands on top of her head.

"Jesus. Do you have any idea how fucking sexy you look right now?"

"Does that mean you'll touch me?"

"Does that mean you'll let me?" She shook her head. "Then it looks like only my lips are getting any action tonight."

His lips pressed into the curve of her throat and she arched back to give him room. When her breasts brushed against his jacket, he stepped back and she moaned.

"No touching," he whispered with a devious smile as his lips fell to her collarbone, then the curves of her breasts. His rich, dark hair was aching for her fingers but she held back. If he could hold onto control, then she could. Couldn't she?

"Mmmm," he murmured against the lace. "Do you like wearing sinful things like this, Princess?"

"Yes," she whispered.

"I wholeheartedly approve. The next time I'm only allowed to kiss you, however, I'll expect you to be naked under your clothes."

"What?" Had she misheard in the haze of lust clouding her brain? Next time?

"For now, though, I'll make do," he said and sucked her nipple through the lace. She moaned at the sheer pleasure of it and arched her back as her body yearned for more. It had been so long since she'd felt a man taste her. Too long. When his teeth lightly bit her nipple, she came off the wall with a cry.

"As much as I love the sounds you make, Princess, it might be best to hold your tongue."

She shifted against the wall again. "I can't help it."

"I know, and it's the hottest damn thing I've ever heard." He shifted to the other nipple and she gasped. Her body clenched tight below, holding off the explosion that was building inside her. It had never bloomed so quickly before, and she wanted to feel him just a little bit more. It had been so long since she'd let herself feel.

"More," she whispered unknowingly.

"Your wish is my command." His lips inched their way down her body. "Spread your legs." After she did, his palms slid down the wall as he kneeled. Arianna could feel the waves of heat from his body, caressing her without a single touch of his hands.

He pressed a few kisses to her stomach before he nuzzled her drenched panties. Using his teeth, he ripped the panties away from her body, and it was easily the most erotic thing she had seen in her life thus far. He shoved the panties into his jacket pocket.

"You like that don't you, Princess? Your body certainly seems to," he said, noticing the moisture that had pooled where her panties had been. Covered only with the smallest strip of hair, she knew everything she had was on display to him.

He gave a long lick and she shuddered. "Your pussy is delicious." He took another lick and she whimpered. "I can tell you're holding back."

She shook her head, though it was the truth.

"Don't hold back from me. You'll give me all of you," he said fiercely and his lips and tongue set to demolish her.

Her hands fisted in her own hair, though they wanted to fist in his and hold him tighter against her. She forced her eyes to stay open and focus on something else in the room, anything to keep her orgasm at bay a little longer. Just a little longer. *Just a few seconds longer.*

Suddenly, she caught sight of how they looked in a mirror across the room. Her: splayed open for him against the wall, her breasts heaving, her face flushed, and her hands as good as tied above her. Him: a head of thick hair shifting against her, her stocking-clad legs spread wide to give him room and access to her body. It was too much.

With a series of gasping breaths, she came hard against his tongue, drenching his lips, which he greedily drank with a groan.

"Yes," she cried. "Yes. Yes."

A knock came to her door and, still in mid-orgasm, she simply said, "Yes."

"Arianna, it's Alex."

It felt as though a rush of cold water had fallen over her. Her hands dropped to her sides as Finn gave her one last lick and stood. Her body still throbbed from his attentions. How long would her orgasm have been if they hadn't been interrupted?

"I'll be there in a minute. I was just changing," she called back hoarsely. "Hide in the bathroom," she whispered to Finn.

Her juices were still on his lips, which curved into an amused smile. "No need for that, Princess. Alex will probably check there first anyway."

"Check?"

"He's going to want to make sure I haven't taken advantage of you." He brushed her cheek with his knuckles. "Have I taken advantage of you?"

"No. You only kissed me, after all."

A broad grin split across his face, and his eyes seemed even greener. Was that possible? "That I did, Princess. One more for the road then." He took her lips hard against his. She could taste herself on his tongue and the flavor only aroused her again.

Finn pulled back. "Does your palace have secret passageways in it?" He reached around her and pressed the wall. If she hadn't seen him do it, she would never have known there was a button there; it blended expertly into the wallpaper of the room.

The wall swung open and Arianna jumped back out of its way. "Our palace does have secret passageways, but they're secured with a fingerprint scanner. Does this mean anyone can come find me?" She couldn't hold back the note of worry in her voice.

He cupped her face. "Of course not. You're safe, Arianna. I would never let anything happen to you."

"Arianna, please, I must speak with you," Alex said from outside the bedroom door.

"Sorry, Alex, I'm coming. Just another minute."

Finn gave her a kiss on the forehead and then stepped into the narrow passageway, brightened only by the dim lighting lining the walls. His eyes raked over her body once more before he smiled and closed the hidden door.

Arianna turned and her eyes widened at the sight of her again. The view of her in the mirror—which a few minutes ago aroused her —now terrified her as she tried to become presentable again. She threw on the robe, realizing as the silk of it brushed her bare skin that Finn still had her underwear. *What had she just done?* If Finn hadn't locked the door, what would Alex have seen? She would have risked her family's respect for her own pleasure again. *Would she never learn?*

As shame washed over her, she stepped out of her shoes and rushed to the bathroom. She threw some cold water on her face, thankful for waterproof makeup, then brushed her hair quickly.

She rushed to the door, turned the lock, and swung it open. Alex stood there fuming with anger.

"What the hell took you so long?"

# *five*

## ARIANNA

"I was undressing, Alex. Not an easy feat in the dress I was wearing. Surely, Rebecca's had similar difficulties." Arianna raised an eyebrow, and Alex scowled but did not reply as he entered.

Arianna shut the door behind him and watched as his gaze raked over the room. "Are you alone?"

"Of course." Arianna was only too happy that old palaces were filled with hidden passageways.

"Then you won't mind if I check?"

"Go right ahead," she said easily as her arm swept through the air. Alex narrowed his eyes, then began searching the closet and the bathroom. His lack of trust in her pierced her well-honed exterior. Would she always pay for past crimes?

Weary, she sat down on the impeccable bed. She and Finn had never made it there, and she was glad. She couldn't believe how she had behaved. If anyone found out, well, she didn't want to think about that.

When Alex strode back into the room, he kneeled down to look under the bed. Arianna rolled her eyes and stood. "Why don't you trust me, Alex?"

Alex stood and faced her. "Let me make one thing very clear. I do trust you. Completely. Don't ever doubt that."

Oh. "Well, then what the hell is all this about?"

"I don't trust Henry, and I'm still considering whether or not to trust Finn."

"What? Why? What happened?"

Alex sighed and gestured to the seats near the window. "Let's sit down for this. I'll make us a drink."

"It's better if I don't have anything this late." She moved her clothes from the chairs so they could sit. She remembered Finn's comment about scenting her arousal and she blushed. She put the clothes on the bed and tied her robe a little tighter. She wished she'd had time to put on some underwear.

"Drink a little if you can manage it." Alex handed her some brandy and then took a sip of his own as he sat down. "Henry's made an unusual request."

She took a sip herself. "So soon? I thought you weren't going to talk politics or diplomacy until tomorrow."

"That's what I thought, too. However, Henry's 'nightcap' proved otherwise."

"What does he want?"

"You."

Her eyes widened. "What?"

"Henry wants you," he said with a twisted expression and took another sip.

"Henry wants me to do what? Sleep with him?" She could not believe what she was hearing.

Alex ran a frustrated, angry hand through his hair. "He wants you to marry him."

"Marry him?" She stood and put down the glass in one fell swoop. "What the hell is he playing at?"

"I know. It's a completely ridiculous request. However, he needs a wife and he thinks you'd fit the bill."

"And what does Valleria get if I marry him?"

"Assistance finding out who conspired against us. He claims to know who it is, but won't give us the information unless we agree to join our two countries through marriage."

"That's, I mean, I just don't know what to say." She sat down again. "Have you told Papa about this?"

"No," Alex said darkly. "Once he hears about it, he'll want to kill Henry, which won't do anybody any good."

"I think you're being dramatic. I don't believe Papa would act that way. Not for me."

Alex gave her a questioning look. "Why the hell would you believe something like that? Papa loves you, you idiot."

"He doesn't love me. At least not like he loves our sisters."

"I'll say it again: don't be an idiot. Of course he loves you. I was there the day you were born, the day all of our siblings were born. Trust me, I know when I see a father's love and he has that for you."

But did she have his respect? She didn't know. "What do you want to do, Alex?"

"I want to speak to Finn about this."

"Finn?" She gripped the lapels of her robe. "Did he have something to do with all this?"

Alex shook his head and took another sip. "That's why I want to speak with him. From everything I've seen, Finn's not involved in running the country at all. However, from the gentle probing both I and our protection agents have done, the public loves him much more than Henry."

"They do?"

"Yes. I found out why he didn't meet us this morning."

"Why?"

"He overslept."

Arianna wondered who he'd overslept with. "A woman?"

"No."

"A man?" she asked but, given his recent behavior towards her, had a hard time believing it.

Alex shook his head. "He overslept because he was out late helping a farmer. Apparently, he is frequently seen talking to and helping the citizens of Brazenbourg on an individual basis."

"I don't understand. If he's so well-liked, why doesn't Henry let him do more?"

"Jealousy is my guess. He doesn't want to take a chance that Finn could usurp his crown."

"That's ridiculous. I mean, you don't worry about that sort of thing. You don't even really care that your twin sister was born thirty minutes after you were, making you and Cat much closer in age than Finn and Henry."

"You're right that I don't care. Though I wouldn't have minded if she'd taken a little more time being born. I only had thirty minutes to enjoy being an only child," he said with a smile.

Arianna smiled back, then frowned when she thought about Henry again. 'What ifs' scrolled through her mind. What if she married Henry? Valleria would get the information they needed, and perhaps her family would respect her more. What if she didn't marry him? Would her life be the same? Would they ever find out who wanted to harm Valleria, before they attacked again?

As the silk of her robe shifted slightly, she readjusted it, keeping her semi-bare body covered. If she married Henry, there would be no more clandestine meetings with Finn. She was a one-man woman.

"What are you thinking?" Alex asked as he put down his glass.

"I'm wondering what would happen if I did marry Henry."

"What?" he asked incredulously as he stood. "Not two minutes ago this was a ridiculous request, and now you're actually considering it?"

She stood again, meeting him face-to-face. "If it helps you and Valleria, why not?"

"Holy hell, Arianna. You deserve to marry for love, not convenience."

Arianna shook her head. "I'll never marry for love, so I might as well marry for convenience."

"You deserve better than that."

*No, I don't.* "It's my choice."

"Not this one. You know Papa will not agree to this."

"He will after I've talked to him about it."

Alex ran impatient hands through his hair. "Why the hell are you doing this?"

"I'm not 'doing' anything. I was just considering it."

Alex gripped her shoulders. "Don't feel you have to sacrifice yourself for me or Valleria. Is this about what happened in the past?"

She shrugged away his hands and stepped back as a chill swept across her features. "The past doesn't have anything to do with this."

"It has everything to do with this, I think. You need to move past it."

"I have."

"You haven't. You think we don't notice it? The family is well aware of it, I assure you."

"Leave me be, Alex. It's my life. While you may not like Henry, you respect his position as a ruler."

"How do you know that?"

"Because if you didn't, you would have punched Henry in the face and gotten us thrown out of the palace entirely when he made his request. Since that didn't happen, I'm assuming you restrained yourself."

Alex grunted but didn't deny it. "That still doesn't mean I want my little sister to marry him. I'm only giving him the smallest benefit of the doubt as it is. If Henry were the second son instead of Finn, well, he would find himself with a busted lip and a swollen eye."

"Look, let's just calm down. Why don't we both try to get some sleep and talk about it in the morning?"

"Papa's waiting for my call."

"So, call him. Tell him the truth, and tell him how I felt about it."

"He would never agree to anything like this over the phone. He'll want to come here to speak with you in person if you decide to go through with this."

"He can't come here; his anniversary party is in a few days. He can speak to me then, although, if I want to go through with it, I will."

"Ari, I just don't know."

She gave his arm a squeeze. "Do me a favor? Talk to Rebecca before you talk to Papa. She may be able to give you another female perspective on this."

Alex softened at the mention of his fiancée's name, as Arianna meant him to. "Yes, all right. God, I miss her. Has it only been a day since I've seen her?"

"It's been less than a day, though I bet you both were video messaging earlier, weren't you?"

Alex smiled but didn't deny it. "Can't you see, Ari? What I have with Rebecca, that's what I want you to have."

Arianna's face hardened again. "That's not in the cards for me, Alex, and I don't think you're surprised to realize that." Before he could respond, she continued. "Please, Alex? Trust me enough to know my own mind."

Alex pursed his lips, then nodded. "We'll talk in the morning."

"Sounds good," she said as she led him to the door.

He paused in the doorway to look at her. "Think long and hard about this, Ari. Marriage should be forever, whether you're royal or not. I know you, even though you don't think I do. Once you make a commitment, you stick with it."

"Some might see that as an admirable trait."

"Not if you're making the wrong choice in the beginning. I don't want you to be sad or regretful later."

*As she once was*, she knew he was thinking. "I said I'd think about it and I will."

Alex nodded and strode out. Arianna spent a few moments watching him walk away, his confident steps receding down the hall, then she turned back and locked the door. She went to pick up her dress from the bed and, as soon as she fingered the silk, she remembered Finn and the dress slid from her fingers.

Her gaze shot towards the wall where she had found such pleasure and where he may still be hiding behind the closed door. Could he hear anything? Had he heard anything?

She walked slowly over and ran her hands over the wall until she found the small button. Instead of knocking, she decided to open the door herself. She pressed the button and then gasped as the door opened.

No one was behind it.

Even while relief swept through her, so did disappointment. She shut the door, then moved a small table in front of it, just in case. While her body would have been glad to meet his lips again, her mind needed to focus on other matters.

~

## FINN

FINN FINALLY MADE IT BACK TO HIS ROOM. ONLY GROWING UP in the palace had given him the time needed to learn all of its hidden passageways, though he doubted Henry had used his time the same way. Tonight, he found his time and effort dedicated to the task well spent.

Finn shut the door behind him and pressed another button to lock it. His brows furrowed as he realized he had not mentioned the locking button to Arianna. It was clear that she and Alex needed to discuss something, and the palace walls were thin enough that he could hear them if he'd strained to. Finn wasn't that sort of man, even if the knowledge might help him one day, so he'd given up and walked away.

Finn stripped as he walked across the room, tossing his clothes heedlessly in his wake. He paused in the doorway to his bathroom, gently pushing off his tight boxers over his stiff cock. Finn didn't think he'd ever been this hard before. Even spending several minutes walking through secret palace halls hadn't diminished it. There was only one way to release his tension now.

Though he usually preferred a bath to set his mood, this time he walked to the tall, spacious, glass-encased shower. He turned the water to blistering hot and stepped under the spray, letting the streams pummel his tense body. He ran his capable fingers through his hair, which was even darker now that it was wet. Water sluiced down his body, over his hair-strewn, toned chest and over his cock, which twitched in anticipation.

Finn lathered up his hands with soap, then groaned as his hand circled his cock. Bracing himself against the tiled wall with the other hand, his feet spread shoulder length apart, he started.

His hand smoothed slowly over his cock and he pictured himself thrusting inside Arianna's body. Her body, which he just knew would be tight and hot, would fit around him like a glove. He would take her bare, skin against skin, when he could. It would drive him mad. It *was* driving him mad.

His hand reached down to tease his balls, and his foot slipped slightly. His milky seed leaked through the tip of his cock. He imagined Arianna's plump lips covering the head, her talented tongue licking him clean.

"Jesus fucking Christ, Princess," he said, as if she were there with him. He thought of reality next, not unfulfilled dreams. He remembered the way her curves had looked in soft lace; the way her nipple had puckered willingly under his lips; the way her body had reacted to every single kiss he had dropped along her silky skin.

He groaned, a guttural noise that he'd never made before. He remembered the way her shaved pussy had tasted in his mouth, a taste he knew he'd never grow tired of or forget. He imagined thrusting inside her again, and his body imitated the movements of his dream.

It was only a few moments later when the orgasm took over and he cried out her name. His cock shot long bursts of his seed into the shower and he slammed his fist against the cool tiles until he was spent.

He'd just had the most explosive orgasm of his life, and he'd had it with just the *thought* of a woman. Of one woman. Of Arianna.

Finn kneeled down in the shower, exhaustion overtaking him. He let the water beat down over him, washing him clean. He and Arianna would talk in the morning. He needed her. He wasn't sure why, but he felt it deep down in his bones. He'd never really had anyone care about him—truly care about him—since his parents were killed in a car accident years ago. Henry never cared for him.

Could Arianna?

He wasn't good enough for her, but he had to try. He didn't want to let her go.

As the water began to cool slightly, Finn stood and pushed his wet hair back as he shut off the water. He stepped out of the shower into a room filled with steam and secrets. He flicked a towel off a nearby rack and ran it carelessly over his body, and rubbed his hair dry.

He threw the towel down and walked back to the bedroom, completely nude. He walked past his clothes, scattered all over the floor; he would pick it all up in the morning. For now, he slipped under his covers, and knew he would dream of her again. His Princess.

# *six*

## ARIANNA

Arianna was ready when the expected knock came on her door the next morning. Dressed in a simple skirt suit of rust orange to match the season, she opened the door to find Alex very upset.

"What's wrong?" she asked as fear slashed through her. "Has something happened? Rebecca?"

Alex took her hands and shook his head. "No, nothing like that. I'm sorry if I worried you."

"Thank goodness." Arianna let out a sigh of relief. Alex gave her hands another squeeze before letting go to step inside. "Well, whatever is the matter?"

"Come sit down." He led her to the same chairs they'd sat in the night before. In the bright light of morning, she didn't blush nearly as much thinking of what she and Finn had done against the wall nearby. She realized after a restless night's sleep that last night was an aberration, and it was one she could not repeat, no matter how sexy Finn was, nor how free she had felt.

"I spoke with Papa this morning," he said after they sat down. "He's concerned."

Arianna had seen this coming. "About the proposal?"

"More about your possible acceptance to it."

Arianna looked down at her hands, which were folded demurely in her lap, before meeting Alex's eyes again. "Would it really be so terrible if I accepted it?"

"Would you be happy with him? Could you be happy with him?"

"What's happiness anyway?" she asked rhetorically with a sigh. "Look, wouldn't it be worse if I didn't accept him? Don't we need his help?"

"We do, but not at the expense of your future."

"That's exactly right. It's *my* future, not yours."

"You know Papa won't agree to anything until he meets Henry, and speaks with you in person."

"So, what does that mean?"

"It means that we'll only be staying another day or two, and that Henry will likely come to Valleria."

Would Finn come with them as well? It didn't matter what he did, she reminded herself. "All right. Do I need to speak with Papa then?"

Alex shook his head. "He wants you to take these days to spend time with Henry, and I agree. I know it will be difficult, since he and I will be in meetings most of the day, but use the evenings to your advantage."

"I can do that. I had planned to do as much anyway."

"We also want you to spend some time exploring the country and meeting the people. If you really want to do this, you'll need the country's acceptance."

"I'll try my best."

Alex reached over and squeezed her hand. "Take care, Ari. Henry does not strike me as the type of man who believes in divorce, and I'm already having my people check on the marriage and divorce laws of Brazenbourg. You have a long life ahead of you, God willing, and that is a very long time to be unhappy."

Didn't she know it? "Thanks, Alex. I promise to consider everything carefully."

He gave her hand another squeeze and then let go as he stood. "Shall we get on to breakfast, then?"

"Yes. They must be waiting for us."

"Then let them wait," he said easily, as he escorted her through the halls. They both remained silent on their way to the dining room, easily lost in their own thoughts. As the scents of toast and coffee grew stronger, Arianna focused on the task ahead of her. She put a small smile on her face just as they rounded the corner into the room, and prepared to greet Henry.

However, the first face her eyes found was Finn's.

Though he had a smile on his beautiful face, his green eyes bored into hers as he stood to greet them. "Alex, Princess. Please have a seat. Henry should be with us shortly."

"Of course," Alex said as he held out Arianna's chair for her, which was inconveniently situated next to Finn again.

"Did everyone sleep well?" Finn asked them both as he took his seat again, though his gaze stayed on Arianna.

"Very well, thank you," Alex said as he took his own seat across the small table.

"And you, Princess? Were you quite comfortable last night? Is there anything you need?"

Arianna was proud of herself for not squirming under his gaze. "I was quite comfortable, thank you. I don't require anything else," she said as she moved to pour some coffee.

"Allow me," Finn said and took the pot from her. When their hands grazed each other's, she felt the same spark she had felt last night. *Focus*, she reminded herself.

"Ah, you're here. Very good," Henry said as he entered the room and took a seat at the head of the table between Alex and Arianna. "I do apologize for being late."

"We've only just arrived ourselves, Henry, so no need to worry," Arianna said with a small smile.

Henry returned a clumsy smile of his own before he gestured for some nearby staff to serve him. It struck Arianna as interesting that Finn easily served himself and others at the table, but Henry didn't even seem to think of it.

"What are your plans for today, Arianna?" Henry asked as they settled into breakfast.

"I would love to see some of your country. Is there someone who could arrange an impromptu tour for me? Nothing formal, I assure you."

"Of course we can easily accommodate you. If your brother and I were not in meetings most of the day, I would be honored to show you around myself."

Arianna smiled brightly. "That is very kind of you."

"Of course, in my absence, I can easily arrange a tour guide."

"I would also be happy to take you around my country, Princess," Finn said casually, though the intense expression in his eyes betrayed him.

Arianna's smile faltered slightly before she recovered. A whole day with just the two of them? "That is a very kind offer. However, I couldn't take you away from your duties."

Henry scoffed. "Finn doesn't do much of anything, do you, Finn?"

Finn's eyes narrowed but, with a tight smile, he said, "It would be my pleasure to show you our country, Princess." He turned to look directly at her, and she found herself falling into a pool of bright green again. "Will you allow me to escort you?"

"Yes," she said without thinking. She cleared her throat. "Thank you."

"Excellent," Finn said. "We can leave after breakfast. While you do look stunning in that outfit, Princess, you may want to change into some more comfortable clothes."

"Finn," Henry scowled in warning.

"It's all right," Arianna said, ever the mediator. "Finn is right to suggest more comfortable clothing. Sightseeing and heels do not often mix," she ended with a smile. Henry nodded, though she could tell he didn't really understand what she meant.

"You'll have to tell me over dinner what you thought about Brazenbourg," Henry said.

"Of course, though I'm sure I'll love it." She exchanged a glance with Alex, whose lips were pursed. She knew Alex was reserving judgment, but she could tell he was itching to say something anyway. Arianna pushed back from the table and stood. Alex and Finn immediately stood as well, but Henry took a moment longer to follow. "I think I will go up and get ready."

"Do you need an escort back to your room?" Finn asked.

Her body wanted to say yes, but her practicality won out. "No, thank you. I'll just ask one of the guards."

Finn nodded, seemingly unsurprised by her response. "Please take as long as you need. The guard will escort you to the East Entrance whenever you're ready," Finn said with a look to the guard, who nodded in response.

Arianna nodded and left for her room again, wondering what she should wear. She wanted to look nice, but not too nice; sexy, but not too sexy. It was a fine line.

She just had to remind herself that Henry was her ticket to redemption, not Finn. No, Finn was a distraction she could not afford if she wanted her family's and her country's respect.

∽

## *FINN*

FINN LEANED AGAINST THE CAR WHILE HE WATCHED THE DOOR and waited for Arianna to appear. He'd changed as well, into jeans and a fitted flannel shirt, for their trip today. It was a stroke of luck, or a curse depending upon how you looked at it, that they would spend the day together.

She walked out with a guard a moment later and he no longer thought of all the terrible things that could happen on their trip. He only thought of her.

She had changed into dark skinny jeans that hugged her curves, and a simple green button-down shirt. A trench coat in dark brown matched the boots she wore and simple pearl studs adorned her delicate earlobes. Her hair was still up, as it had been at breakfast, and he set a goal of seeing it down before the end of their day together. He could just picture her as she had been last night: caramel-colored hair, lightly damp with the sweat of desire, streaming down over her full breasts and peaked nipples.

Finn shook his head, his cock already growing just at the thought of her again. He had to remain in control.

"You look lovely, Arianna."

"Thank you," she said as she slowly approached him. Was she nervous to be with him all day? "You look very nice, too, though aren't you cold?"

He chuckled as he glanced at his rolled-up sleeves and the jacket he had thrown carelessly into the back seat of the car. "I'm rarely ever cold, Princess. I seem to have a furnace burning hot inside me most days."

"I see," she said softly.

"Your chariot awaits," he said as he opened the passenger door for her.

"You're driving?" she asked as her eyes widened. "What about security?"

"I am an excellent driver, so don't worry, and security is following behind us." He gestured to another car some ways away. "One of your men is with us, too."

"My men?"

"One of your Vallerian Royal Protection agents. Alex insisted upon it, not that I minded, of course."

"Didn't you?"

He gave her a curious look. "Why would I mind? Does it make you uncomfortable to have him here?"

"Don't be silly," she said as she sat down in the car.

Finn shook his head again as he shut her door and walked around to the driver's side. He gestured to the security staff that they were ready to leave, and they slipped into their car as well.

"So where are we going?" she asked once he'd sat down.

"Oh, here and there."

"Finn."

With a smile, he decided to elaborate, at least on most of their trip; their final stop would remain vague. It was, after all, one of his special places, and he never took anyone there. Not even Henry knew about his frequent visits.

"Apologies, Princess. It's just so fun to tease you."

"I don't like being teased," she said in a soft voice.

Finn put a hand over hers. She gasped and tried to pull away, but Finn wouldn't let her. "I would never laugh at you or make fun of you, Arianna," he said in an even, clear voice. "I can't resist teasing you, it seems, but I don't mean it as an insult, and I certainly never mean to hurt your feelings. Do you believe that?"

After a moment, she said, "Yes. Yes, I think I do believe it, though I'm not sure why."

Finn let the comment go. He kissed her palm before reluctantly letting go of her hand to start the car and drive off the palace grounds. "There are a lot of places you could see while you're here, but I don't want to overwhelm you."

He thought she mumbled, "You do that already," but wasn't sure.

A safe topic, that's what he needed. "Do you know much about Brazenbourg?"

"Some. There's always some research done before visiting another country, though you'll never know as much about the place as the locals do."

Finn nodded in agreement. "Well, we're a small country, as

you know, with a total size just under one thousand square miles. A lake is centered north of the capital, and I'll take you there last today, no matter where else we go. I'd like for you to see it."

"Then I will."

Finn smiled while he let out an internal sigh of relief; he wasn't sure what he would have done if she had said she wasn't interested. It would have been as good as saying she didn't want his heart, though she likely didn't want that anyway. His heart didn't have much to offer anybody.

"I'll take you around the capital first, which I know is confusingly named the same as the country."

"Is there a reason for that?"

"Lack of imagination, I suppose, on the part of my ancestors. Terrible, but true." She chuckled and the sound seemed to jump across his skin. He cleared his throat.

"Anyway, there are rivers that stream down from Brazenbourg Lake and cut the country into ten districts. Because we're a constitutional monarchy, unlike Valleria which is a more traditional monarchy, each district has a mayor, who reports to Henry, or whoever is the current reigning monarch. When the constitutional monarchy was put in place, it was decided by the people that no one would hold the title of King, so that's why Henry will forever be a Prince."

"Does that bother him?"

"I'm going to tell you the same thing I told Alex; I'll be as honest as I can be when it comes to my brother. In my opinion, he'll never be happy just being a 'Prince', despite the fact that he is the leader of this country."

"I see."

Finn noticed her brows were furrowed, as if she were trying to figure something out.

"What about you? Are you happy being just a 'Prince'?"

Finn struggled with how to respond, but decided the truth was best. "To me, that's just a title. Henry wishes I didn't have it, and I certainly don't need it."

"You don't help Henry with any state business?"

"Our family's not like yours, Princess. We're not like most other royal families."

"Does that mean you don't want to?"

Finn sighed. He forgot how hard it was to stay diplomatic at times. "Look, Henry's not interested in help. It's his way or no way. I'm not like that."

"Do you think Henry's philosophy is the same in all aspects of his life, or just politics?"

Finn gave her a curious look. "I couldn't say."

Arianna nodded, then noticed the passing scenery. "Where's our first stop in the capital?"

Pleased to be back on neutral ground, he said, "We've got a lot of the standard tourist fare: old churches, ruins, monuments, and the like. But I thought you might like to visit some of the places the locals love, perhaps meet some of them."

She clasped her hands together in front of her. "Oh, that's perfect actually. I'd love that."

A ridiculous surge of pride swept through him. "I'm glad." He felt happy for getting something right for once, and wasn't that just ridiculous? The problem was that he had spent too many years listening to Henry tell him he was useless.

A few minutes later, Finn pulled into an empty spot near an incredibly busy pedestrian area, his security finding places nearby as well.

"I can't believe you found a spot so close." Arianna stepped out from the car, Finn holding the door for her.

Finn reached up to scratch the back of his neck. "Well, the locals sort of unofficially keep it open for me."

"Really? That's very nice of them. You and Henry must come out here a lot then."

"They do see the royal family out here from time-to-time, it's truc," Finn said in a half truth. He wasn't sure why he was defending Henry just then, but he was still his brother, after all.

They slowly walked down the street, Finn greeting various shop owners and street vendors by name. He loved this part of the capital; it had seen a great resurgence over the last several years, led by Finn's quiet efforts. Henry would never have approved.

"You certainly seem well known," Arianna said after hearing 'Prince Finn' shouted in greeting yet again.

They turned a corner onto a solely pedestrian street. "I am their Prince."

"It's not just that. It's like you're a friend. That's how they're greeting you."

"They are my friends," he said easily, because it was true. "I don't think of them as citizens I rule over. That's Henry's job. I grew up with these people, and they grew up with me. Brazenbourg is a small country, and we're all a part of the same community. At least, that's how I see things."

"What is this place?" Arianna asked with wonder in her voice. The pedestrian-only cobbled street was filled to the brim at barely eleven in the morning. The thick, rich scents of cooking meats, vegetables, and more filled the air along with smoke from grills and outdoor stoves. While food trucks and stands lined one side of the street, the other was lined with outdoor stalls where merchants sold everything from homemade jewelry to clothing to housewares.

"It's locally called Food Street," he said, unable to hide the pride in his voice. "It's one of my favorite places in the city."

"I can see why. Has it always been here?"

"It was built hundreds of years ago. Many years back, there was a movement to rip it up and turn it into a more modern street, with standard pavement. My father couldn't bear to see it go, though, so he campaigned for it to be saved."

"Well, who would want to destroy it?" Arianna asked as she took a sample of grilled sausage one vendor offered her. "God, this is delicious."

"George is one of the best," Finn said as he slapped a hand on the man's shoulder.

"You're not so bad yourself, Prince Finn," the bear of a man said. "And who's this lovely miss with you?"

"George, this is Princess Arianna of Valleria. She and her brother are visiting us."

"Oh! I beg your pardon, Princess," he said as he dropped into a clumsy bow, which caught the attention of the people nearby.

"Oh, please, there's no need for formality," she said, but it was too late. As a crowd formed around them, Finn wished he could pull her against him and keep her safe in his arms. Since he couldn't in public, security was the next best thing and he gestured for them to come closer. He didn't think anyone would hurt Arianna, but he'd rather be safe than sorry.

Finn could tell Arianna was overwhelmed as his fellow countrymen and women came to greet her. He watched a wide smile grace her face as a little girl gave her a flower, and she kneeled down to speak to her eye-to-eye.

"How long are you here for, Your Highness?" one voice called. "Are you dating our Finn?" asked another.

Finn clapped his hands a few times and calmed the crowd. "Everyone, thank you so much for giving the Princess such a warm welcome. I told her she'd be charmed by Brazenbourg and its people, and I was right."

"Have you charmed her, too, Prince Finn?" a young boy, no more than five years old, asked and everyone laughed. *Out of the mouths of children,* he thought. Arianna was blushing, and he didn't want her to feel embarrassed.

"I am simply showing the Princess our lovely country, and I am being a perfect gentleman," he said as he playfully tweaked the young boy's nose. When everyone chuckled, Finn said, "Okay, so maybe not a perfect gentleman, but pretty close."

George spoke up in defense of Finn. "You don't need to worry, miss, I mean, Princess. Our Finn here's a scamp, but a better man you'll never know. He's always one to lend a hand if you need it." A murmur of agreement swept through the crowd.

"Thank you, all," Arianna said as she affixed the small flower the little girl had given her into her upswept hair. "Prince Finn has been a gentleman, and you are all very kind. I won't forget how lovely and welcoming you have been."

Finn could feel the pride sweep through the crowd. Brazenbourg may be a small country, but pride in their homeland was never determined by the size of the country, only by those who lived within it. After a few more remarks, Finn dispersed the crowd.

"They love you," Arianna said.

"What's not to love?" he said with a broad smile as he slid on some sunglasses.

Arianna laughed. "You know what I mean. Do they feel the same way about Henry?"

Finn's smile faded. "Henry's a different man than I am."

"So, he expects more formality."

Finn gestured for her to keep walking. It wasn't safe to speak of such things in public; Finn knew Henry always had someone tailing him or hiding in the crowd. "Henry expects quite a lot, from everyone," Finn simply said. "Are you hungry?"

"Starving. Who wouldn't be in the midst of all this?"

"Savory or sweet?"

"What?"

"Would you prefer something savory or sweet?"

After a moment, she said, "Why not both?"

Finn threw his head back and laughed. "A woman after my own heart. Let's go. I know just the place."

They walked down the street, which encompassed several blocks. Finn pointed out things she might like, and regaled her with stories about some of the characters behind the food and wares being sold.

"You talk about them as if they're your family," she said when they finally sat down. The entire food side of the street was covered with picnic-style tables and benches for everyone to enjoy.

"They are my family," Finn said as he gestured to one of the owners of a pop-up café on the street. Finn didn't mention that sometimes his fellow citizens felt more like his family than his brother did. "I told you that I love Brazenbourg, and I meant it. This is my home, and I won't give it up without a fight."

Arianna gave him a long look; he knew his last statement sounded odd. What Arianna didn't know, and neither did anyone else, is that Henry would only be too happy to have Finn exiled from the country.

Before Arianna could comment, a woman came out bearing a large tray of food. Arianna's face broke into an easy smile of greeting; she was a natural with people.

"What is all this?" she asked and took a deep breath. "Mmmm. It smells heavenly."

The sound she made reminded him too much of last night, which they had very studiously avoided discussing thus far. "It's a number of local dishes." Finn gestured to the pixie-like woman who had carried the tray. "Linda is from America originally, but she cooks almost as good as my grandmother did."

Linda blushed. "Thank you for the compliment, Prince Finn."

"How long have you lived here?" Arianna asked as she loaded up her plate. To Finn, it was good to see a woman unafraid to eat and, from his first-hand experience, he loved her curves.

"I did a backpacking trip through Europe after college," Linda said. "I ran out of money here in Brazenbourg and planned to stay just long enough to earn my way to the next stop on my trip."

"What happened?" Arianna asked as she lifted a spoonful of a hearty meat and vegetable stew to her lips.

"Oh, I raised the money easily enough, but I had fallen in love with the place. This country, its people, they just felt like home to me. So, I stayed."

"And our stomachs thank you for it." Finn rubbed his stomach and Linda laughed.

Linda winked at Finn. "Still a charmer, aren't you?"

"Well, have I charmed you enough for your world-famous tea and cake?"

"Oh, I think you've charmed me just enough. I'll bring it out when you've finished with your meal."

"Thank you, Linda."

"It's no trouble at all. It's my honor to serve you and the Princess." Linda curtsied to Arianna before walking away.

Arianna blew out a deep breath. "Tea and cake? After all this?"

"You need to keep your strength up," he said as he loaded his own plate to the brim. "We've got a long day ahead of us, and I'm afraid we'll miss afternoon tea at the palace."

"You do afternoon tea in Brazenbourg?"

"Not historically," he said as he tore off a chunk of bread and offered it to her. She nodded her thanks and took it with one graceful hand, immediately dousing it in the stew. When she licked her fingers clean—a very un-Princess-like move—he had the urge to help her. *Focus*, he reminded himself.

"It was our mother," Finn said as he tore off another chunk of bread and dipped it just as Arianna had done. "She was British and brought the custom with her. The people loved her and started the custom to make her feel at home here."

Arianna shifted her stew around without taking a bite, deep in thought. "That was a very sweet thing to do. Are they always so welcoming?"

"Yes, that's Brazenbourg. I think everyone got used to having afternoon tea, so they never stopped it, even after my mother died. She was like me, and often came out to visit people personally. People often served her tea because they knew she liked it."

Linda came out and set another tray on the table, this time filled with a tea service and two large pieces of cake covered in powdered sugar and slivers of almond. "Linda served my mother tea many a time, didn't you?" Finn asked her.

"Oh my, yes. She was a lovely woman."

"She was. Thank you, Linda." Finn shook her hand, slipping her twice as much money as the bill required while he did.

She held onto his hand and tried to give the money back. "None of that, if you please. It's our honor today."

"Please, Linda?" Finn knew her husband was having some health problems and could certainly use the extra money. "Make me look good in front of the Princess," he whispered.

"Oh, all right," she whispered back. "You let me know if you need anything else. It was a pleasure to meet you, Your Highness."

"Oh, the pleasure was all mine. The food was wonderful, and I can already tell that cake will melt in my mouth."

Linda laughed and thanked her for the compliment before turning away.

"I'm going to gain five pounds a day at this rate," Arianna said as she pushed away her now empty plate and reached for the cake.

Finn laughed. "You're gorgeous, Princess. Trust me, a few more curves will only make you sexier in my book."

"Finn," she said in a warning tone.

He held his hands up in surrender. So, it seemed they were still avoiding the subject, at least for now. He poured Arianna some tea and then reached for his own cake.

"This tea's sweet," she said after taking a sip of creamy brew.

Finn nodded. "It's how my mother drank it, and it's the only way you'll usually find it made from a street vendor like Linda. Milk and sugar pre-mixed with the tea, so you only need to pour it into a cup. Linda is actually one of the few who really does make it as my mother liked it."

"Don't get me wrong, it's delicious and goes very well with this almond cake. We've got a version of this in Valleria, only a little bit sweeter."

Finn nodded. "I'm glad you're enjoying it. After we finish up here, we can walk a little further down before we turn back. Are you looking to do any shopping while you're here?"

"I hadn't really thought about it, but it might be good to pick up a few things for my sisters."

"There are nine of you aren't there?"

Arianna nodded as she took a sip of tea. "Nine siblings all together. Five boys, four girls. I'm right in the middle at number five. Of course, with Alex getting married, and Marcello as good as engaged, that means I've got two more sisters."

"What's it like in a family that large? Do you resent having so many siblings?" He wasn't sure why he'd asked such a bold question. He only knew he resented having Henry as an older brother.

Arianna pursed her lips. "No, of course I don't resent it. The community that you feel with your fellow countrymen and women, that's how it is with us; we're our own little community, too." She looked down and started playing with her cake instead of eating it.

"What's wrong, Princess? I'm sorry if I offended you."

"You didn't. It's just that, well, never mind. It doesn't matter."

"It matters to me." He wished he could reach across the table and hold her hand. Unfortunately, too many eyes were watching them.

"I suppose I just feel as though I don't always fit in with them, that's all. But we all love each other very much," she added quickly.

Finn was stunned. He felt as though he never fit in with Henry, who never even really liked him, as far as he could tell.

"It's stupid. Forget I mentioned it."

"I'm sorry, Arianna," he said softly. "It's not stupid at all. I've felt the same way about Henry, and I'm sorry to hear that you have, too."

"It wasn't always like that." She took a long sip of her tea.

"What changed?"

"Everything," she sighed.

The crash of a tray falling nearby reminded him where they were, and he decided to move the day along. If he lingered with the Princess too long, he may very well find himself falling in love with her. He'd already had to resist kissing her and touching her for the last two hours, and they had a long day ahead of them.

# seven

## ARIANNA

A rianna strolled easily beside Finn, who waved and greeted vendors as they passed. Word had spread that a Vallerian princess was with him, and many came up to bow or curtsy as a sign of respect. Arianna noticed that few greeted Finn the same way, but she could see it was not from a lack of respect; Finn seemed to prefer it that way.

From what he had told her, these people were more of a family to him than Henry was. Arianna was sure he was exaggerating. She may feel like she didn't fit in with her siblings, but they were always there for each other. She shook her head, unable to believe that she had actually told Finn her fears about fitting in with her family. What was it about him that seemed to strike something in her? She didn't trust easily, certainly not with her past, but she sensed something in him that she kept hidden in herself.

Sadness.

"Are you ready to head back, Princess?" he asked.

She didn't seem to mind when he called her 'Princess', though she loved the way 'Arianna' slipped from his talented lips as well. "Yes. I just need to use a powder room if there's one available." One of the trickiest parts of being a princess was finding a delicate way to say 'restroom' or 'bathroom'.

His brows furrowed as they approached a public restroom. "Will you be all right without a guard? I didn't think to bring a female one today."

She placed a hand on his warm, toned arm. "I'll be just fine. No need to worry." Finn nodded and she stepped inside.

She was just finishing up in the stall when she heard a pair of female voices giggling near the sinks.

"Prince Finn is so dreamy," one girl tittered.

"I know," the other one sighed. "If only he were looking for a bride."

"What makes you think he'd go for you?"

"Why wouldn't he? I'm gorgeous."

In the stall, Arianna bit her lip to hold back the laughter. She'd only known Finn a short time and, though his reputation said otherwise, she had the feeling that good looks without substance behind them would not hold his interest long-term.

The first girl spoke again. "If you want to be a princess, you should go after Henry."

The other girl scoffed. "Just how would I run into Henry? He never mingles with the crowds like Finn does. Besides, what makes you think Henry's looking for a wife?"

"Well," the first girl said conspiratorially. "A brother of a friend of mine works in the palace. He said that they've heard rumours that Henry needs to marry soon to secure an heir."

"Henry's not as good looking as Finn."

"No, but if you're a princess, you could probably put up with it."

"That's true. And I could be closer to Finn."

"I wouldn't bet on Finn being there."

"What do you mean?"

"Well, I heard that as soon as Henry gets married, Finn is out. Henry doesn't want him around, and he'll stop at nothing to do it."

"You are so dramatic. What makes you think he could get rid of Finn? Everybody loves him."

"That's true. I don't know. The guy I know at the palace said Henry was planning to get rid of him. That's all I heard."

"Well, half of what you hear isn't true anyway. Are you done primping yet? I want to see if Finn's still outside."

"Yes, come on, let's go."

Arianna waited until their chattering voices had faded away before she opened the stall door. As she washed her hands, she wondered. Was the gossip she'd just heard true? And, if it was, what should she do about it?

She was lost in thought when she stepped outside.

"Everything all right, Arianna?" he asked, his face a study in concern.

"Oh, yes. Just fine. Sorry if I took too long."

"One thing my mother taught me was to never rush a woman. No, I was just worried that maybe some of the food disagreed with you."

"Oh, no. Nothing like that." As she glanced around, she noticed a few of the vendors with concerned faces of their own. She put a bright smile on her face, to reassure them as well as Finn. "I'm perfectly fine."

Deciding again to shuffle propriety aside for the moment—something she only seemed to do with him, she realized—she wound her arm through his for the walk back to the car. He felt warm and solid next to her, like an anchor she could hold on to and have total faith that she would never drift away.

They remained in companionable silence for most of the walk, except for the few instances where Arianna stopped to purchase something or other. A pair of earrings here, a scarf there. She saw a beautiful vase and immediately thought of Nonna, her grandmother, and picked it up. Christmas would, after all, be here before she knew it.

Every time she made a purchase, one of the security agents took the bags and she linked arms with Finn again. She knew she shouldn't, especially if she were even considering things with Henry. She sensed one man was her past and the other her future; was she making the right choice?

"Where are we going next?" she asked as she cuddled in the car; she hadn't realized just how warm Finn's body had been keeping her.

"We'll leave the capital now and see some of the countryside." He pulled out, security following in a car close behind. "There are a few places farther north I'd like to take you."

Arianna flicked on her seat warmer and rubbed her arms against the chill. Glancing at Finn, whose sleeves were rolled up to his elbows and whose jacket was still in the backseat, she said, "I can't believe you aren't cold yet."

Finn chuckled. "I seemed to have been born with a fire in me. While others get cold, I never seem to. We Brazenbourgians are used to it. Doesn't it get cold in Valleria?"

"Of course it does. It's only October, though, so the chill hasn't really set in yet."

"Tell me about Valleria. What do you love most about it?"

"Tell me what you love about Brazenbourg first," she said, deflecting the question. She loved her homeland, but she wanted to know more about Finn. She also wanted to gauge how Finn would react if she told him what the gossiping girls had said in the restroom.

A genuine smile of adoration swept across his face. "There are few things I *don't* love about Brazenbourg. I love the people, the places, the food, as you just saw. I love the mountains and flatlands and farmlands. I love the lake and the rivers streaming from it, pumping life and livelihood into our districts."

"Sounds like true love."

"It is. My parents loved these lands." His hand swept through the air, gesturing to the fields outside. "Even my English mother.

She loved my father, but she could have easily resented having to move to a new country to make their home here. She didn't. She fell in love with this place, these people, and I suppose that trickled down to me. Nothing's perfect in this world, not even our little country. I'm under no illusions about that. However, that doesn't mean I won't live for Brazenbourg, and die for it, if it comes to that."

She could see Brazenbourg through his eyes. The love, the duty, the respect he had for it, and the truth of it all; that was what a true leader had. Hadn't she seen the same thing in her father growing up, and now Alex? Considering her experience thus far, she could see why Brazenbourg was so easy to love.

"If you had to leave Brazenbourg, where would you go?" she asked.

He considered for a moment before answering. "I don't know. If I had to leave, perhaps I would go to England. My mother's family is still there, and I keep in touch with them." He shrugged. "It doesn't really matter in the end, though, does it? My heart will always be here."

Further conversation was cut short by their arrival at some ruins. Finn showed her around, telling her about the history behind the broken walls of stone. He held her hand through most of it, guiding her over fallen walls and through overgrown brush. She had to admit, she didn't mind the simple gesture.

She was more afraid that she liked it a little too much.

The rest of their day went similarly, Finn either stopping at various historic sites or pointing them out on their drive. The sky had turned a gloomy gray as the day had progressed, so when she checked the time hours later, she was surprised.

"Should we head back soon? I don't want us to be late for dinner."

"Just one more stop, Princess, then we'll go back."

"The lake?" she asked as the large body of water came into view in the distance.

"Yes. It's one of my favorite spots. I'd like to share it with you," he said softly, eyes straight ahead.

"I'd like that," she said with a shy smile. "Why is it so special to you?"

"I'll tell you when we get there."

A few minutes later, they followed a curve in the road and the lake came fully into view. She gasped. "It's beautiful."

"I know." He pulled the car into an unofficial parking lot on the side of the road. The gravel crunched underneath her boots as she stepped out of the car without waiting for Finn to open it for her. Finn met her at the front of the car and took her hand in his.

The water was a crisp, clear blue, and seemed to stretch towards the horizon. Nearby, there was a very small, white church with a dark red roof. The remains of a fading, white fence line dotted the landscape in various places, and a makeshift gravel path led through it to the church.

"What is this place?"

"The White Church at Brazenbourg Lake." When she looked at him with questioning eyes, he just laughed. "I know. I know. We're terrible at naming things. I'm sure the church had another name long ago, but it's been lost now."

He tugged her hand and they walked along the path. The brisk breeze off the lake was sharp and cool, and Arianna shuddered as it swept over her. Finn simply let go of her hand to pull her tight against him, the heat of his body warming her up quickly, in more ways than one.

"My parents were married here," he said as a bird called out in the distance.

"Really? A royal wedding? Here?"

"That wedding was just for them and their parents. It's actually a not-so-secret tradition."

"What do you mean?"

"All of the royals have been married here first. Someone long ago wanted a simple ceremony, with just friends and family, so they came here. As you see, it's very much out of the way. These lands are actually now owned by the royal family, so it's technically trespassing if you come here, not that we usually mind visitors."

"Not on your wedding day, though."

"No, definitely not on your wedding day. Anyway, my ancestor was married here first, then they had a more formal ceremony at the palace. Since then, it's always been done that way."

"And the people don't mind? They don't try to crash the party?"

Finn shook his head. "Tradition is important. My people wouldn't do that, though the foreign press have been known to attempt sneaking in. I'm not sure how we'd handle it in today's age with all the long-range cameras and the like; they didn't have to worry about it at the last wedding when my parents were married."

Finn used a key he had with him to unlock the church door and open it for her. As she stepped inside, she felt as though she stepped into another, simpler world.

The scent of dark, rich wood aged by the sun mixed with the scent of the lake nearby. Though it was small—only four windows and four rows of pews on each side—it was lovely. A simple stage was set up at one end, and there was a small set of stairs near the door leading up one level to the church bell. There were a few doors leading away to smaller chambers, but it didn't seem to be lacking in anything. She could easily see a young bride wanting to be married here in the cool and quiet. She could almost see herself there, too.

"It's charming." She turned in a circle and watched the light play through the windows. "Completely charming and romantic. I can see why it's a favored spot for a wedding." She turned to Finn, who had taken a seat in one of the pews. His face looked stricken. "What is it?" she asked as she rushed the few steps to him. "What's wrong?"

Finn shook his head, and his face seemed to clear. "Nothing. Sorry. Nothing's wrong."

"Are you sure?" she asked and he nodded. "Well, can you tell me why this place is so special to you, besides the obvious?"

"I come here to think sometimes."

"Oh? Well, everybody has a place like that."

Finn nodded. "We royals need to have a place like that, don't we? This has been mine since as long as I can remember. My father or mother would come here, too."

"Henry?"

"No, he never came. He's been here, of course, but this place doesn't mean as much to him as it does to me."

"Because of your parents? I'm sure you must feel close to them here." She felt close to them, and she'd never even met them before.

"Yes, that's part of it. Soon after the car accident that took their lives, I came here. I had my own funeral for them here even while they laid in state at the palace."

"I'm sorry," she said as she took a seat in the pew next to him. "I can't imagine losing my parents, and so young."

Finn took her hand and she let him; she sensed he needed the comfort. "It's barely been ten years now. I'll never forget it."

Who could? "Would you like to talk about it?"

Finn shrugged. "There's not much to say. Drunk driver drove through a crowd. He killed several citizens before he rammed our convertible."

"What do you mean? Were you in the car with them?"

He nodded. "Henry and I both were. My parents and Henry were thrown from the car, I was thrown across the seat. Henry had injuries but he managed to survive."

She squeezed his hand. "I'm sorry, Finn. I imagine that no matter how many years go by, you'll still miss them. There's no shame in that."

"No, there isn't." He lifted their joined hands to his lips for a kiss. "Thank you, Arianna." He kissed her hand again.

Tingles of warmth spread from her hand and coursed through her body. Without breaking eye contact, he pressed a kiss to the inside of her wrist. Could he tell her heart was beating faster because of him?

He stood and tugged her up with him. He wrapped his long arms around her and brought her close. His musky scent, undimmed by the crisp lake air, filled her senses.

"I need to kiss you, Princess." Needed, not wanted. Was there a difference right now? She shook her head, unsure of what to do.

"Please, Arianna," he said, bringing her closer. She gasped as his arousal pressed against her and she fisted her hands in his shirt. "Please let me kiss you."

He sounded almost desperate, and so was she. In a haze of increasing lust, she breathed out, "Yes."

He moaned and his lips fell to hers, a swift clash of needs ensuing. His tongue demanded entrance, and her mouth—which remembered only too well how talented a tongue it was—opened without hesitation. As their tongues explored, her hands shifted to his back and roamed lower to his ass. God, he had a fantastic ass. When she squeezed it, his foot slipped and he stumbled.

Instead of falling, however, he used the momentum to move them, and soon she found her back pressed against a wall.

"Finn," she whispered on a gasping breath.

"Yes, Princess?" His hands delved underneath her layers of clothes. Her jacket was easily pushed aside, and one hand moved into her hair while the other undid her jeans.

"Finn." She pulled at his shirt so tightly that two buttons popped off. She gasped when she saw what she'd done and time seemed to stop. Though Finn didn't seem to mind—his look was one of amusement—she pushed away from him.

God, how could she be so stupid? She was falling for the wrong man again. Physical chemistry wasn't enough for her, not anymore. She ran a frustrated hand through her hair, which now hung loose, thanks to Finn. The flower the little girl had given her that morning had fallen to the floor.

"What's the matter, Arianna?" he asked behind her. "Did I hurt you?"

She zipped up her jeans and turned to face him. "No, of course you didn't," she said, upset but not at him.

"Then what is it?" he asked as he took a step towards her. He didn't try to touch her again, and while her head was happy with that, her heart wasn't. Why couldn't they get on the same page?

"We shouldn't be doing this, anything like this."

"Why? Is there someone else?"

She didn't respond right away. How should she tell him?

"There is, isn't there?" he said resigned, and ran a hand over his face. "Someone back in Valleria?"

She shook her head. "Do you know why Alex and I are really here in Brazenbourg?"

"What? No, not really. Henry doesn't involve me in those types of discussions. What has that got to do with you?"

"I'm not sure how to tell you."

"Just give it to me straight."

"It's Henry."

"Henry? What about Henry?" Realization dawned on his face. "The other man is Henry?" She nodded. "Jesus. How long have you been seeing him? He's kept it very quiet. So have you."

"It's not like that," she said shaking her head. She sighed and sat down in a pew. "Henry wants to marry me."

"What? What the hell are you talking about?"

"He told Alex he wants to marry me. He won't help us, that is, Valleria, unless I do. Or maybe he won't think about helping us until I do."

"And you're marrying him?" he asked, his body stiff with tension.

"I don't know."

"That means you're thinking about it." He ran an impatient hand through his hair. "Then why didn't you stop me today? Or even last night? I wouldn't have—"

"I know," she said, interrupting him. "I wanted it, Finn. I wanted you."

He sucked in a breath, then let it out slowly. "But you don't want me anymore. You want Henry."

"I don't know about Henry, but I do know that I still want you. I can't seem to help it," she ended quietly, the admission surprising even herself.

"Arianna," Finn said gruffly as he sat down next to her. He tilted her chin up to face him. "I'd never push you to do anything you didn't want to do."

"I know. I'm just afraid that I'll end up pushing myself instead."

His hand fell away. "And regretting it? Do you regret what we did last night?"

Her lips quirked in a half smile. "As I recall, you didn't do much of anything last night. You only kissed me, after all."

He returned her smile. "You have no idea, do you?" he said in a husky voice. "You have no idea just how fucking sexy you looked last night."

"You shouldn't say things like that in a church."

Finn huffed a laugh. "People have done worse here. One of the rooms over there actually had a bed so the bride and groom could consummate their marriage before they headed to the palace for the formal wedding."

Arianna's eyes widened. "Well, still though." She cleared her throat. "Besides, I think it's you who doesn't know how sexy he looked last night."

"Is that right?"

She nodded. "I was practically naked and you were dressed in that lovely suit, ordering me around."

"You liked that, didn't you? When I told you what to do?"

"I didn't think I would, but I didn't feel like I was losing control. I felt powerful." She hadn't felt like that in a long time.

"Good," he said as he brushed her hair back behind her ear. "You are powerful. Even last night, you were telling me what to do." He dropped a kiss just behind her ear. "And it was fucking amazing," he whispered.

"Finn."

He sighed and pulled away. "Sorry, Princess. Let's get out of hcrc. All I can think about right now is being with you, and that's not an option, so let's go."

She put a hand on his arm to keep him from standing up. "Why isn't it an option?"

"You just told me you might marry Henry."

"*Might* being the key word there."

"But you're still considering it. I haven't been able to stop thinking about you since we met. It's not a good idea for us to be together."

She understood how he felt; didn't she feel the same way? But she also liked the way Finn touched her—like she mattered. She hadn't felt that for a very long time. "I know what you're saying, Finn, but Henry and I haven't even spent any time alone together. I've barely spoken to him beyond the meals we've shared with you and Alex."

"Arianna," he said, and she could sense his resolve wavering.

She cupped his face. "Kiss me again, Finn. Kiss me like you mean it."

"I always mean it with you. But I can't. We can't."

She straddled him. "It's my choice. These are my lips and I want them to touch yours again." She rested her forehead against his. "Please?"

After a few moments, he groaned. "God help me," he said and crushed his lips to hers.

Unlike last time, this was a hard crash of their mouths against each other. Both of them taking and taking more, then giving back to the other. Her hands buried themselves in his dark brown hair while his hands gripped her ass and brought her against his erection.

Moans filled the small space and her hands shifted to find skin. She slipped her hands through the portion of his shirt she'd ripped open and sighed at the feel of his chest hair covering a toned, masculine chest. His hands slipped underneath her jeans, cupping her ass and sliding his finger through the cleft to find her wet in the front.

Her lips broke free on a cry and she arched her back. "Do you like that, Princess? Do you like it when I touch you?"

"Yes. God, yes." She shifted against his probing fingers and groaned in frustration when he pulled his hand away. "Why did you do that?"

"This isn't the time or the place, Princess," he said and coated her lips with the moisture on his fingers. "Open," he ordered and she took the fingers into her mouth, sucking her juices clean from his talented digits.

He pulled his fingers out and she licked her lips, too. He groaned and pulled her in for another deep kiss.

"I'm sorry," he said when they broke away.

"What for?"

"I shouldn't have let it get that far."

"I wasn't complaining, Finn. We were both at fault, if you want to look at it that way, but I don't."

"But you might marry someone else."

"Listen. Somebody has asked my brother a question meant for me. That somebody has not spoken to me directly about it, or even asked me that question. Until they do, I don't think we're doing anything wrong."

He rested his forehead against hers. "Who are you trying to convince?"

"Both of us, I imagine."

Finn sighed. "I want you. I've never wanted anybody like this before."

Her brows shot up. "Really? But you have, well, quite the reputation."

"It's mostly just gossip, and you can't trust much of that."

Arianna briefly wondered about the things she had overheard earlier that day, and decided to dismiss them. If there was one thing she knew as a royal, it was that you couldn't trust everything you heard.

"So none of it is true then?"

"I'm not saying I was celibate or anything. I have a past, but I'm not that person anymore. Rumours of my prowess have been greatly exaggerated."

She chuckled. "From what I've seen, perhaps the quantity was exaggerated but the quality seems to be on point."

He smiled. "Glad it's to your liking."

They spent the next few minutes just wrapped in each other's arms in the quiet room, listening to the sounds of the lake crashing gently against the shore outside. Eventually, Finn sighed again. "We should get going if we're going to make it to dinner on time."

Arianna's gut clenched. "Dinner. Right." She stood and Finn followed, both of them arranging their clothes as they did. Arianna fixed her hair and picked up the fallen flower on her way out.

After locking up, Finn pulled her against him for the walk back to the car. Their security agents, who had been stationed outside, also prepared to leave. Arianna blushed as she wondered if they had seen or heard anything. Since Finn didn't seem too worried, she decided not to be, either.

She had enough to worry about with dinner that night.

### FINN

FINN WAS LOST IN HIS OWN THOUGHTS ALL THE WAY BACK TO the palace, and so, it seemed, was Arianna. He'd been honest with her about his past and what he felt. Hell, when he'd seen her in the church, a smile on her face as she took it all in, it had been only too easy to imagine her as his bride, and it had thrown him for a loop. However, in the end, what he felt may not even matter.

Now there was the possibility that Henry was the groom in that vision, not him.

He couldn't believe Arianna was thinking seriously about the proposal. If she was only marrying Henry to help Valleria, perhaps there was something he could do. But, if she was marrying Henry for some other reason, and he sensed she was, then he may have to let her go. He wasn't sure he would be able to, if that time came.

The way she fell apart at his touch, the way she smelled, the way she moved, the way she seemed interested in what he had to say—he felt needed and wanted by a woman for the first time in his life. He'd been with women, sure, but they had wanted to be with a prince.

She was the first who seemed to want to be with him.

He dragged his hand through his hair as the capital came into view. A few minutes later, he was working his way through the various palace security gates. A few minutes more, and they stopped in front of an entrance.

Arianna waited for him to open the door this time, and gave him a long look and a soft smile when she stepped out. "Thank you for the lovely day."

"You're very welcome, Arianna. Believe me, the pleasure was all mine." Finn kept the car door between them; it was the safest thing to do. Otherwise he'd be tempted to kiss her hard and there were too many eyes watching them now.

"It's about time you two made it back," Alex said as he walked casually towards them. He gave Arianna a pointed look. "Dinner is in an hour."

"So it is," Arianna said smoothly. All signs of the passionate woman who had been in his arms earlier had disappeared, and the polished princess was now in her place. "Walk me to my room, Alex?"

"Of course. How did you enjoy sightseeing?"

A bright smile lit her face. "Oh, it was wonderful. Brazenbourg is a beautiful country."

"I'm glad to hear you enjoyed yourself. I'm only sorry I couldn't join you." Before Alex and Arianna walked away, Alex turned to Finn and said, "Your brother would like a word with you, Finn."

"I'll go straight there. Thank you for telling me."

Alex nodded. "See you at dinner." As Alex and Arianna

disappeared into the palace, Finn finally shut the car door and took a deep breath as he walked inside. How was he going to make it through dinner? And what the hell did his brother want?

A few minutes later, Finn found himself at Henry's office door. After a brisk knock, he entered without waiting for Henry to respond. As Finn usually did, he strolled over to take a guest chair and propped his feet on Henry's desk. Henry, who was standing near the window, scowled.

"Did I say you could come into my office?" Henry snapped.

"Alex said you wanted to see me. Since you so rarely request my presence, I figured it was an emergency."

Henry narrowed his eyes but didn't say anything. Instead, he took his seat across from Finn and cleared his throat. "Valleria and I are in some delicate negotiations."

"About?" Though Finn already knew.

"That is none of your business."

"You made it my business by calling me in here. Spit it out."

"Don't you have any respect for my position?"

"I have a great deal of respect for your position, brother dear." *Just none for you,* he didn't add.

Henry shook his head. "I'm going to marry Arianna."

"So you've already asked her? Funny, she didn't mention she had agreed to marry my brother on our trip today." That much was true.

Henry faltered slightly. "I haven't formally asked her yet, but I've spoken to Alex about it. We're negotiating it."

"So, does she have any say in who she marries? Or did you both just decide for her?"

"See? This is why you're not engaged in matters of the state or politics. You don't understand any of the nuances involved."

Finn understood this 'nuance' all too well. "That's where you're wrong. So, what does Valleria get out of this deal?"

"Information."

"About?"

"That, too, is none of your business."

"And that, too, is where you're wrong. You may as well tell me the facts now, so I can spin it for reporters."

"What reporters?"

"They're always around, especially when I'm out meeting with the citizens."

Henry harrumphed. "You'll do anything for attention, won't you?"

Finn merely smiled. It wouldn't make any difference if he tried to correct Henry.

"Fine. We have information that Valleria wants."

"So? Why don't you just tell them what they want? Why do you have to make everything so goddamn difficult?" If only he'd tell them, Arianna wouldn't even have to consider this ridiculous proposal.

"Watch your language. I hope you weren't speaking to Arianna like that today."

Finn just shook his head, not wanting the conversation to get off track. "Why won't you just give them the information?"

"Because it's time I found a wife anyway. She's already a princess and understands the duties that would be required of her."

Arianna was complicated, frustrating, and fucking sexy, but a duty she was not. At least, not to him. In that moment, Finn knew that to Henry, Arianna would never be anything more than a duty. A burden. A means to an end. She deserved more than that, more than Henry. She even deserved more than Finn.

"Is that how you talk about the woman you want to marry? Mother would have slapped you for that."

"Well, she's not here, is she?" he said with a sneer. "And let's be thankful for that."

"Henry, what the fuck? Are you glad our parents are dead?"

"Don't be ridiculous. Who would be happy over that? I'm merely saying that our mother had a way of planning events that I disagree with, and I'm glad I don't have to fight with her while planning my wedding."

Finn wasn't entirely convinced of Henry's answer. "I'd rather have annoying and alive than dead, but then I miss my parents. Anyway, you just told me Arianna hasn't even agreed to this. Why are you planning the wedding already?"

"It's a foregone conclusion, as far as I'm concerned. The information I have is incredibly valuable to Valleria. They will trade it for Arianna."

"She's a human being, not a commodity."

"She's a princess, which makes her as good as a commodity. What else would she be useful for, but for this?"

"You asshole," Finn said as he stood. "She's smart, talented, and, yes, beautiful. Our people loved her today. She can rule Brazenbourg with you."

Henry stood, his eyes blazing across the wide desk at Finn. "No one rules this country but me. Not you, not her, no one. It's mine."

After a long, charged moment, Henry broke eye contact and spoke first. "I'm having dinner with Arianna tonight. Hopefully, by the end of the evening, she'll be convinced."

"I can't believe that Alex would approve of this, or her father."

Henry scowled. "They don't at the moment. If all goes well tonight, then I'm to meet their father, King Gabriel. Alex said there will be no wedding unless he approves."

"King Gabriel's known to be a fair man." Hopefully a savvy one, too, for Arianna's sake.

"Yes, well. I couldn't care less for the man. Arianna is just what I need to follow through on my plans. Believe me, no one, not even her father, will stop me."

"What the hell are you planning? And Arianna is a 'who' not a 'what'. You can't treat her like a possession. I spent the day with her. Believe me when I tell you that she deserves better than that sort of treatment."

"What did you do?"

"What do you mean?"

"Clearly, you must have said or done something to come to this conclusion."

"I said nothing of the kind. I spoke to her like a human being and asked her questions. Do the same at dinner tonight, and you'll come to the same conclusion."

"Perhaps," Henry said. "But you are to go along with whatever happens."

Finn cocked an eyebrow. "So you need my help, is that it? I never thought I'd see the day."

"Neither did I," Henry mumbled.

"You want my help, you need to give me more. What information does Valleria want?"

"It's irrelevant."

"Clearly not. It's the purpose behind this entire scheme."

"If I say it's irrelevant, then it's irrelevant, and that's final," Henry said loudly and banged his fist on the desk.

Finn shook his head. He knew from experience that Henry would not give into anything in this state. Finn would just have to pry the information from Alex.

"Are we clear?" Henry asked.

"Crystal," Finn said, then turned and walked out. It was time to get ready for dinner.

# eight

**ARIANNA**

Arianna was giving herself one final look in the mirror when the clock in the room chimed. She had not been on a date for a very long time and had debated what to wear for ages before selecting something. Should she wear a more formal floor-length gown? A sexier knee-length cocktail dress? She was only considering the latter, she had to admit, because she wanted Finn to see her in it.

Since Finn wouldn't be at her dinner with Henry, she decided to go with the long, oyster gray silk dress. The halter neck-style dress draped elegantly on her body, and the neck, which formed a circular band, was encrusted with sparkling costume diamonds that glimmered in the dim light of the room. A pair of long, real diamond earrings and bracelet were paired to match and add to the sparkle. A silk sash was tied in a graceful knot around her waist, and her back was bare. The sash accentuated her wide hips, but she recalled that Finn didn't seem to mind her curves; perhaps his brother wouldn't either.

She sighed and shook her head. She shouldn't think of Finn, not tonight. Oh, what had she done? She was falling for Finn and it just wouldn't do. Finn was just like the last man she'd fallen for: dangerous, sexy, and charming. That was the kind of man who would betray and hurt a woman. She just couldn't go through that again.

She took a few deep breaths and centered herself and her thoughts. She would go to dinner, and then she'd think about what to do next.

She grabbed a small matching purse, also embellished with costume diamonds, and left her room. One of the guards escorted her down to dinner and she gave a brief glance at Alex's room as she passed; he would be having dinner with Finn while she dined with Henry.

The dining room she was escorted to was different from the ones she had seen so far. It was much smaller, much more intimate. A fire was lit, sending heat and light dancing through the room. A table for two had been arranged, complete with candlelight.

"You look beautiful, Arianna," Henry said from the shadows before stepping forward. "Stunning."

"Thank you," she said with a small smile. "You look quite handsome yourself." He did, she had to admit. Henry didn't have Finn's raw sexuality, but he looked dashing in an expensive black suit with his hair slicked back and his mustache trimmed slightly.

"You are too kind," he said and helped her to sit. After she had arranged herself and her dress, he spoke again. "Some wine?"

"Please," she said and accepted the glass a waiting servant poured.

"Do you mind if I get straight to the point?"

Arianna blinked, surprised at his desire to skip small talk before easing into such a difficult conversation. "No, please go ahead."

"I assume your brother has told you about my proposal?"

Arianna flicked a gaze to the waiter, whose face remained impassive. Perhaps the waiter already knew? Or perhaps he was just used to strange situations in the palace?

"Don't worry about the staff," Henry said easily. "They're paid to hold their tongue, else I cut it off for them." Henry laughed at that, and Arianna chuckled awkwardly in return. She couldn't tell if he was serious or not, but surely he wasn't. "Have you considered my proposal?"

"Yes, though I must admit I was surprised by it. We've barely met and you've decided you want to marry me."

"You'll want for nothing as my wife, Arianna. You can see that while we may be a small country, we are not a poor one. I have business interests aside from my role as ruler of Brazenbourg that do very well for me personally."

"You've just told me you can provide financial security, but you haven't mentioned anything about yourself. I'd like to learn more about you."

Henry gave Arianna a long look before answering. "Are you a romantic, then? I must admit that I didn't anticipate that after meeting you. You seemed to be as practical-minded as myself. I thought you would be happy to serve your country in this way."

Practical. Yes, she was proper, practical Arianna, at least to the outside world. She wasn't practical with Finn, though was she? *Stop thinking about him*, she reminded herself.

"I am always honored to serve my country," Arianna said evenly, belying the turmoil within. "I was born into a royal family, same as you. I understand the responsibilities that come with the role of a princess."

"Excellent. Things are different here in Brazenbourg, of course, than what you may be used to in Valleria. I want an easy marriage and a non-political wife at my side. I won't have my wife involved in state affairs, and that's final."

Arianna wasn't sure if he was just clueless or hoping for things beyond the achievable. She wasn't sure an 'easy' marriage existed. Her own parents, who were deeply in love with each other, certainly had not had what could be termed an 'easy' marriage. "Those seem to be very clear cut terms, Henry," she said, and wondered why even his name felt wrong on her tongue. "Are you stating those terms unequivocally? Do you not believe in negotiation or compromise?"

"Of course I do," he said casually. "Who wouldn't? Tell me, Arianna: what is that you want from a marriage?"

Love was the first word that came to her mind, but she dismissed it. Love could come with time, she hoped. "Children, of course. If I did agree to this, though I would call Brazenbourg my home, I couldn't dismiss my family or Valleria. I would still see my family and visit them."

His mouth flattened into a thin line. "That seems a natural request."

"As to politics, I've never been fully involved in Valleria's unless needed, though I would not be content to simply stay in the palace. I would use my position to help people, if I could."

"Anything else?"

She felt like she was on the end of a business deal. She needed a personal connection with him. Changing the subject slightly, she said, "Finn told me a great deal about Brazenbourg and its history as we toured today. He also told me a great deal about your parents."

"Did he?" Henry murmured. "And what exactly did he say?"

"Only that they were beloved by the people, and that losing them was very difficult. I'm sorry for your loss."

"Thank you," Henry said and reached across the small table to take her hand. His soft hand had a slight chill to it, as though it could never be fully warm. "That's very kind of you to say. It is very difficult to lose one's parents, and then also take over running the country at the same time."

Arianna squeezed his hand. "I'm sure."

"Finn's lucky he didn't have that burden as well. I only pray you do not have to live through such an ordeal."

"I do, too. Logically, I know that I may outlive my parents, but the thought of losing them is unbearable."

"You're practical, as I said." He lifted her hand to his thin lips for a kiss. His lips were cold, too. "I think we'll make a perfect fit."

Henry let go of her hand as the appetizers were served. Throughout the meal, conversation was kept to general topics. She felt as though Henry were interviewing her, determining how she felt about certain things. In a way, she was doing the same with him.

After dessert was finished, Henry dismissed the servants. He turned on some soft music from a hidden console and walked back to her.

"May I have this dance, my lady?" he asked, holding out a hand to her.

"Yes, of course," she said, charmed unexpectedly. She stood, placing one hand in his while gathering her dress with the other.

He brought her into his arms, keeping one hand on the small of her back, brushing against her bare skin. She thought of Finn again, remembering how his hand had grazed her back before he had zipped up her dress.

"Are all your dresses like this?" he asked.

"What do you mean?"

"Are they all this revealing?"

Arianna's eyes widened in surprise. If he thought this was revealing, she was glad she had not worn the shorter dress she'd been considering. "This isn't that revealing."

"With your hair up, your entire back is bared for anyone to see," he said and skimmed his fingers along her spine. She felt warm where he touched her, but it wasn't the spark she felt with Finn.

"Does that bother you? This is fairly demure for a modern royal gown."

"If we marry, I'd prefer you wear revealing clothing only for me," he whispered.

"I thought that's what I was doing tonight."

"There were servants," he said against her ear after he pulled her flush against him.

"There are always servants," she replied against his ear. His scent was stronger than Finn's, and had an edge to it she didn't care for. It certainly wasn't as addictive to her as Finn's scent was. *Stop thinking about him*, she reminded herself again.

They shifted softly against the sway of the music, Arianna's jewelry catching the light and sending color dancing on the walls from time to time. It was comfortable in his arms. Not exciting or new, but it wasn't awful, either.

He pulled back slightly and his eyes dipped to her lips. She knew it was coming and prepared herself. His thin lips were weak against her plump ones. He wasn't demanding, at least not yet. She realized that with Henry, there may be heat, but no passion. Could she live with that? It wasn't the most terrible thing in the world.

When he pulled back, his black eyes glittered in the firelight. "Well, that was very nice, wasn't it?" he asked as he ran a hand over his lips, removing any lipstick she may have transferred.

"It was nice."

"I think it could be more," he said as he pulled her close again. "I think we can be more. I could make you happy, Arianna, if only you'll let me try."

"I just don't know," she said honestly and felt his hold tense around her. "I need more time. I can't make this decision in a day, and there are my father and brother to consider."

Henry let out a sigh of exasperation and stepped back. "Are they more important than your feelings? Are they to be there on our wedding night, too?"

"Henry," she warned.

"I'm sorry, I'm sorry," he said as he held a hand up. "I didn't mean to get upset. I only wish we could move things along. This is right, Arianna, and you know it, too, if you're honest with yourself."

"I need time, both with myself and family as well as with you. Perhaps we could spend some time together tomorrow, if your schedule permits it."

"Of course it does," Henry said with a smile and walked over to take her hands. "I'll always make time for you."

"Then let's discuss it over breakfast tomorrow."

"We could discuss it in my room tonight."

Arianna unconsciously stepped back and saw Henry's eyes narrow and darken. "I don't think I'm ready for that."

"Of course. A lady such as yourself would wait until her wedding night. Even better."

"Henry," she started, about to let him know that she was no virgin.

"Say no more about it," Henry said, cutting her off. "Let me walk you back to your room then."

"All right."

As they walked back, Henry pointed out various things about the palace. She noted that while Finn had mentioned similar things with affection, Henry mentioned them with little affection at all. He could be charming when he chose to be, and she was not sure which side of him was the true one. Perhaps both were.

When they reached her door, he said, "Tomorrow I'll show you around the palace. If it's to be your home, you should become comfortable here."

Did the man never listen? "I haven't agreed to anything yet, Henry."

"I know, but once you've thought about it, you'll see it's the best thing for everyone."

The best for Valleria, maybe, but she wasn't convinced it was the best for her. "Perhaps."

He leaned in to kiss her and again she felt heat but no spark. When he pulled back, he gave her a smile and wished her good night.

She entered her room and let out a sigh as she locked it, glad the evening was over. She knew she wouldn't sleep just yet—there was too much on her mind—so she decided to run a bath. As she made her way through the bedroom, however, she let out a gasp of surprise.

She wasn't alone.

～

## *FINN*

WHEN FINN MADE IT TO THE SITTING ROOM, WHERE HE WAS TO meet Alex before dinner, it was to find Alex already nursing a glass of wine.

"I'm sorry if I kept you waiting, Alex," Finn said as he went to fix himself a glass of something stronger than wine; he needed something to take the edge off his thoughts, which were currently consumed with Arianna.

"You didn't keep me waiting. I came down early," Alex said from his perch on a chair by the fire.

"Oh?" Finn said as he took a seat across from him, unbuttoning his suit jacket as he did so. "Checking on your sister?"

Alex quirked an eyebrow. "Something like that. You know she's having dinner with Henry?"

Finn nodded. "She mentioned it to me earlier."

"And what do you think about the pair of them?"

Finn swirled the amber liquid of his scotch around, watching as it played against the light of the fire and the crystal of the glass and ice. "May I speak plainly, Alex?"

"Please do."

Finn dismissed the servants in the room, who also closed the door behind them when they left.

"You must have some fervent opinions to dismiss your staff before speaking in front of them. Don't you trust them?"

"No," he said simply and watched surprise flicker on Alex's face. "They're Henry's servants, not mine."

"I see."

"Tell me, Alex. What information are you willing to trade your sister for?"

Alex stood, fury flashing on his face. "How dare you ask me that!"

"How dare *you* bargain with your sister's happiness!" Finn stood as well, meeting him face-to-face.

"I would never do that. I've been trying to talk her out of this."

Finn staggered back, the fuse of anger dying quickly. "What? You don't want this marriage?"

"I want my sister to be happy. She deserves it. She hasn't had the easiest life, and she thinks she's got to sacrifice herself to prove something."

Finn had come here to confront Alex, but perhaps now they could be allies instead. "Sit down. Please," Finn added.

Alex sat back down a moment later and Finn followed. "I apologize. I thought you were the impetus behind all this. Arianna deserves better than a marriage of convenience."

"How do you know what my sister deserves?"

"I spent the day with her. That's not a lifetime, I know, but she's a remarkable woman. Anyone like that deserves the best." *Which didn't include him.*

"At least on that, we agree."

"My brother has been tight-lipped, always is with me. He only told me about his proposal this afternoon after Arianna and I returned. Tell me what information you need. Perhaps we can find another way to help you and Valleria, without a wedding needing to take place."

Alex drank another sip of wine, giving himself more time before answering. "It's an interesting idea. However, you told me yourself that you aren't involved in state business. How could you possibly have the information I need?"

"I probably don't," Finn answered honestly. "But what I do have are connections. I'll do whatever I can in my power to help you and your sister."

"And go against the wishes of your brother and your own country?"

"I would never go against or sell out my country," Finn said with a fervency that couldn't be denied. "But what Henry wants isn't right. Arianna wouldn't be a wife to him, she'd be no more than a piece of furniture."

"That's a very harsh statement to make."

"It's harder still to make it when speaking of one's own brother."

They remained silent for a minute, while each thought through what to do next.

Alex spoke first. "You like my sister, don't you?"

"Of course. She's a wonderful woman. I can't imagine anyone not liking her."

"Are you also in love with her?"

Finn's gut clenched. Was that true? Had he fallen in love with her? "I don't know about that."

"I do, even if you don't realize it yet. You have the same tortured look on your face that I had on mine a few months ago."

Finn's lips lifted in a half-smile. "Perhaps, but I know your sister also deserves better than the likes of me."

Alex sat back in his chair. "You know, for a prince, you're not overly confident, are you?"

Finn huffed a laugh. "I'm also a second son. You may not know how that feels, but you can guess. Our family's not like yours. If my brother could exile me and get away with it, he would."

"That's very drastic."

"That's truth. I work with my hands most days. I'm savvy with the financial markets, so I'll never want for money, but my life isn't going to be a formal one in a palace at this point. It'll be out in the countryside, getting my hands dirty."

"Is that what you wish for, then?"

"I don't wish for anything anymore." *Except her.* "I just do what I think is best. I think I can help you."

Alex finished off his glass and put it down on a side table. "I think you can help us, too. All right. Do you remember the news about a month ago regarding Gardar Rus?"

"You mean when Valleria had Vlad, the leader of Gardar Rus, one of the largest countries in the world, arrested? I remember it."

"The International Police Force arrested him. We just provided them with some evidence," Alex clarified.

"What really happened?"

"We received word that Gardar Rus was planning to invade three of its neighbors: Estoria, Byelorus, and Litva. Those three asked for our help."

"Military help?"

"Diplomatic help, actually."

"Vlad was never known for diplomacy."

"We knew that. However, we were approached to lead the diplomatic mission. Truthfully, the opportunity was also beneficial to show the world Valleria was still powerful."

"There was doubt about that?"

"You really aren't involved in politics at all, are you?"

Finn shrugged. "I told you."

"So you did. Well, I won't go into specifics except to say that security at the Vallerian Royal Palace was breached. Rebecca, who's now my fiancée, was kidnapped. One of my brothers, Marcello, is head of our national security and defense and took the breach very personally. He offered to go on the diplomatic mission to Gardar Rus, to help restore our reputation and his own."

"It was a setup, wasn't it?"

Alex nodded. "We expected that going in, though, so Marcello was prepared. What we weren't prepared for was the treachery of two of our supposed allies."

"Which ones?"

"Byelorus and Litva. They formed an alliance with Gardar Rus to destroy and take over Valleria and Estoria. Marcello and Estoria's security head managed to thwart their plans in the end, but it was dicey."

Finn could tell from Alex's voice that Marcello must have had a close call. He wondered what it would be like to have a brother who loved him as much as Alex seemed to love his. "So what information do you think Henry can get for you?"

"During the confrontation in Gardar Rus, someone let slip that another country was also intent on destroying us, specifically Valleria, and wanted us to suffer even more. We never learned who it was, and the prisoners we captured that day haven't said anything during the multiple interrogations we've held."

"And you think Henry knows who that country is?"

"That's what he has told us. Whether or not I should believe him is another story. He hasn't shown any proof, yet demanded my sister in return for it. Neither my father nor I will go for that kind of deal, no matter what my sister decides."

"Would she go against your wishes?"

"No, she wouldn't. At least, I don't think she would."

Finn finished his scotch in one long gulp and put the glass down. "I don't know if Henry's telling the truth or not, but I can find out."

"How?"

"I've got an idea, but let's discuss the details over dinner." Finn stood and held out his hand to Alex. "You won't regret trusting me, Alex."

Alex stood and shook Finn's hand. "I don't believe I'll regret it, either." Alex gave him a quick slap on the shoulder and they headed into dinner.

Finn wondered if Arianna and Henry had started dinner yet. Finn also wondered what she was wearing, and how she was feeling. He wondered if her hair was up or flowing down and free.

With a sigh, Finn wondered if Alex was right and he was in love for the first time, and then wondered what the hell he could do about it. He only knew he had to see her tonight, and hoped she wasn't spending the night with Henry.

# *nine*

## *ARIANNA*

In her room, Arianna gasped, then staggered in relief as Finn stepped out of the shadows.

"Finn, what are you doing here?"

"I had to see you," he said as he stalked closer. The only light in the room was from the bathroom, which Arianna had left on before heading down to dinner. To Arianna, his bright green eyes were like a beacon in the dark, drawing her closer.

"I put a table in front of the secret door. How did you get past it?"

"It wasn't that heavy, Arianna. It moved easily when the door opened."

"Oh, well, you still should have waited before entering. What if I hadn't been alone?" she asked boldly and he halted his progress across the room.

"Then there would have been a problem, wouldn't there?"

Arianna sighed. "Finn, please."

Finn took a deep breath. "Do you want me to leave?"

Her fingers were toying with the sash of her dress. "I might. Would you leave if I asked you to?"

Finn stepped closer and brushed his knuckles down her cheek. "I'll always give you what you want, Arianna, if it's in my power to do so. You look beautiful, by the way. Stunning and unbearably sensual."

"I do?"

"Oh, yes. I'd like to peel that dress from you and lick each inch of your skin."

She swallowed, her skin heating from just his words.

"But I won't." He sighed and stepped back.

"You won't?" She hoped the disappointment wasn't evident in her voice.

"Not unless you ask me to. I would like to talk to you, though I'll leave afterwards if you'd like me to. Will you sit with me? Please?"

"Oh, well, yes, of course." She put her small purse on a side table and made her way over to the chairs near the window, flicking on a few of the lamps along the way. Finn poured them each a glass of water and joined her.

"Thank you," she said as she accepted the glass. "What did you want to talk about?"

"How was dinner?" he asked genuinely.

"It was fine. Nice. It was nice."

"Boring, you mean."

"No," she bristled. "It was a nice evening. There's nothing wrong with nice evenings."

"No, I suppose there isn't. I suppose some women like that sort of evening."

"Yes, they do." Arianna wasn't sure why she was getting so defensive. "Why do you care?"

"I'm not sure," he murmured and looked down at the glass in his hands. "I care about you, that's all I'm sure of right now."

"You care about me?" It was the grandest declaration she'd heard in a very long time. Even the last man, Huck, whom she had almost lost everything for, had never said anything so simple, yet so moving. He had been all about the grand gestures, and she had fallen for each one. A little like Henry, she realized.

"I do care about you, Arianna, but that doesn't matter if you don't feel the same about me. I didn't even mean to tell you, really."

"Your feelings matter."

"Not really. Definitely not right now, anyway. Listen, that's not why I came. I spoke to Alex at dinner."

"I assumed you would speak to each other. Dinner without talking makes a very long and dull few hours."

"I meant, Alex told me everything," he said as he put down his glass.

Arianna stiffened. Had Alex told him about Huck? "What do you mean?"

"He told me why you're really considering this sham of a marriage."

Arianna sat up straighter. "A marriage of convenience doesn't have to be a sham. Not everyone has a passionate, love-filled relationship."

"Baby, you ooze passion from every pore. There's no way you could be happy with that kind of marriage."

"Oh? And I suppose you'll say I'd be happier with you?"

"No."

Arianna blinked. "No?"

"No, I don't think you'd be happier with me. I don't have enough to offer you."

"What do you mean?"

Finn shook his head. "Look that's not why I came here. I came up with a plan that I think can work. I think I can find out what Alex needs without you needing to marry Henry to get it."

She opened her mouth to speak and then shut it again.

"I know it might be a shock. If you still want to see Henry, we know we can't stop you." Why did Finn sound so resigned?

"But if you don't really want to do this," he continued, "then you don't have to. You don't even have to consider it anymore."

"I am still considering it, even after what you just said."

"For God's sake, why?" he burst out as he stood and began pacing.

"I need to do this."

"Explain it to me. Please."

"I don't owe you any explanations." As soon as she said it, she regretted it. Finn shut down, the anger and passion in his eyes dissipating in one quick pop.

"You're right. You don't. I'm sorry to bother you. I won't take up any more of your time." He strode quickly towards the door, but Arianna didn't want him to leave.

"Stop. Finn, wait," she said as she stood and walked after him as fast as she could in heels and a long silk dress.

He stopped with his hand on the doorknob. "You're right. I should use the secret passage I came through. No one should see me leaving your room." As he walked past her to get to the secret door, she grabbed his arm.

"No, that's not what I meant. Please stay. I didn't mean to be so abrupt."

His face was turned away from her, as though he couldn't bear to look at her. "You're right. You don't owe me anything." He tried to shake her hand free.

"Oh, will you just stop? Please. I'm sorry. I'd like to explain. It's just that, well, I haven't talked about this in years. I don't know where to start."

He finally turned to face her, his mask still in place. She didn't like him like this; he seemed a fake shell of his real self. Arianna wondered if that's what she looked like, as she tried to hide her true self every day.

"Please sit down," she said softly. He nodded and they both walked back to the chairs and sat down. "I suppose the best place to start is with Huck."

"Huck?"

"Well, that's not his real name. That's just the name he used with me. I don't even remember his real name anymore."

"But you remember Huck?"

She sighed. "It's hard to forget."

"Tell me," he said gently and held her hand.

"I met Huck when I was much younger and still at university. I hadn't had much luck with boys at that point—because of the princess thing—and he was the first one to pay any real attention to me."

"Were all the boys at your school blind? You're fucking gorgeous."

She smiled even though the bad memories were swirling inside her. "Thank you," she said with a squeeze of his hand. "But when you're a princess, people automatically think you're off limits. Since some of my brothers were attending university with me, it made it even more difficult."

"Did they chase them off?"

"A little bit, but it was more that they were around in the first place. I told you I was the middle child in the family; I always had older siblings and younger ones around me. Don't get me wrong," she said quickly. "I love them very much, but they weren't the best for a girl wanting a social life."

"How did Huck get past the defenses?"

"We were in the same class, and ended up being assigned to a group project together. We were forced to work together, and my brothers couldn't say anything about that."

"He asked you out?"

"Yes, eventually. He became a sort of friend first, and even my brothers got used to seeing us together studying. Once they got to know him better, they didn't deter us when he finally asked me out."

She could still remember how excited she was, and embarrassed; not many women had their first dates in college.

"He was my first everything."

"Everything?"

She nodded. "First date, first kiss, first boyfriend, first lover." She wasn't sure why she was sharing this with Finn, but it felt right, and she felt safe with him.

Finn's hold tightened on her hand. "He took advantage of you, didn't he?"

"Yes. How did you know?"

"I don't mean this in a bad way, baby, but you looked like an easy target."

"I know you don't, and you're right. I was. Too easy."

"I'm sorry. I shouldn't have said anything."

"You speak the truth, Finn. It's one of the things I like about you." At his startled expression, she smiled. "Yes, I do like you, Finn."

"That was news to me. Very pleasant news, though." He kissed her hand. "How did he hurt you?"

"He betrayed me, my family, and my country in the end. We were together for about two years. He had even met my father by that point. Papa didn't approve of him, exactly, but he didn't force me to break up with him. I wish he had."

She wondered how much to say about the next part of the story. "About the same time I was with Huck, one of my older brothers, Marcello, began seeing a woman, too. He'd actually gone deep undercover with the woman, who was a secret agent from America named Julia. I can't give you the details of that. I hope you understand."

"Of course I do. I wouldn't want you to be in an uncomfortable position."

She nodded. "Well, what I can tell you is that Julia betrayed Marcello. She was a double agent, not even working for America, when she sold Marcello out. He managed to make it out alive, and he completed the mission to boot, but he was injured. Only a few of us know about that."

She paused, gathering her courage for what she had to say next. "It was my fault. I'm the one who almost got Marcello killed."

"What? How?"

"It was Huck. He was working with Julia, and we never knew. Huck used what he found out about the royal family, palace, security, you name it, and passed it along to Julia. She used that information to position herself as a candidate for Marcello's dangerous mission. It worked."

"I don't understand. What was their endgame?"

"Valleria. They wanted to destroy us, though I have no idea why."

They remained silent for a few minutes, while Finn thought it all through. She knew it was a lot to take in all at once. "How did you figure out they were connected?"

"When Marcello came back unharmed, Huck became erratic and unreasonable. He spent quite a lot of time at the palace at that point, since my duties as princess had increased once I graduated, and our Royal Protection agents found him more than once trying to break into locked rooms and offices."

"What was his excuse?"

"That he'd left something inside or got the wrong door. It was always something. He made one of these excuses in front of Marcello once, and that was all it took. Apparently, Julia had used the exact same phrase during their undercover stretch. He made the connection."

"I'm so sorry."

"So was I. I still am, really. I still blame myself."

"Your family can't blame you for that."

"They don't, but they should. I was completely clueless. Two years we were together and I never knew."

"What happened to them?"

"He's in maximum security prison in Valleria. So is Julia, though they're kept in separate prisons. Marcello told me they've both been interrogated numerous times, but they've never told anybody who they were really working for. I suppose at this point, we'll never find out."

"And this is why you feel like you need to marry Henry? To redeem yourself with your family who doesn't even blame you for what happened?"

"I blame me." She wrenched her hand from his as she stood, then made her way quickly across the room, eventually stopping in front of the dresser.

"Why? Why are you torturing yourself for something that happened years ago?"

She looked up, her gaze locking with his in the mirror atop the dresser. He was now standing just a few steps behind her. "I don't know. I just feel useless, I suppose. I've never done anything good."

Finn closed the distance between them and whipped her around to face him. "How can you say that? You're everything that's good and decent in the world."

She just shook her head. "I know I'm not a bad person. I meant I haven't made a difference like my parents or siblings have. They're all amazing at something. I never found out what I was good at. When I met Huck I thought maybe that was how I would leave my mark, as the first to marry and have children."

"There's no shame in that. Being a mother and wife is a very important job and you'd be wonderful at it. But there's so much more to you. Don't you see it? Look." He turned her around again, and forced her to look in the mirror. "You don't see yourself. Look, please," he pleaded.

She looked and locked eyes with herself. For the first time in a long time, she really looked into her own eyes. She'd looked in mirrors to check her makeup or put in earrings, but she hadn't really used it as a chance to look at herself.

Her eyes were wide, the caramel color even darker now that they were filled with emotion. Her lips were trembling slightly and, she noticed, so were her hands.

"Finn," she started, but wasn't sure what to say. What did you say when you were truly faced with yourself for the first time in years?

"Shhh." His hands slipped down her arms and locked with

hers, holding her steady. "You're worth so much more than you think you are. Don't you see? So many people love you and want you to be happy. But that doesn't matter if you don't want that, too."

"I do," she said almost desperately. "I do want to be happy."

"When was the last time you were happy, Arianna?"

She turned to face him and his arms wrapped loosely around her, giving her the choice to step away or hold on to him. "The last time I was happy was with you, Finn."

"Arianna."

"It's true. Today, with you, was one of the best days I've had in a very long time."

"I'm glad you enjoyed yourself. I want you to be happy." His hand came up to cup her cheek, his thumb idly brushing her soft skin. "If Henry will make you happy, then do it. But don't agree to his proposal out of some misguided notion of your worth. You're worth everything."

The mention of Henry had reality crashing back to her. She still wasn't sure she would agree to Henry's proposal; the need to help her brother and country still warred with her personal needs. If she did end up marrying Henry, then she and Finn would have no other time together but tonight.

"I want you, Finn."

Finn tensed and his hand fell away. "What do you mean?"

"Stay with me tonight?"

Finn let out a breath and Arianna wondered why sadness was in his eyes. "You want me for the night. Arianna, I didn't come here tonight to seduce you."

"I know. I know you didn't. This is about me, and what I want. I want you."

"For a night." He turned away from her.

What had she said wrong? Before she could ask, he was facing her again. "I'd never deny you anything you asked for, Arianna. If you want me, you've got me, for however long you want."

"Finn," she said stepping towards him, but he held his hand out to stop her.

"Just a minute. I want you to know, you can stop at any time. You say the word and I leave. You'll never have to see me again if you don't want to," Finn said, choking on the last few words.

Arianna stepped forward and laid her hands flat against his chest. "Thank you for that." She pressed a soft kiss to his cheek. "Thank you for today." She dropped a kiss to the other cheek. "Thank you for tonight." She pressed a chaste kiss to his lips.

Finn pressed her tighter against him and deepened the kiss. She moaned as his demand grew and her mouth opened, as eager to taste him as he was her.

"Are the doors locked?" he whispered when he pulled the smallest bit away.

"Yes. The secret passage?"

"I locked it, baby, don't worry." He covered the gap between them once more and covered his lips with hers.

Her hands, slightly unsteady, were fisted in the lapels of his jacket. His hands, warm and steady, were plastered against her spine, and began shifting upwards. He buried them in her hair, tugging loose pins while directing her mouth into another angle.

The ends of her hair tickled her bare back as it fell, and she felt her earrings tug as they became tangled in the flowing strands.

"Wait," she said in a husky voice.

He pulled back, searching her eyes. "Change your mind, Princess?"

She shook her head. "My earrings. I need to take them off. They're a family heirloom."

"You can still change your mind if you want to," he said, his hands still buried in her hair. "You've been through a lot tonight. I won't take advantage of you."

"I thought I was taking advantage of you." She kissed the inside of his wrist as she pulled his hand away.

"Baby, you can take advantage of me anytime you want. Just make sure it *is* what you really want."

"I'm not sure about much right now, Finn. I don't know what will happen tomorrow. Maybe it's reckless what we're doing, maybe we should wait or not be together at all. I just know it feels right to be with you tonight. I don't know much more than that."

"Arianna," he said with a tortured groan. "How am I supposed to resist you when you say things like that?"

"You're not," she said simply. "Unless you've changed your mind."

"I haven't. I couldn't even if I tried."

"Then let me take this jewelry off first."

"Let me," he said, his voice dropping lower. His able fingers began to massage her ears and she closed her eyes against the sensation. When his fingers shifted down to her lobe, he undid the clasp one-handed. She shuddered thinking about what else his nimble fingers could do.

As he slid off the earrings, she felt the heavy weight of them disappear and sighed in relief. She sensed him place the earrings on the dresser behind her.

With her eyes still closed, she gasped in surprise when he touched her again. This time, his mouth was soothing her sore lobe. Her head tilted back to give him more room.

His lips trailed down her throat until he reached the jeweled band of the dress around her neck. He continued kissing her while his hands undid the meager clasp. The heavy weight of the band caused the top of the dress to fall easily away, leaving her breasts bare. Finn took her mouth again, this time slow and steady while he pushed the dress over her wide hips, causing it to fall in a soft swish to the floor.

Her nipples tingled as she felt a flush of cool air against her skin, and Finn's hands rubbed idly along her back, warming her up. "How are you, Princess?" he asked as he gazed into her eyes. She was clad only in panties, stockings, garter, and high heels, but his eyes never left her face.

"I'd be better if I wasn't the only one naked."

A sly smile lit across his face. "You're not naked, not yet anyway. Why don't I rectify that?"

She squealed when he unexpectedly lifted her up and tossed her softly on the bed. She landed spread eagle, and lifted herself up on her elbows to see him. This time, he wasn't looking at her face.

Just one look from Finn set her body on fire. Her nipples were already erect and her breasts seemed to grow tighter. Her curves, which stayed no matter how much she exercised, didn't make her feel unattractive. Instead, she felt voluptuous and desired. With her legs spread apart, she had no doubt he could see everything through the thin lace of her thong, and it aroused her even more.

He walked around the bed to the front, now facing her. Her breath was already shallow and they'd barely even started. The raw heat in his gaze was enough to make her panties wet and she moaned and fell back against the bed. She'd never felt so wanton in her life, not even with Huck.

As the hot bite of shame washed over her, she turned away from Finn and curled up on her side. Finn was sitting behind her on the bed barely a moment later.

"What's wrong, Princess?" His hand was caressing her back in soft, soothing motions. How he could go from raw sensuality to searing gentleness so quickly was beyond her.

"I'm sorry."

"You've got nothing to be sorry for. What are you thinking about?"

She picked at a nonexistent spot in the bedcovers. "Do you think there's something wrong with me?"

His hand gently pushed her shoulder so that she was lying on her back, and her gaze caught his. "What are you talking about? There's nothing wrong with you."

"You don't think I'm wanton or anything?"

He chuckled. "I'm sorry, I don't mean to laugh. I'm absolutely not laughing at you. Even if you are wanton, who the hell says there's something wrong with that?"

Her forehead crinkled. "But I was getting aroused just from the way you looked at me. We barely know each other and here we are."

"Don't we know each other, Princess?" he asked as he brushed back a lock of her hair. "You know me better than anyone else ever has. Don't we recognize something in the other, something that makes this attraction impossible to ignore?"

There was truth in his words. From the first sensually-charged moment they'd met, she had been drawn to him, despite herself.

"Let me ask you something. When was the last time you made love with a man?"

"Not since Huck, almost five years ago."

"So, you've only had sex with one person before this in your entire life, and even the last time with him was five years ago? And you think that makes you some kind of 'loose' woman?"

"When you put it that way."

"When I put it any way. You have no idea how passion just oozes from your every pore, Princess. At dinner the other night, I almost came just watching you eat."

Her mouth dropped open in surprise. "Really?"

"Really. I don't know what that asshole you used to date said to you, but you are a beautiful, vibrant woman." He slid down on the bed and took her in his arms. "And tonight, you're *mine*."

He pulled her against his fully-clothed body and kissed her with urgency. One of his hands slid to her thigh and pulled it over his hip, bringing her against his substantial erection. "Do you want to stop?" he asked in a raspy whisper.

She was tired of denying what she wanted, what she needed. She needed Finn. "No. No, don't stop. Oh, be with me, Finn," she said as she brought his lips back to hers.

He groaned and pulled her tighter against him for several long

moments before shifting over her and then pulling back. "I seem to
recall something about undressing you," he said with a half-smile.

"Only if I can undress you, too," she said, wanting desperately to
feel his skin against hers.

"Not this time, Princess." He stood on his knees, which were on
either side of her hips. "This time you can just watch me. No
touching."

He unraveled his tie and slid the silk over her flushed breasts and
peaked nipples, waiting until she squirmed from the sensations
before tossing it aside. He undid his cufflinks, tossing them deftly on
the nightstand, before slowly undoing each button of his shirt.
Arianna bit her lip to keep from crying out, and her body shifted
impatiently underneath him. His eyes never left hers.

He took off his jacket and shirt and tossed them aside, revealing a
delicious chest covered with rich, dark hair that ended at his
collarbone. This was a man toned from working outdoors, virile, kind,
and strong. When he undid his belt and slid it away, she gripped the
bedcovers to keep from reaching for him, and willed her body to stop
squirming.

He unzipped his pants, but didn't take them off, choosing instead
to put his hands to better use.

"Don't touch me, not yet," he whispered in a low voice and she
moaned in dismay and arousal. "Don't worry, Princess. I won't make
you wait much longer."

His hands fell to her breasts and she arched her back the
moment he touched them. Hands and lips, teeth and tongue, all
tortured her nipples before he kissed down her body. He nuzzled her
panties, taking a deep breath, before his tongue licked her through
the lace.

Her hips jumped off the bed, and his hands went to her waist to
hold her still. He found her nub and nibbled, causing her muscles to
contract inside her in anticipation. When her panties became
drenched, he slowly slid them off and tossed them aside, too. He slid
two fingers inside and teased her even more, widening her tight

channel. He continued to tease and torment her until her orgasm washed over her, hot and fast.

When her body stopped trembling, she noticed his fingers were still inside her and she was still partially dressed. "My stockings?" she said in a husky voice.

"Those are staying on, baby, at least the first time."

First time? Holy hell, she wouldn't make it through the night. When Finn laughed, she realized she'd said that out loud.

"Trust me, Princess, I would never do anything to hurt you. You're safe with me."

She locked eyes with him and felt the truth in his words. She nodded.

He slid his fingers out and gave them a long lick before he stepped off the bed. He kicked off his shoes and socks, and his pants and skin-tight boxers followed soon after. Arianna groaned at the sight of his thick, hard cock standing proudly against him.

"Like what you see?" he asked as he stepped onto the bed once more.

"Yes," she said as she spread her legs even wider to accommodate him. He positioned himself over her, keeping most of his body away from her by propping himself up on his hands, his arms rigidly straight.

He pressed his cock against her, coating it with her ample wetness. "Fuck," he said but didn't pull away.

"What?"

"Condom. I don't have one."

"I'm on the pill."

He paused against her. "Are you sure? I'm clean. No matter what you may have heard, I haven't been with anyone for over a year."

Her eyebrows shot up. "Oh. Well, yes, then I'm sure."

"Fuck," he said again and dropped his head down.

"What?"

"I don't have any control where you're concerned. I don't know if I can hold back with you."

Letting go of her fierce grip on the bed, she lifted her hands to cup his face. His eyes, now a deep, dark green, stared back at her. "Then don't."

"It's been a long time for you," he said, his voice strained. "I don't want to hurt you."

She writhed underneath him. "Please, Finn. Please don't hold back for me." Her hands trailed down his back to his ass and pushed him forward, forcing him to enter her in one hard thrust. She cried out and arched her back, the feeling of him inside her full and glorious.

"You okay, baby?" She nodded. "Open your eyes, Princess. Look at me."

Her eyes blinked open and stared straight into his. For several long moments they simply stared at each other. Her body began to stretch and accommodate his, but he didn't move. She simply stared into the darkening green depths of his eyes, breathing heavily, while he did the same with her. She didn't even like looking into her own eyes in the mirror, but she felt as though she could stare into his for hours.

Her body heated while they remained still, his cock throbbing inside her, their eyes linked in a way she'd never thought possible. It was almost unbearably erotic, and one of the most intimate moments of her life. It felt even more intimate than the physical bond they currently shared.

"Arianna," he said eventually and took her mouth in a demanding kiss. His cock refused to be ignored any longer, and he pulled out and thrust inside her again. Their lips broke apart when he groaned.

"Yes. God, yes. Please don't stop," she said as her hands gripped his ass, encouraging him to continue.

"Hold on, Princess," he said and thrust again and again. It was just his cock filling her over and over again, and the power of their heat and passion made it hard for her to breathe. Had she convinced herself she didn't need this? Didn't want this? Didn't want him?

"Now," he said, almost begging. "Now."

Her vision splintered into a thousand pieces as her orgasm washed over her, hotter and fiercer than ever before. She heard him call out her name, just as she cried out his, and felt him filling her as his own orgasm burst free. She collapsed onto the bed, her stockings feeling unbearably hot, and she wanted to rip them from her body. As soon as she got any energy back, she would.

Finn's hot, sweaty body fell on top of her while his breathing evened. A few moments later, he kissed her neck, then cheeks, and ended by giving her a long, deep kiss. She could already feel him hardening inside her again.

He gently pulled out of her, her body aching at the rough reintroduction to sex she'd just had, which she'd loved every minute of. He slid off the bed and walked to the bathroom, returning a minute later with a wet washcloth that he'd also used on himself, if his glistening cock was any indication.

"You don't have to," she said as he walked over to the bed and slid in beside her.

"Yes, I do," he murmured and gave her a sweet kiss. She gasped when the warm cloth touched her body, but he didn't stop kissing her while the towel caressed, cleaned, and soothed below. She sighed when pulled back and threw the towel on the floor.

When she moved to sit up, he stopped her. "Where are you going?"

"I was just going to take off my stockings," she said as she kicked her heels off, which landed with a soft thud on the carpet below.

"I'll do that. Just relax," he said and kissed her forehead.

As he moved down the bed, she realized she still had her diamond bracelet on and removed it, setting it beside Finn's cufflinks on the nightstand. She wondered why the two looked good next to each other, as though they complemented each other.

When she was finally naked, he shifted to lie down beside her, and pulled her into his arms.

"How are you, Arianna?"

"I'm good. Wonderful, really."

"Sore?"

"A little."

"I shouldn't have been so rough. It'll be even worse tomorrow."

"Nothing a hot bath won't cure."

"Do you want me to make you one?"

"No," she said, tightening her grip on him. "I'll have one in the morning. Right now, I just want to lie here with you."

He kissed the top of her head. "Happy to oblige your every need, Princess."

A few words from his lips and her body seemed ready for round two. "Finn?"

"Hmmm?"

"How are you doing?"

He chuckled, the sound reverberating through his chest and against Arianna, who was currently nestled against it. "Oh, I'm just wonderful, too."

"Really?"

"Really."

"May I ask you something?"

"Anything you like."

"You said you hadn't been with anyone for over a year."

"That's not a question."

"Well, why?"

Finn sighed. "I told you that tales of my exploits were exaggerated and it's true. I've been with women over the course of my life. I treated them with respect while we were together, but never promised them any more than I could give."

"Why?"

"Why what?"

"Why haven't you gotten married or have a girlfriend or anything?"

"I never met anyone I wanted to be with long-term until recently."

She tensed. "Recently?"

He kissed her head again, and rubbed a soothing hand down her back. "I meant you, baby."

"Oh."

"But don't worry about that. I'm not anybody to fuss over."

"Why do you say that?"

"You deserve better than me. I know that."

She shifted to look into his eyes. His face was determined to remain passive, but those emerald green eyes of his betrayed him. "Why don't you think you deserve me, or anyone for that matter?"

He shrugged. "I don't have much to offer, even with a 'Prince' title attached. I want a simple life with my people. Most women want more than that."

"What do you mean by a simple life?"

"Ideally, I'd just love to be one of the district mayors. Personally, I'd love to oversee the Brazenbourg Lake district, and grow something useful in some rich Brazenbourg soil. I've never aspired to anything else."

"Do you love farming? Is that why?"

Finn shook his head. "I'll tell you the truth. I do love the land and outdoors, but I honestly think it's the only profession my brother would let me get away with."

Henry, the man she may marry. Although, after Finn, she didn't think of it as a real possibility. "Why doesn't he want your help running the country? There are nearly a dozen of us doing various royal duties in Valleria and we can barely keep up."

"Henry's different," Finn said simply, and Arianna had to agree; she had never seen two brothers more night and day than Finn and Henry. She sighed.

"What's wrong, Arianna? Do you regret what we did?"

"No, of course not," she said as she brushed her knuckles against his cheek.

He took her hand and brought it to his lips for a kiss. "Then what are you thinking about?"

"Reality."

He nodded. "Well, we've still got the rest of tonight, don't we?"

"Yes, we do," she said as she nestled against him once more, and heard the steady beat of his heart underneath her ear.

"Are you tired?"

"A little bit, but not that tired."

She could tell he was smiling without even looking at him. He dropped a kiss to the top of her head and held her tighter against him. "Get some sleep, Princess. You're too sore for anything else."

"Do you promise not to leave without saying goodbye?"

"I promise, Arianna," he said and tugged the covers over them.

Soft and warm against him, she fell into an easy sleep.

# ten

## FINN

Finn woke up first. Truthfully, he had barely slept. He'd spent hours just watching her sleep, her slow, even breathing eventually lulling him into dreams. Sometimes those dreams were filled with Arianna and he woke suddenly, hard and wanting, only to find her cuddled next to him and blissfully unaware. She was apparently a very sound sleeper. For some reason, he liked knowing that about her.

It was still fairly dark outside, though he could see that light was beginning to break through. He would need to leave soon.

He didn't want to leave her.

He'd never become this close with a woman before. Physically, yes, but emotionally, no. He'd told her things he'd never told anyone else, and he'd never really enjoyed cuddling before. With Arianna, he never wanted to stop.

He rubbed her back idly, while his other hand brushed back some hair that had fallen over her face. When she nuzzled against his chest, he paused, but then she sighed into sleep again.

He wondered how sore she was. He shouldn't have taken her so hard last night. He'd never lost control like that before. He'd felt like a rutting animal as his need to claim her had consumed him. She deserved to be treated like a, well, like a princess.

Finn shifted on the bed, positioning her against the pillows underneath them, her hair fanned out beneath her soft, delectable body. She deserved a little soothing.

Finn slid quietly from the bed and into the bathroom, where he arranged a blisteringly hot bath. By the time he woke her up, it would be a little cooler and the perfect temperature for her.

Naked and aroused, he willed his cock to tamp down the orgasm brewing inside him, just at the thought of her naked and wet. He walked back to the bed and slid in again, dropping a soft kiss to her lips, like a prince in a fairy tale.

She sighed but didn't wake, so he continued dropping kisses down her throat and between her breasts. He dropped a particularly wet kiss to each of her nipples and her torso shifted slightly. He smiled; she was still asleep. He would just have to work harder.

Finn slid down the bed until he met the juncture of her thighs. A few well-placed licks later, he finally sensed her waking up. With a moan, her eyes blinked open.

"Finn." Her hands delved into his hair. The bite of pain from her fierce grip only spurred him faster. "Please, Finn. Please don't stop. Please." Her body bowed on the bed while she pleaded with him.

When her body began to shift against his mouth more urgently, his thumb began to toy with her clit. It was only a few moments later when she cried out his name and gushed in orgasm.

He continued to suck and lick until her body collapsed against the bed and her grip on his hair loosened. Then, he crawled up the bed and hovered over her so they were face-to-face.

"Morning, Princess," he said and gave her a long, sweet kiss.

"Morning," she said in a husky voice when he pulled back and situated himself on the bed beside her.

"How are you feeling?"

She turned towards him and her fingers began to play with the hair on his chest. "I'm feeling surprisingly relaxed at the moment."

He chuckled. "I meant are you feeling sore? Did I hurt you last night?"

"No." Her hand cupped his cheek. "I mean, I am a little sore but you didn't hurt me. I loved it."

"You're surprised by that, aren't you?"

She nodded. "I never thought I would. I mean, I know I'm not very experienced or anything but I didn't know it could feel like this."

"Baby, you don't need experience." He brought her palm to his lips for a kiss, then linked it with his against his chest. "You've got more passion in one little finger than most people do in their whole body."

"I guess you would know more about these types of things."

"For the record, what I've felt with you, I've never felt with anyone else. Not physically or emotionally."

She gasped. "Really?"

"Really." He pulled her flush against him, his cock still aroused and hopeful. "God, what is it about your damn lips? I just can't resist them." He pulled her in for a demanding kiss. Their arms shifted to wrap around each other, while their legs and bodies tangled below. When she started to grind against him, he groaned and pulled back.

With his face buried in her neck, he whispered, "You're sore, baby. Let's go take a bath instead."

"I'm all right."

"And I know better."

"So, you know my body better than me, do you?"

"Yes, I do," he said in a low voice. When his cock twitched, he reluctantly pulled away from her and slid from the bed. He laughed when he saw the pout on the face. "Come on, Princess. Time to start the day."

∼

## *ARIANNA*

Arianna took Finn's outstretched hand and got out of bed. They walked, both naked, to the bathroom where Arianna was surprised to see a tub of steaming, fragrant water waiting. "When did you do this?"

He tested the water temperature with his hand and nodded. "Just before I woke you up."

She smiled; it had been a very pleasant way to wake up. "You've had a busy morning, haven't you?"

He cupped her cheek. "I almost didn't want to wake you. You looked like my own private angel sleeping beside me."

"Why did you wake me then?"

"I promised I would before I left. I keep my promises, Arianna." He placed a sweet kiss on her lips and then lifted her into his arms.

"What are you doing?"

"Helping you into the bathtub." He carefully stepped in himself and eased down.

"I could have gotten in myself."

"But then I wouldn't have had the pleasure of your naked body in my arms, would I?"

When they settled in, her back against his strong chest, she asked, "How much longer can you stay?"

"Not much longer." He pushed back her hair and used his nimble fingers to twist it into a messy bun to keep it from getting wet.

"I guess reality couldn't stay away forever."

"Neither can I, it seems."

"What do you mean?"

"This is probably the wrong time to bring it up."

"You can tell me anything, as long as it's the truth."

He waited a few long moments before responding. "Arianna, are you still considering Henry's proposal?"

Reality crashed like a wave of cold water over her and she

shivered. Finn rubbed his hands down her arms, which did nothing but remind her of the choice she faced. "I don't know."

"I know you have a lot to consider, with your family and your country, but will you give me some time to find the information your brother needs? Just a little time before you make a choice you may come to regret?"

In the breaking dawn of day, she had to admit that Henry's proposal didn't appeal to her. If she were honest with herself, it had never really appealed to her, except as a way to prove herself to her family and country. It would also have been a very good way to hide her true self even longer, something that seemed impossible after what she and Finn had shared last night.

If only marrying Finn were an option, she realized, she may not have had so many qualms about it.

"I'll give you time, Finn," she said, and felt him release a breath on her neck. She turned, some of the water sloshing over the side, and situated herself against him. "I have to admit that Henry's proposal doesn't look that great to me this morning."

Finn's brows furrowed in concern, and he cupped her face. "I didn't sleep with you to change your mind, or seduce you into something you don't want to do."

"First of all, I believe we slept with each other." When his lips quirked she continued. "Second, I know you didn't. I don't believe you're that kind of person." Her fingers toyed with his glistening chest hair for a moment before she said, "It's hard for me to trust people after what happened to me."

"I know. I understand that."

"It's going to take me some time, but I know you mean well. If Alex trusted you enough to tell you what was going on, that's good enough for me. Right now, anyway."

He gave her a soft kiss on the lips and brought her head down to rest in the curve of his neck. She couldn't help but notice another part of him twitching underneath her and she wiggled against him.

He growled in a low voice. "Don't move around so much."

"I'd like you to move around a lot more." She leaned up and whispered in his ear. "Especially inside me."

"You're dangerous."

"Only with you," she admitted and slid her wet body against his. Finn's eyes closed as his head tilted back. She used the opportunity to taste the cleft in his chin and his long, lean neck. The stubble on his face would surely leave a mark—on her face as well as down below where he had pleasured her earlier—but she couldn't bring herself to mind.

"Stop, baby."

"No," she said simply and gripped his cock under the water.

With a gasping breath, he said, "Princess."

"I want you, Finn." She guided him to her entrance and then pushed down over him. They both gasped.

"You feel so good inside me," Arianna whispered, a little bewildered. She may have only been with one other person before Finn, but she never expected sex to feel like this.

"Fuck, baby. You feel goddamn amazing around me." With heavy-lidded eyes, he watched her rise and fall against him. His arms were draped along the rim of the tub, while her hands used his chest for support.

"Touch yourself," he rasped and she blinked. "Show me how you touch yourself."

"I don't," she said unconvincingly.

He huffed a laugh. "All that heat inside you needs a release. I think it's sexy, baby. Show me how you do it."

As a blush swept over her cheeks, she swallowed. With wide eyes, a little unsure, she shifted her hands from his chest to her own, filling them with her full breasts.

She closed her eyes as she continued to ride him, kneading her breasts and playing with her nipples at the same time.

"I want to see your eyes," he whispered through the steamy air, his hips shifting slightly as his cock grew even larger inside her.

She opened her eyes and, keeping one hand on her breast, she lowered the other one below the water line. She touched where their bodies met before shifting to find her clit.

She bit her lip to keep from crying out as she toyed with her nub. Usually, it took several minutes of concentrated effort with a vibrator to orgasm, but not with Finn.

Her muscles clenched inside her, close but not quite there. She gasped and pleaded with herself, begging herself to come as she often did while alone. She drew out the torment as long as she could until she saw Finn's jaw fraught with tension and his hands fiercely gripping the edge of the tub.

She gave him a pleading look and he said, "Now, baby. Now."

With a few shuddering gasps, she exploded. Her body clenched around his, over and over and over again, and her hands went to his chest once more for support. His hips pumped into her in earnest, hard but not rough. She collapsed against him as soon as he finished.

He kissed the top of her head. "Are you all right? Was that too much?"

She shook her head. "It was lovely."

He smiled. "It was fucking hot, is what it was."

"You like to curse, don't you?"

He brushed a stray lock of hair behind her ear. "Does it bother you?"

"No, actually, it doesn't." For some reason, his loss of control, whether in words or physical expression, simply aroused her.

The distant sound of a ringing phone broke into their secluded bath.

"It's my phone," Arianna said with a sigh as she sat up. "It's Alex. I can tell by the ringtone."

"Then I'd better leave before he decides to pay a visit. Will you be all right?"

She nodded. "Will you be at breakfast later?"

"Wouldn't miss it," he said and gave her a swift kiss.

They untangled their bodies and Finn stepped out to dress while Arianna took a quick shower. When she reemerged into the bedroom dressed in a robe, she noticed all of her clothes were now draped over a chair.

Finn stood near the secret entrance clad in his suit again and was checking his own phone. She had to admit, he looked sexy in that suit but she much preferred him naked. The thought made her blush.

"What's got you so red, Princess?" he asked with a gleam in his eye.

"Nothing," she said softly.

"I bet that's not true."

When she walked over to him, she wrapped her arms around his neck. "You're right, it's not true. I was thinking about you naked."

"Funny, I was thinking about you naked, but those kinds of thoughts are dangerous when I need to leave."

She pulled his mouth to hers, taking a long, heady kiss to last her through the day. When she pulled back, she said, "I'll see you soon."

"Count on it," he said in a husky voice. He gave her a last look before he pulled away and disappeared into the secret hallway.

Finn disappeared not a moment too soon, as a knock came to her door right after he left. Arianna quickly fixed the bed, hoping to make it seem less 'passionate' and then glanced frantically around the room for anything that might give her away. She noticed Finn had left his cufflinks on the nightstand, so she quickly scooped them and dropped them into the pocket of her robe.

After a last look, she went to the door. "Who is it?"

"It's Alex. Open up, will you?" Alex rushed inside the moment she opened it. "What took you so long?" he asked with a grim expression.

"I was in the bath," she said, her steam-dampened hair providing evidence of her statement. "I thought I heard you calling. What is it?"

"You never called me back last night. You're lucky Rebecca talked me out of storming into your room last night."

"Yes, you are lucky that Rebecca talked you out of it. She seems to be the only one besides Papa who can keep you sane."

Alex ignored her last comment. "Why are you happy that I didn't barge in here? Were you with Henry?"

"No, I was not," she said as she put her hands on her hips. "You can ask the guards if you don't believe me. Henry walked me to my door and left."

Arianna knew she'd won the argument when Alex only grunted and asked, "So, how did it go last night?"

"Stop glaring at me and I might tell you." After she gave him a stern look, he ran a frustrated hand through his hair and nodded.

"Good." She indicated for him to sit down and, after she took a seat herself, said, "It went okay, Alex."

"Just 'okay'? Not good or great?"

Arianna fiddled with the tie to her robe. "It was okay. He seemed to be singularly focused, but I don't know if it was towards me."

"Did he talk to you about his proposal?"

She nodded. "He seems to think it a foregone conclusion that I'll accept, but I just don't know."

"You don't want to do it?"

"I don't know."

"You seemed very sure of yourself yesterday."

"Yesterday was a different day. For the record, I was never sure of myself about this. I did want to go through with it, to help Valleria, but now I'm not sure. I suppose you're disappointed in me."

"Let's get one thing straight here and now. I have never been, nor will I ever be disappointed in you."

"You can't say that with such authority, Alex. I could screw things up for you. I've done it in the past."

Alex muttered a curse. "You made a mistake before. Hell, so have I. So has Papa, and all of our siblings. We're human beings, for Christ's sake, of course we'll make mistakes. That doesn't mean any of us will stop loving you or believing in you."

Her eyes welled up despite her efforts to hold them back. "Thank you, Alex."

"Don't thank me for being your brother. I quite enjoy it, you know." She huffed a laugh while she brushed away some loose tears.

"Now, tell me," he said as he looked her straight into her eyes. "Can you see yourself with Henry? Forget everything else. Can you see yourself as his wife?"

"I just don't know."

Alex nodded. "I'm working on getting the information through other means. I don't know if we'll be successful. However, you should know that no matter what happens, this marriage need never take place."

She knew the answer but asked anyway. "How are you getting the information?"

"I suppose it won't hurt to tell you, but keep the information to yourself. We've got our own Vallerian spies looking into it, but Finn's also helping us."

"You trust him, don't you?"

"More than Henry, that's for sure."

"Then I'll follow your lead, Alex."

"We'll have to be careful at breakfast today. I've already told Henry that we won't even entertain the idea of a marriage until Papa meets him."

"So, what's the plan?"

"I need to head back to Valleria today, and I'd like you to come with me. Mama and Papa's fortieth anniversary ball is tomorrow night. I'm going to invite Henry to come for the ball and meet our parents then."

"And if Finn finds the information we need before then?"

"Truthfully, our spies could have it even before Finn but, if that happens, we'll deal with it when the time comes."

Arianna nodded. "All right. Like I said, I'll follow your lead. Will you invite Finn to the ball, too?"

Alex quirked an eyebrow. "Would you like to?"

"If we did, he'd be closer to you if he found out what you needed." *And closer to me,* she didn't add.

"I don't know that he'll be able to come, but I think you're right that we should invite him. In fact, we'll make it conditional."

"What do you mean?"

"I'll say Papa wants to meet them both before making a decision."

"If you think that's best."

"I do. Here's what I propose we should do at breakfast," Alex said and proceeded to outline his plan. After a few tweaks, Alex left Arianna to finish getting ready.

It would be a long few days.

# eleven

## FINN

As soon as Finn had made it back to his room, he had quickly showered and changed before leaving the palace entirely. He only had a short time before breakfast, and he had promised Arianna he would be there.

He made his way quickly through the quiet streets of the capital. With the days growing shorter, more and more shop owners and vendors had switched to winter hours: opening late and closing early. No one was around, which was just what he needed.

Finn parked a few blocks from his destination and jogged quickly to a small café, barely open with only one person behind the counter setting up a display of morning pastries. Finn slid in the door, which chimed his arrival.

"Jacob," Finn said.

"Finn," Jacob said with a tone of surprise. Jacob was one of the few people who didn't call Finn by his title, even in endearment. There was too much history between them for that. "To what do I owe this visit so early in the morning?"

Finn glanced around. "Are we alone?"

Jacob's eyes narrowed. "I take it this is not a visit to taste my newest pastry?"

"No. This visit involves your old life."

Jacob nodded. "Let's head to the back. I'll lock the doors. Where did you park?"

"A few blocks away, in front of an office building."

Jacob nodded and went to lock the doors while Finn proceeded to the back. Jacob's office was small but organized and functional. As a former spy for Brazenbourg, Jacob was used to making the most of small places and few amenities. Though Jacob had left that life long ago, some habits were too ingrained.

"What's going on?" Jacob asked as he walked in and gestured for Finn to take a seat. Finn just shook his head and leaned against the man's desk instead.

"I need information."

"Regarding?"

"Henry, in a way."

"I see." After a searching look, Jacob asked, "What's going on?"

Finn, who knew Jacob could be trusted, told him what information Valleria was seeking, but didn't mention what Henry wanted in return for it.

"So, you want to know who's got it out for Valleria and their royal family."

Finn nodded. "Time is of the essence here."

"When is it not?" Jacob muttered. "You know this isn't my job anymore. I left that world behind."

"I know you did, but you still have contacts in that world. I would never ask you if I wasn't desperate for help."

"Desperate, huh? First time I ever heard you say that word."

"But it's not the first time I've felt it," he said, and Jacob nodded. Finn knew Jacob was remembering the day of the fatal car crash that killed his parents; Jacob had been the one to pull him from the car afterwards. They had grown close after that.

"Will you help me? Or lead me to someone who can?"

After a charged few moments, Jacob said, "I'll help you."

Finn let out a visible sigh of relief; if Jacob hadn't agreed he wasn't sure what he would have done.

"The Vallerian royals are visiting right now, aren't they?"

"Just the heir to the throne, Alexander, and one of his sisters."

"Yes, I seem to recall some pictures in the paper this morning of you with a beautiful woman."

"What?" he burst out as he stood. "Do you have the paper? May I see?"

"Behind you on the desk," Jacob said, and Finn turned to see his face staring up at him. Walking and smiling next to him was Arianna, as they strolled down the Food Street speaking with various vendors. How had missed this when he'd first walked into the office?

Crushing the newspaper in his hands, unaware of the ink coating his fingers due to his fierce grip, he scrutinized the picture. He knew Henry would see it, so Finn gazed at it as someone who was looking for something untoward. After a minute of staring at the black and white image, nothing seemed improper. Arianna was holding a scarf in her hand, while Finn's hands were tucked casually in his pocket. It was a simple scene. Finn hoped Henry would see it as such, too.

"There were other pictures," Jacob said, and Finn remembered he was in the room.

"What other pictures?"

"Others that may appear in the tabloids soon."

"Damn it." As Finn threw the paper down, he wondered if he could intercept Henry before breakfast, but dismissed the idea. In today's hyper-connected world, Henry could just as easily access those images on his phone, or from one of his spies.

"I doubt the Princess will be bothered overmuch by them," Jacob said as he crossed his arms over his chest. "She's likely to understand about these things, having grown up a royal."

Finn wondered if that were true. She held so much uncertainty and doubt inside her because she found it difficult to let go of the past. Arianna may seem polished on the outside, but Finn already knew she felt things acutely. The tougher the shell, the softer the heart.

Finn was momentarily blinded by the headlights of a car flashing as it parked nearby, and checked his watch. "How soon can you have something for me?" Finn asked as he carefully folded up the newspaper; for some reason, he wanted to keep their photo.

"Come by first thing tomorrow and I'll give you an update."

"That's pretty ambitious."

"That's why I'm the best," Jacob said with a wide smile.

Finn laughed. "So you are, my friend. I'll sneak out the back, if you don't mind."

"I prefer it, actually. I'm trying to keep a low profile here."

"No problem." Finn shook Jacob's hand. As Jacob went to assist his customers, Finn went out the back door of the office, exiting behind the cafe. In the growing dawn of day, few noticed him skirting through the alleys and between buildings, and only one or two may have glanced at him when he revved his engine and sped away.

~

## ARIANNA

ARIANNA AND ALEX WALKED INTO THE DINING ROOM TO FIND Henry already there. Since there was a buffet awaiting them today, they all greeted each other, plated some food, and sat down. Arianna's stomach gave a little flip as she wondered where Finn was; she hoped she could keep a calm demeanor after a night of passionate sex with him.

She was wrong.

Finn strode in barely a moment later, his hair windswept and his air hurried. Lust curled sharp and swift inside her. By the way his gaze raked over her, she guessed he was having a similar reaction.

"Sorry, I'm late," Finn said as he plated some food for himself and took an empty spot beside her, managing to put his chair as close to her as possible in the process.

"Really, Finn," Henry said with a frown. "You should show our guests more respect."

Finn merely cocked an eyebrow, and why the defiant look had Arianna's blood racing was beyond her. "I had some business to see to this morning. I do apologize if I offended either Alex or the Princess."

Did anyone else notice how Finn's voice had softened when he said her name? Or was she merely imagining it?

"You didn't offend me," Alex said casually as he reached for his coffee. "I believe I can speak for Arianna when I state you didn't offend her, either."

"You didn't offend me," she agreed, her voice huskier than she intended. She reached for her glass of water just as Finn's hand came to rest on her thigh, teasing the edge of her knee-length dress. His hand felt like a fire against her skin.

Henry pursed his lips but didn't say anything further about it. Switching topics, he asked, "Arianna, my dear, what are your plans for today?"

"We wanted to discuss that with you," Alex interjected as he put down his cup; the fine china made nary a sound as it was placed on its saucer. Arianna, who knew what was coming, reached down and placed her hand over Finn's.

"We'll be heading back to Valleria today," Alex said, his eyes fixed on Henry's shocked reaction. Finn's hand tightened around hers; she wished she'd had time to explain their plan to him.

"Today? But we have not finished our negotiations. You cannot leave yet."

"I'm afraid we must. As I mentioned, there is the anniversary party for our parents that we must attend, and several family members are due to arrive for it."

Henry glanced furtively at Arianna, who hoped she was keeping a straight face. "Arianna, my dear, surely you would like to stay behind, at least one more day?"

Arianna cleared her throat. "I'm sorry, but I must go back with my brother. I do hope you understand."

"Oh, well, yes, of course. I had hoped you would want to stay in Brazenbourg a little longer, if it is to be your home."

Finn's hand was gripping hers fiercely; she couldn't bear to look at him just yet. "Nothing along those lines has been decided yet, as you well know."

"Indeed," Alex said with narrowed eyes. "You would do well to remember that, Henry."

"Of course, of course. I was merely hopeful, that's all," Henry said with an awkward laugh.

"In any case," Alex said, "we would like to invite both you and your brother to the Anniversary Ball. I know it is rather short notice, but my father would like to meet you both."

"Both of us? Surely only myself," Henry said.

"Do you doubt my and my father's word?" Alex asked as he leaned back against the chair.

"No, no, not at all. Not at all," Henry said quickly. "Of course, if your father wishes to meet us both, then he shall. Would you like us to come down with you today?"

Alex shook his head. "We'll be far too busy today to arrange the meeting. I'll have my chief of staff, Tavin, contact your assistant; he'll give you all the details."

"With a ball tomorrow, won't a meeting be difficult?"

Alex smiled. "Not at all, I assure you. A few minutes before the ball is enough for introductions. We can discuss more the day after, if needed." Turning to Finn, he asked, "Will the short notice be a problem for you, Finn?"

"Not at all. I'm very honored by the invitation. I do have some business to attend to in the morning, but if you'll have Tavin contact me with the details for our meeting, I'll make sure I'm there. On time," Finn finished with a pointed look at Henry.

"Excellent," Alex said with a smile.

Unable to resist anymore, Arianna looked at Finn, who gave her a broad smile. She blushed and smiled shyly back.

Henry was looking less and less appealing.

# *twelve*

**FINN**

After Henry and Finn had seen Alex and Arianna off later that morning, Henry had forced Finn into the first empty room they'd found after returning to the palace.

"What the hell is your problem, Henry?" Finn asked as he put some distance between them, moving to stand near a fireplace.

"My problem is you. I have no choice but to bring you on this trip, but you're not to make a fool of me, you understand?"

"That's not my intention and you know it."

"You made plenty a fool of me at breakfast."

"What are you going on about? Breakfast was fine."

"Really? Did Arianna think it was fine while your hand groped her underneath the table? Don't try to deny it."

"I didn't grope her, for Christ's sake." Not that he hadn't thought about it; however, just holding her slim hand and remembering how she'd used it on his body had done plenty to him.

"Arianna is too much of a lady to draw attention to your

lechcrous ways," Henry said; Finn wondered what Henry would think if he knew what she was really like in bed.

"You're imagining things and blowing everything out of proportion, as usual," Finn said, brushing off his comments. "Relax, would you? Don't you think if I had been doing anything untoward, that Alex would've kicked my ass for it?"

Henry paused, letting those words sink in. "Yes, that's true. Still, I don't want anything to go wrong in Valleria."

"Nothing will go wrong." *Unless I want it to.* He still couldn't believe marriage was on the table, but he'd do whatever it took to prevent it. It was becoming harder for him to imagine a world without Arianna by his side.

Henry huffed, a disbelieving sound Finn had heard most of his life. With a wave of his hand, Henry dismissed him, and Finn left to follow-up on some more leads; Jacob wasn't the only contact he had that could be trusted.

~

## ARIANNA

ARIANNA WAS EXHAUSTED BY THE TIME EVENING CAME AROUND. After arriving at the Vallerian Royal Palace, Alex had been rushed off to see to pressing business and Arianna had been ushered into preparations for the ball. She'd constantly checked her phone though, as she and Finn had traded numbers before she'd left Brazenbourg. He'd messaged only once, letting her know that he was thinking about her while he chased down leads on the information Valleria needed.

She missed him.

It was almost dinnertime when she entered her apartments in the Royal Wing of the palace. The majority of her siblings had slowly trickled in that day, with only Ethan, Marcello, and Grace left to arrive early tomorrow. Tonight was another famed family dinner, which she usually loved, but today the thought of it only made her tense.

As she made her way to her bathroom, she began to strip off the sky-high heels and business dress she'd worn for most of the day. She needed at least a bath before dinner, even if it made her late.

A woman whose future may soon change deserved to be a little late to dinner, didn't she?

Arianna tucked in her hair, which was still pinned up from the long day. There was a low throb at the base of her neck, and she was contemplating leaving her hair down for dinner. It would be out of character for the persona she'd adopted, but maybe a small change wouldn't draw too much attention to her.

She sat down into the achingly hot water and sighed. She flexed her toes under the water, letting the steam and heat soothe her tortured feet. The image of another bath, and an addictive man, drifted into her mind.

Finn.

She was growing to like him, she realized. No, that wasn't true. She already liked him; she wouldn't have slept with him otherwise. No, it was the other dreaded 'L' word that had her heart stuttering.

Love.

Arianna was growing to love Finn. His sharp, quiet mind, the pain hidden below that she could recognize in herself, and his body, oh my, his body. Just the thought of it had arousal blooming and a gasp escaping her lips.

Her wet hand slid beneath the perfumed water and followed the line of her body to settle between her legs. While one hand gripped the side of the tub, the other tortured her below. She imagined not her own, but Finn's deft fingers arousing her. She remembered his cocky smile and darkening green eyes just before her fingers slipped inside. She remembered his clenched teeth as he held back his release until she found her own. *Now, Princess. Now.*

The memory felt real, as though he were whispering the words into her ear, and she came fast and hard, water shifting dangerously against the edge of the tub. She cried out his name as her body became impossibly hot, and then fought to cool itself in the still-heated water. She fell limp against the tub, rubbing herself idly until the tremors stopped.

She blinked her eyes open—when had they closed? —and took in the steam-filled room around her. A moment of disappointment pinged through her when she realized she was alone, but it passed. As her eyes swept the room, an absent glance at the clock had her sighing. Time to face the family.

She stood, letting the water sluice down her flushed skin. She stepped out carefully, and dried herself tenderly. As she walked back to her bedroom, she wished Finn were there.

It was harder and harder for her to imagine marrying Henry, since Finn was so much on her mind and invading her heart. Was it the same for him? When he'd held her hand at breakfast, emotion had tugged at her, and she'd felt, for the first time in a long time, that she wasn't alone.

She hoped Finn had found a way to get what Alex needed; she wasn't sure she could go through with the wedding now. Duty and honor warred in her heart with her growing feelings for Finn. If she was forced to choose, what would she do? How could she turn her back on her country facing an unknown threat? Was her happiness such a high price to pay for the safety and security of her whole country and the rest of her family?

She sighed again as she began to pull out a simple dress for dinner. She hoped Alex had some news.

# *thirteen*

## ALEXANDER

Alex walked through the secret corridors within the palace, going from his set of offices to the Queen's. Though he loved his mother, his main goal was to see his fiancée, whose office was now situated within the Queen's set of offices. Fortunately, his mother was busy dealing with last-minute preparations for the ball tomorrow, so Rebecca should be alone.

Just how he liked it.

After checking the peephole to make sure she was alone, he used a special fingerprint scanner to access the door to her office. The scanners were installed in all the secret corridors of the palace—both here in the offices and on the other side of the palace in the Royal Wing.

The door opened, and he entered to find her on the phone. Her back was turned to him and one hand held the phone to her ear while the other feebly massaged her shoulder. Alex's eyes narrowed; he didn't like to see her hurt or upset. The memory of her kidnapping a few months ago rose like bile in his throat but he pushed it back. She was safe now, and she was his.

He shut the door behind him, and it seamlessly blended into the wall; no one would know it was even there. He walked up behind her and used his strong hands to massage her shoulders. She gasped at his touch and turned around, then sighed in relief when she saw it was him.

"No, no I'm all right," she told whoever she was speaking to. "Listen, I've got to go. Are you sure you're all set for tomorrow?" A pause. "Good. Yes, all right. Love you, too, Mama. Bye."

Rebecca dropped the phone in her purse nearby, then tilted her head back against the chair. "You startled me, Alex."

He smiled, then bent down to kiss her forehead. "I apologize, Miss Campo. What's wrong with your shoulders?"

"Oh, it's just tension I suppose. I'm nervous about the ball."

Alex stopped massaging her shoulders and walked around to face her. The antique chairs used in the palace offices were beautiful, but not made for swiveling. "Why are you nervous?" he asked as he leaned against the desk and placed one of her slim hands in his. Just the feel of her skin against his—really, just the thought of her—always sent his blood racing. Some days he still couldn't believe they were really engaged, and that he would get to spend the rest of his life with her.

"I'm nervous because it's our first ball together. What if I trip or make a mistake? I wouldn't want to do anything to embarrass you or Valleria."

He felt a surge of pride; Rebecca was often concerned about Valleria and its citizens. It was just one more reason why she was perfect for him, and perfect as the future queen. "You won't do anything to embarrass us, I assure you." He gave her hand a kiss, his lips lingering a moment too long, or perhaps not long enough. "You did brilliantly last month when we visited the British royal family, didn't you?"

"Only because you and Cat were there to help."

"Darling, it was you." He pulled her up and into his arms; she fit perfectly against him.

She wrapped her arms around his neck and pressed her delicious, curvy body against him. "You're almost my husband. You have to say that."

Alex growled. "I wish I was your husband already. Some antiquated law is forcing us to stay engaged for a year." The Marriage of Royal Heirs Act of 1702 forced any heir to be betrothed for a year before the marriage could take place, which was aptly named the Royal Marriage Notification Year.

"You're my husband in *almost* every way that matters," she said softly and rested her forehead against his. "I love you, Alex."

"Rebecca." He was once again overcome as the declaration fell from her lips. They said it to each other several times a day— sometimes with actions instead of words—and each time made his heart flip. "I love you, my darling fiancée."

She giggled. "You'd better. I'm going to be Rebecca Frances Santoro di Valleria soon."

"Don't you mean *Princess* Rebecca Frances Santoro di Valleria?"

"Hard to forget that part, but that's not my name yet."

"Don't remind me. It will be your name in nine months, two days, ten hours, and thirty-three minutes." She laughed, and the movement of her breasts against his chest gave him other ideas. He nuzzled her neck. "Let's go back to our apartments, darling."

"Think you can make it all the way to the other side of the palace?" she asked as her breath grew short and her eyes shut.

"Probably not." He took a nibble just behind her ear and she let out a soft moan. Primitive instincts roared inside him and he wanted to shove everything off her desk and take her then and there. Only the camera situated in the corner of the room kept him from doing so.

"Alex, please."

He felt her body heating under his attentions, and took a deep breath to steady himself. He inhaled the soft lavender scent of her hair, a scent that followed him wherever he went, and happily so.

"Are you finished with work for the day?" he asked, still holding her close.

"I don't have time for anything else anyway. We've got the family dinner tonight."

Alex groaned; he'd forgotten about that. He had hoped that the two of them could enjoy a private dinner in their apartments, followed by several hours in each other's arms. He hadn't made love to her for days, not since the morning he left for Brazenbourg, and was aching for her now.

"It won't be so bad, Alex."

"My plans for the evening did not involve anyone but you," he said as he stood and put a few inches of unwanted distance between them.

She smiled; it was a smile just for him and filled his heart to bursting. "We'll have time later," she said as her hands shifted up to tangle in his thick, black hair. "I promise." She pulled his face down to hers and let the heat of her tongue and lips cement the vow she'd just made. Alex tangled his own hands in her rich, chestnut-colored tresses, which hung in soft waves down her back.

"Becca," he moaned as he pulled away, using the nickname that usually came out when they made love.

"Sorry," she said, clearly not sorry at all. "I couldn't resist your lips any longer."

"A fine excuse." He took a deep breath and stepped away from her, hoping to get his erection under control before they walked the long path back to the Royal Wing.

"Oh, it was much more than 'fine', don't you think?" she asked, then giggled.

Alex huffed a laugh. He couldn't argue with her there. The physical intimacy he shared with Rebecca was definitely more than 'fine' and, coupled with their emotional connection, made it the most explosive experience of his life. Even a mere kiss had him hard in seconds.

"Come on," he said a minute later, holding out his hand for her.

She picked up her purse and linked her hand with his; her slim fingers fit perfectly between his longer, stronger ones.

"How did everything go today?" she asked as they made their way down the ancient halls, Royal Protection agents trailing ahead of and behind them. He loved these moments with her at the end of the day, both of them together and sharing their burdens and fears.

"I'm not sure." His shoes and her heels tapped softly against the floor as they walked. "Papa's still against Arianna marrying Henry, but that's the father talking."

"I don't think that's true. As a modern king, I don't think he'd believe in sacrificing a woman's happiness for the sake of the country."

"Perhaps." Did the needs of the many outweigh the needs of the one? Alex wasn't sure. He didn't think he could ever force his sister to marry, even to benefit Valleria, and it made him wonder what kind of king he might make one day. He decided not to worry about that now; becoming king was not in his immediate future, anyhow.

"Well, if nothing else, your father can delay any sort of official announcement from happening."

"That's true, and that's what we're planning for. Arianna seemed less sure of the idea when I spoke to her this morning. I'm going to try to have a word with her tonight."

"Leave her be, Alex."

"Why?"

"If she's unsure, she needs to become sure of the decision she wants to make. You hounding her for an answer won't change that."

"It might."

Rebecca bit back a laugh. While she loved the possessive, demanding side of Alex—at least sometimes—she knew his siblings cared little for it, and weren't really affected by it. "If you say so."

"That didn't sound convincing."

"It wasn't meant to be."

"All right, I won't hound her. I can't say the same for Papa, though."

"He's a father; it's different. Have you heard back from Finn yet, or our own spies?"

Alex shook his head. "Marcello said our people don't have any leads yet. As far as Finn is concerned, I received a message from him letting us know that he'd have more information in the morning."

"Maybe it'll be good news."

"Maybe. I just wish I knew what Arianna was thinking. Why would she even consider this? You spent the day with her prepping for the ball; do you have any ideas?"

"Oh, Alex. I didn't need to spend the day with her to know. She's lonely."

"Lonely? With eight other siblings, nosy parents and grandparents, and a palace full of staff?"

"You can be lonely in a crowd full of people. The crowd only makes it easier not to get noticed, but it doesn't change anything. Didn't you say you were lonely before we got together?"

Alex considered that. "Yes, I suppose that is true."

"Having a large family doesn't mean you aren't lonely for someone to share your life with. She's had a difficult past from what I've gathered, and it's probably hard for her to move past it. She might see this as the only way she could marry."

"But that's ridiculous. She's an intelligent and beautiful woman; she could marry whomever she wants."

"Alex, darling, you may have to reconcile yourself to the fact that it could be Henry she wants."

Alex shook his head. "I don't think it is. I think she might actually prefer his brother."

"Finn?" Rebecca said with raised eyebrows. "Because you caught him in her bedroom, helping her with her dress?"

"I was actually thinking of breakfast this morning, though I'm sure there was more to that little dress incident than she mentioned."

"What happened at breakfast?"

"I think they were holding hands under the table."

"That's interesting," Rebecca said with a broad smile.

"Why do you look so happy about that?"

"Woman's intuition, that's all."

Alex groaned. "Not this again."

"Yes, this," she said as she bumped her shoulder against his. "You doubt my intuition, but it was my intuition that told me it was a good idea to marry you. Was it wrong?"

"So, it was right once. Doesn't mean you're right again."

"You can trust your intuition, but I can't trust mine?"

"Exactly. So happy you've finally figured that out, darling."

"Care to wager on it?"

He stopped in the hall, only a few strides away from the entrance to the Royal Wing. "What sort of wager?"

She turned to face him, a bemused expression on her face. "If I'm right, and Arianna really likes Finn and ends up with him, then you'll be at my beck and call for an entire week of my choosing." She trailed her fingers up his tie to his chin.

Lust, which he had viciously chained up earlier, broke free. As domineering as he could be in bed, he just as much enjoyed it when his fiancée took control. Though she'd been a virgin when they met, he'd very much enjoyed teaching her and reaping the rewards.

"And if I win, which I will, because I don't believe Arianna wants Finn long-term?"

She stepped up onto her tiptoes and whispered in his ear. "Then I'll be at *your* beck and call, my dear." Her hand slipped around his neck and her fingers teased the ends of his hair.

He growled and pulled her close. "And if we're both wrong?"

"I'm sure we can think of something." She dropped a kiss just below his ear, a spot he hadn't known could feel erotic before her.

"Get inside, fiancée." He nodded to an agent nearby and they opened the door for him. He didn't like having his private moments witnessed by anyone, but a future king didn't always have a choice. Especially if they were near-constantly aroused by their future wife.

She smiled and walked inside, her broad hips naturally shifting side-to-side in the skirt and heels she wore. Who cared if they were late to dinner? He needed Rebecca like he needed his next breath, and he would have her.

He followed her laugh down the hall towards their private apartments. As soon as they stepped inside, they tore off each other's clothes and he took her hard and fast against the door. They would definitely be late to dinner.

# *fourteen*

## ARIANNA

Arianna arrived late to pre-dinner drinks, but hardly anyone noticed except her father, who gave her a pointed look as she entered the sitting room. The entire space was filled to the brim with siblings, and she noticed Alex and Rebecca were missing. It certainly wasn't the first time they'd shown up late, and they all knew it wouldn't be the last.

She envied them.

After pouring herself a glass of wine, she went around and greeted everyone she hadn't met earlier that day. Her younger brother Lorenzo, who lived in the coastal town of Masillia, and her younger sisters—Carolina, who was currently working on her art in Paris, and Sarah, who was the Vallerian ambassador to Italy—had arrived just an hour ago. Catharine was teasing Nathaniel, who worked on the Royal Council as Minister of Finance and Treasury. The others arriving tomorrow included Ethan, youngest of them all, who served as a doctor in the Vallerian Royal Navy, and Marcello, who would be arriving from England with his lady love, Grace, who still had a home there.

She loved this time with family. Even if she didn't always fit in with her clever, strong brothers, or sophisticated, artistic sisters, she loved them all very much. They all watched out for each other, even her, and she knew she would be the center of attention if Alex or Papa revealed what was really going on with Brazenbourg.

"Arianna," her father said as he walked up to her, "come talk with me for a minute."

"Yes, Papa," she said, and he walked away towards a corner without waiting to see if she followed.

"What did you do? Papa seems upset with you," Carolina said as she gestured with her drink-filled hand, her numerous bracelets chiming against each other while she did.

"It's nothing." Arianna turned to go but Lorenzo put a hand on his arm to stop her.

"It doesn't look like nothing." Lorenzo gave her one of his searching looks. Arianna knew it was an inherited trait; she'd seen the same looks on her father, Alex, and Marcello, too.

"You'll know soon enough, I'm sure, if there's something to tell." Arianna easily broke free of the hold and walked away towards their father.

$$\sim$$

## CAROLINA & LORENZO

"I bet it has something to do with a man," Carolina guessed, then took a sip of cold wine.

Lorenzo's mouth dropped open in surprise. "Arianna? She hasn't been with anyone since you-know-who."

"So, it's about time, isn't it?"

"As if you would know. When's the last time you had a date?"

"I go on dates quite regularly, thank you very much."

"What?" Lorenzo's older brother instincts were coming out in full force. "With who? Tell me their names."

Carolina laughed. "Oh, no, dear brother. Don't worry about me."

"Like hell I won't. Are you seeing anyone right now?"

"No, I am not. No man has been able to catch my attention long enough for a relationship." She sighed. "Men are idiots."

"Thank you very much."

"Present company excluded, of course."

"A fine concession."

"What about you? You're known for playing the field quite a bit. Both you and Nate do. I don't see why I should be held to a double standard."

"Because you're our sister."

"And you're my brother. Do you have a steady someone?"

"No," he admitted. "Though I think Nate might."

"Nate? Really?" She started laughing, drawing the attention of others in the room. "Tell me more, Lorenzo. Tell me everything."

## ARIANNA

ARIANNA WATCHED CAROLINA LAUGH FROM ACROSS THE ROOM, envious of her easy, carefree laugh and attitude.

"Are you listening, Arianna?" her father, King Gabriel, asked.

"Yes, Papa. I know you're ambivalent about this."

"He's not the only one," Alex said from behind her. She turned to see the same serious expression her father held echoed on Alex. She noticed Rebecca was greeting the others in the room, giving them a wide berth for the moment, just as her mother had. Rebecca must know about the situation, then.

"Let's hope our own agents or Finn find something first."

"And if that doesn't happen?" her father asked.

"Then I'll do my duty for my country."

Her father stood even straighter, if that was possible. "At the sake of your own happiness? I won't allow it."

"Neither will I," Alex agreed.

"Stop it. Both of you. Everyone in the room knows that you're bullying me about something; they keep looking over here and soon they'll just happen to 'pass by' so they can eavesdrop. Would you please keep this conversation outside of our family gatherings?"

Gabriel's stance relaxed a little. "Of course, my child." He kissed his daughter's head, inhaling the scent of his child that was uniquely hers. "But do take care. A marriage without respect is not one at all. Be sure you can respect and look up to the man you choose to share your life with. Otherwise, it will not only be a long and difficult road, but a treacherous one."

Finn's beautiful face came to her mind, but she pushed it back, at least for now. Instead, she smiled and gave her father a hug, who easily returned it. "Well, it's not my fault I can't seem to find someone as decent as my Papa, is it?"

Gabriel chuckled and gave her another kiss. "Nice try, daughter. Nice try."

Dinner was announced a few moments later. Alex left to escort Rebecca inside, while Gabriel left to do the same with their mother, Genevieve. Everyone else followed behind them, chattering away and catching up. Though modern technology made it easy to stay in touch these days, there was always something to be discussed, and something to tease or torment someone else about.

A month ago, Marcello had been the center of the teasing for falling in love with Grace. The month before that, it had been Alex, who had admitted a longtime love of Rebecca. She wondered what her siblings would have to say if they knew that she, too, may be married soon, and to a man she didn't love.

When Finn came to her mind again, she tried to push thoughts of him aside, but goosebumps rose on her skin at the thought of seeing him. He would be at the ball tomorrow night. Would they dance? Could she hope for a life with him?

As she sat down to dinner, some of her siblings probed her for information, but she remained tight-lipped. If there was something to tell, tomorrow would be soon enough. She knew she would barely sleep until they heard from Finn in the morning, and she fortified herself for the long night ahead.

# *fifteen*

## FINN

Finn strode back to his room in Brazenbourg Palace, a man quite upset with his brother. Henry was forcing Finn to travel with him to Valleria. It wasn't for Finn's company, oh, no. Finn was going along because he was being treated as a teenager alone in the house for the first time. Henry had just made it very clear he didn't trust Finn.

But then, Finn didn't trust Henry, either.

Finn entered his room and went straight to his closet. He pulled out his suitcase and began throwing clothes inside; they could be ironed later if needed. All he really wanted to do was stay behind a little longer and gather more information. Jacob had pushed their meeting back to noon, as he was following a hot lead and needed more time. Finn couldn't leave the country now, but he would have to.

Finn ran a frustrated hand through his hair just as his phone vibrated in his pocket. He pulled out his burner phone; he'd learned years ago that Henry had begun tapping his given phone, so he'd used a burner for any personal business.

Alex had messaged him with another request for an update. Didn't he know that Finn would tell him as soon as he knew? He typed the same thing he had that morning and sent it back, only adding that Henry had requested his presence for an early departure. Finn was only half-worried that once he left the country, Henry would find a way to keep him out for good.

He prayed this was not one of those times.

Just in case, however, Finn took a small, pre-packed bag from a hidden panel in his closet. It was filled with money and a few mementos he'd tucked away of his parents. Finn might hope for the best but, when it came to Henry, he prepared for the worst. After grabbing everything, including a suit for the ball, he made his way out the door.

He also sent a quick message to Jacob letting him know what had happened. Tense though he was for Jacob's call, the only bright spot would be seeing Arianna again. Just the thought of her caused an ache inside. He hoped they could have at least one dance together.

## *ARIANNA*

ARIANNA FLUFFED THE LAYERS OF HER FULL SKIRT AGAIN IN front of her mirror. It was customary for all members of the royal family to wear something in a dark shade of purple, the royal color of Valleria, to most of the balls they held, the exception being their annual Holiday Ball in December. With her Mama, three other sisters, and two future or potential sisters-in-law as well, finding something to wear took massive amounts of coordination.

Arianna's dress was a vision of elegant purple and gold in a wide spiral across her dress, each stripe streaming from a point on her right shoulder and growing larger as it fell down by her left foot. The fitted waist would enhance her God-given attributes on the top, and the layers of skirt would hide her God-given curves on the bottom.

The asymmetrical neck made a necklace obsolete, but she paired the dress with the same emerald and amethyst earrings she had worn in Brazenbourg. If things did need to move forward with Henry, it would be the proper thing to wear. If things worked out otherwise, well, she would just have to deal with some comments in the papers about her ability to color-coordinate.

She picked up her tiny purse and began the journey towards the family room, where they would all gather before heading to the ball. The Royal Wing of the palace made it easy for the royals to have their own space as well as communal ones. The secret hallway that led from her bedroom could lead straight towards the communal family room, but it would be impossible to maneuver those passages in this dress. So, she was taking the long route from her royal apartment, down several hallways, to where the family would meet.

As the sounds of voices grew louder, she could feel the excitement in the air, and Arianna couldn't help but smile at it. A ball was always a fun occasion, and one celebrating their parents, even more so. They'd all teamed up on a surprise present for them; she hoped they liked it.

As she entered the room, she was lost in a crowd of purple silk and black tuxedos, and momentarily blinded by the heavy jewelry all the women were wearing. Though some of it was fake, extra Royal Protection agents had been assigned to them all individually as well as to the ball; nothing would happen if they could prevent it.

Her parents, Gabriel and Genevieve, were the last to arrive. Genevieve looked resplendent in her own strapless gown of plum purple and rich gold, which came with a small cropped jacket that also shimmered in the light. Genevieve's dark blond hair was wrapped in a sleek bun at the base of her neck, perfect for the crown she was to wear tonight. A crown was only worn for special occasions, and this was definitely one of them.

Gabriel looked just as amazing and powerful as her mother did.

He was dressed in a tuxedo and royal cape, complete with a crown as well. Arianna knew that her father would have preferred to wear his dress military uniform, as her brother Ethan currently was, but it could not be worn with the crowns her mother had insisted they wear.

Arianna could just picture them as they had been decades ago when they married. They had aged so well it seemed as though no time had passed, but for her father's peppery hair and her mother's curvier form, the result of nine children in eight pregnancies.

"You all look beautiful," Genevieve said. "Positively beautiful."

"We're handsome, not beautiful," Lorenzo said, puffing out his chest.

Genevieve walked over and gave him a gentle kiss on the cheek, careful not to transfer her lipstick. "Lorenzo, dear, you're beautiful. You're my beautiful son, and you always will be."

"Geez," he said, looking abashed. "All right."

"All right, what?" Genevieve asked with a smile.

"All right, I'm beautiful." Everyone laughed. "Oh, shut it," he told his brothers and sisters. No one listened.

"I, too, second your mother. Everyone looks radiant. We have been very blessed, dear wife."

"That we have, dear husband."

"Is everyone ready to go? Are we waiting on anyone?" Gabriel asked as he surveyed the room, mentally checking off each of his children he saw to glean if anyone was missing.

Everyone turned to Catharine, who didn't like the attention for once. "What are you looking at me for?" Cat asked as she put her gloved hands on her hips. "I am here on time."

"You'll have to forgive us for being surprised by your punctuality, Cat," Marcello said. He stood nearby with Grace tucked under his arm.

"Yes, my twin," Alex said from where he similarly stood nearby with a smiling Rebecca. "You are not known for your timeliness.

Even at our birth you showed up late." Everyone chuckled at the long-standing joke.

Cat narrowed her eyes but wisely bit her tongue. "Well, I am here now, on time, and waiting for all of you to get going."

"Hot date tonight, Cat?" Nate asked. "How much longer did Mama give you to get married?" Genevieve had given Cat an ultimatum when Alex and Rebecca had gotten engaged: Cat had to be at least engaged by the time the wedding came around, or else.

"Nathaniel," Genevieve warned. "First of all, how did you hear about that? Secondly, leave your sister alone."

"Mama, how am I supposed to leave something that good alone?"

Cat smacked Nate on the back of the head. "Like that. If you start thinking about it again, just smack yourself in the head, or let me know and I'll do it."

A number of voices rang out at once. "Can I?" "I'll do it." "I want to smack Nate."

"Quiet," Gabriel said in an even voice and the room quieted immediately; he had a talent for that sort of thing. "Leave both your brother and sister alone. Tonight is a night for celebrating, and that is what we plan to do."

"Before we begin the celebrations, we have a gift for both of you," Alex said and gestured to a pair of servants nearby, who brought out a very tall, thin box.

"What is this?" Genevieve asked as tears glittered in her eyes. "We weren't expecting anything."

Alex smiled. "We know. That's why it's called a surprise, Mama. Go ahead, please open it."

With trembling fingers, both Gabriel and Genevieve carefully pulled out the prize with the aid of the servants. They both gasped when they saw it.

It was a painting of the whole family, including Gabriel and Genevieve. Rebecca and Grace, who were considered family, even if it wasn't official yet, were also in the work of art.

"We didn't pose for this," Genevieve said.

Carolina, the artist in the family, spoke first. "You didn't have to. It's hard to get all of us together, so we gave the artist pictures of everyone when we needed to. Do you like it?"

"You didn't paint this?" Gabriel asked his talented daughter.

"No, but a friend of mine did. I felt I couldn't be objective enough."

"It's beautiful. Amazing. Oh, I can't wait to see what it looks like above the mantel in the dining room," Genevieve said. The dining room always featured a portrait of the royal family and, since Alex and Marcello had found the loves of their lives, the painting had needed updating.

"I'm so glad that everyone's in the painting," Genevieve said with a look to Rebecca and Grace.

Grace dabbed at the tears in her eyes, and pushed back strands of her long blond hair which were delicately styled around her face. "I'm so honored to be included. I know Marcello and I aren't engaged." Grace was a widow whose first marriage had been abusive, to say the least. Though she and Marcello were deeply committed to each other, she just wasn't ready to take that step yet, and the family completely understood.

"As if that matters, my dear," Gabriel said as he walked over to her. "You're family, whether or not you sign a paper stating so." He dropped a kiss to her head, then walked over to Rebecca. "You are family, too, my dear."

Rebecca's eyes were shining brightly, as were the eyes of her parents nearby. "Thank you."

Gabriel smiled. "Thank you very much for the very thoughtful gift. We love it almost as much as we love all of you." As he looked around the room, his gaze stopped on Arianna's. "Why doesn't everybody start heading out. Alex? Arianna? A word, please. Rebecca, dear, please head out with your parents; Alex will be there shortly."

As everyone else filtered out, Rebecca escorted by her parents,

Gabriel, Arianna, and Alex remained in the room with Genevieve. A sense of dread filled Arianna's stomach.

"Prince Henry and Finn are here," Gabriel said, his eyes fixed on Arianna. "Alex and I greeted them when they arrived."

"I assumed they'd arrived by now, but why didn't you want me to greet them when they did?"

"I wanted to meet them without you. However, it was clear that one man was very disappointed you were not in attendance." And it hadn't been the man Gabriel had expected; it had been Finn, not Henry.

"Oh?" Arianna asked, slightly hopeful. She wanted to ask who, but didn't dare. "Well, did you have a chance to speak with them?"

"Unfortunately, nothing more than a greeting. We may step away from the ball sometime during the evening, or just wait until tomorrow. We may also ask you to join us, depending upon how that conversation goes."

Arianna nodded, then turned to her mother's searching gaze. "Mama?"

"You do know that we only want the best for you."

"Is that what you told Cat when you gave her an ultimatum? That you only want the best for her?" Arianna noticed Gabriel was very uncomfortable at the mention of Cat's dilemma.

"I didn't give her an ultimatum. I just strongly encouraged her to find someone, and soon. Besides, Cat's situation is completely different and you know it."

"Perhaps," Arianna said, holding back her tongue against her mother's meddling. She loved her mother, but a finer meddler there never was.

"Enjoy tonight, my child," Gabriel said as he put a comforting hand on her shoulder. "This situation is a worry for another day, not tonight. Nothing will be decided right now."

"Any news?" Arianna asked Alex, who shook his head.

"We didn't have a chance to talk to Finn before the ball. I'm going to pull him aside before we talk to Henry. By the indications he was giving me, he had managed to learn something."

"Will you let me know as well?"

"I'm sure Finn will dance with you at some point; ask him then. Just be discreet when you do. You never know whose ears are nearby."

"Yes, all right. Don't worry, I won't say anything revealing."

"Good," Gabriel said. "Now that we're all on the same page, let's go have some fun. Come, my beautiful wife; your party awaits."

# sixteen

## FINN

Finn glanced around the tasteful and historical Grand Ballroom at the Vallerian Royal Palace. Delicate chandeliers hung sparkling near the ceiling, sending just the right level of light around the room, burnishing it in a soft gold. Everybody and everything seemed to shine like a jewel: the women, along with their dresses and jewelry, the table decorations, and even the men and the food lining the tables.

The Vallerian royals had yet to make an entrance. Though he had business with a few of them, it was only one he truly wanted to see: Arianna.

He'd been disappointed when Arianna hadn't greeted their arrival earlier. Oh, Henry had put up a good front, feigning disappointment, but as King Gabriel had searched Finn's eyes, he was sure the man knew what Finn felt for his daughter.

Finn reached for another glass of water, forgoing alcohol until he'd spoken with Alex, at least. He needed a clear head, especially if what Jacob had told him was true. Someone was indeed out to sink the royal family, but it was one of their own allies. Jacob was working now to find out who it could be; he had a short list, Finn knew, but it must be terribly shocking for Jacob to keep it so close to his vest.

A trumpet sounded and the noise in the room dimmed. A man Finn recognized as Tavin, Alex's chief of staff, announced the royal family as they entered; he had been there to welcome him when he'd arrived earlier that day.

All of the women were in stunning gowns featuring the dark purple of Valleria. When Arianna was announced, Finn lost his breath. She wore layers of dress that he wanted to peel off, and even from some distance away he could see she wore the same jewelry she'd worn in Brazenbourg. Had she done it for him? Or Henry?

Wishing his water was something stronger, Finn took a few long, unroyal-like gulps. As the icy chill settled in his stomach, it seemed to calm him.

Alex and his fiancée, Rebecca, were announced, to the great delight of the crowd. Vallerians certainly loved their next generation of rulers. In fact, to Finn, it seemed as though the crowd cheered even louder for them than they did for King Gabriel and Queen Genevieve, who came out next.

"Finally," Tavin began, "we wish to inform you that Her Royal Highness, the Former Queen Victoria, was unable to join us this evening." Finn knew Victoria was Arianna's grandmother, her Nonna as she called her, and mother to King Gabriel.

"Queen Victoria has been waylaid by the Medicane, which is the rare tropical-like storm that has settled in the Mediterranean. The storm made travel difficult from Her Highness's home on the island of Ilva, but rest assured that she is safe and well, and wishes our King and Queen another forty years together."

When the applause died down, both Gabriel and Alex gave a brief statement welcoming everyone, then kicked off the party. As the band began to play, most of the royals made their way off the stage and began mingling. The King and Queen opened the dancing, and

Alex and Rebecca followed soon after. Halfway into the dance, others began to join in.

Alex was holding Rebecca close, both with ridiculous grins on their faces; they were clearly very much in love. The King and Queen, having raised nine children and spent forty years together, were also clearly in love but slightly more reserved about it in public. It was an interesting dichotomy to witness: new lovers and established lovers, side-by-side. Finn wondered if he would ever make it to forty years as a married man. There was only one woman he could ever consider for that position now.

As if she sensed he needed to see her, Arianna came into view. She, too, was dancing, but Finn didn't feel threatened by the man holding her, as he knew it was one of her brothers. Finn had told Henry he wouldn't embarrass him, but seeing Arianna so beautiful and seemingly unattainable, made him want to claim her right then and there.

Finn gulped down the rest of his water before setting the glass aside, and slowly made his way through the crowd. Most of the guests were Vallerian or related to the royal family in some way; there were only a few dignitaries from other countries, as he was, so he didn't really know anybody or need to stop and chat along the way.

His mind and his focus were on her. She was like a beacon calling out to him, saving him. Could he save her, too?

Finn put on the mask of formality as he reached them. "Your Highnesses." Finn bowed to them for appearance's sake. "Prince Lorenzo, allow me to introduce myself. I am Prince Finn de Bara of Brazenbourg."

"Of course," Lorenzo said as he held out his hand and Finn shook it. From the side of his eye, he noticed Arianna blush, but she was otherwise composed. "We are happy you could join us for such a delightful occasion."

"We are honored to receive an invitation, thank you. Princess Arianna, I wanted to claim you for a dance this evening, at your earliest convenience."

She smiled. "Of course. I'm afraid the next dance is spoken for, but please find me after that."

Finn bowed again, hating the formality that went with being a royal sometimes. "Thank you, Princess," he said and saw her blush deepen. "Prince Lorenzo." Finn shook his hand again and walked away. He'd have Arianna in his arms in maybe ten minutes, and that was all that mattered.

As Finn strode away from the dance floor, he caught Alex's eye. Finn nodded and headed toward a darker corner of the room to bide his time. It didn't surprise him when Alex found him barely a minute later.

"We'll have to make this quick," Alex said, after they, too, had bowed to each other for form's sake. "I had planned to hold my fiancée all night long and this is interfering with those plans."

"You seem to be quite in love, Alex. Rebecca is a lovely woman, and you're both very popular with the crowd, it seems."

The pride on Alex's face couldn't be hidden, and neither could his broad smile. "I'm a damn lucky man, I know. I found the perfect woman for me and my country." Finn wondered if he had, too, in Arianna.

"Well, this shouldn't take long," Finn said, and proceeded to tell Alex about his initial findings.

"One of our allies?" Alex said, his eyes narrowing. "How can you be sure?"

"I trust this source with my life, and I don't trust easily. It doesn't look good for you. My contact is searching for more proof now before confirming who it is."

"Even if they have proof, how will they prove it to the world? I can't think of any of our allies who would want us dead or destroyed this much."

"Neither can I, but you'd know best. My advice is to go and enjoy the night with your fiancée, and leave the worrying to the rest of us."

"Will you be dancing with Arianna later?"

"As soon as the next dance is done."

Alex nodded. "Give her a discreet update, if you can. There are a number of ears listening and nothing is safe."

"Not even this conversation?"

Alex's face spread into a smug smile. "I'm not worried about this conversation, as we're standing far enough away from other people. Besides that, I've got a jammer in my pocket which disables any electronic devices nearby. We finished testing it a week ago, and it came through with flying colors."

"Top secret stuff. Why are you telling me?"

"So you won't worry next time we speak. None of the others, save Marcello and my father, have a jammer on them most of the time."

"I'll remember that."

The next song started and they turned towards the dance floor. Finn knew Alex was searching for Rebecca, but Finn's breath caught when he saw Arianna's dance partner: Henry. How had Henry found her so quickly?

"Ah, there's Rebecca," Alex said, sounding almost relieved.

"Afraid someone else will want to dance with her?"

Alex pursed his lips. "Of course not. I just want to ensure we have plenty of time together, that's all."

Finn laughed and slapped Alex on the shoulder. "Well, what are you waiting for? Don't let me hold you up. I'll find you if something comes up."

Alex nodded and shook Finn's hand before walking back towards a smiling woman who seemed as eager to be in his arms as he was to be in hers.

Finn spent the rest of the song analyzing—overanalyzing, really—every movement Arianna and Henry made. Was her smile at him real or forced? Did she keep her distance from him for propriety's sake, or because she didn't want to be near him? He just didn't know.

When the song ended, Finn made a beeline for her. Henry would see them dancing anyway, so there was no need to try to hide it.

Arianna's lips were in a thin line. "Thank you for the dance, Henry."

"Let's dance again. We're to be married soon, anyhow," Henry said.

Finn stepped up to them and spoke in a low voice. "She hasn't agreed to that, and you should learn how to hold your tongue. If anyone had overheard you and spread that comment as news, the Vallerian royal family would have been most displeased with you."

Henry's eyes glittered with anger, but he didn't respond.

Finn took hold of Arianna's slim hand. "Besides, she's dancing with me next."

"Is this true, Arianna?"

"Yes. Prince Finn asked me and it would be inconsiderate considering the current negotiations between our countries."

"Yes, yes. Of course," Henry said quickly, not wanting to offend her or her family. "Please, by all means. Dance together."

Finn saw annoyance flash in her expression and completely understood; Henry made it seem as though he'd given her permission to dance with Finn, when she didn't need his permission at all.

"Come, Princess," Finn said, leading her deeper onto the dance floor.

He twirled her once and then settled her in his arms, in a loose but close grip. They were certainly closer than she and Henry had been, but Arianna never complained. While they stared into each other's eyes, Finn could feel Henry's eyes fixed upon them, even from his perch some distance away.

There was tension in her body he didn't quite like. Was that because of Henry? Or him? "What's wrong, Princess?"

She was quiet for a moment before she spoke. "I don't think Henry likes you very much."

"I don't, either. Did he say something to you?"

"I won't repeat it, but he seemed to think that you weren't very loyal to Brazenbourg."

That bastard. "It's not true."

"Of course it isn't. I told him so."

Finn's eyebrows went up. "You told him he was wrong? About me? I would have loved to have seen that."

Arianna bristled. "Yes, well, it wasn't true. I had to defend you."

Hope budded in his chest, along with an emotion he'd rarely felt before: love. No one had ever defended him to Henry since his parents had died. "Thank you, Arianna."

Her eyes were soft. "You're welcome, Finn."

He seemed to remember they were on a public dance floor and cleared his throat. "How are you this evening otherwise?"

"I'm very well, thank you. How are you?"

Finn didn't like the proper mask she'd just slid into place again. "You're being very polite."

"Shouldn't I be polite to you?"

"Well, I've been thinking about doing something to you that's not polite at all."

She swallowed. "Oh?"

"Oh, yes." He leaned in closer and whispered in her ear. He remembered Alex's comment about who may be listening in and revised what he originally thought to say. "Let's just say there's something very appealing about your lovely dress."

"Is there?"

"Yes. The beautiful woman inside it is very tempting." He held back the urge to bite her ear or kiss her throat.

She cleared her throat and Finn put some small distance between them again. "Have you found out anything yet?" she asked, clearly changing the subject.

"I have learned a great many things, but some knowledge still requires research."

"I see."

"Do you?"

"You can't say any more?"

"Not here."

"Then I guess that's that." She sighed.

"Are you done with me then?" Finn asked, irrational anger bubbling inside him. Did she want him gone so badly?

"What do you mean?"

"I don't have the answers you need so you're ready to push me aside."

"I'd rather push you inside me, is the thing." She gasped at her brazen words and put a hand over her mouth. Realizing her gesture made a scene, she gave a few feeble coughs before her hand dropped away. "I'm sorry."

"I'm not," Finn said with a smile. "That was one of the hottest things anyone's ever said to me."

"Really?"

"Really. I'd like to make it happen."

"We shouldn't."

"Probably," Finn conceded and leaned close again as the music slowed even more. "I can't stop thinking about you, Arianna. I can't stop dreaming of you, and tasting you. You haunt me."

"Finn."

"Couldn't we have tonight? All hell could break loose tomorrow, but we have tonight."

"Yes, we do," she said softly. After another minute of dancing, she spoke again. "Where is your room?"

"Not in the Royal Wing."

"Then you'll be in the North Wing. It's where we usually house foreign dignitaries who don't stay in our section of the palace."

"Is there a way to you?"

"I'll find you this time. Don't worry. Tonight, after the ball."

"Keep your dress on when you come."

He almost laughed at her startled expression. "I can try, but I can't make promises."

Finn nodded. "Just so you know, I'm leaving the ball right after this dance. I couldn't bear to see you dancing with other men all night."

"I wish I could dance with just you," she whispered.

"So do I," he whispered back.

For the rest of the dance, they stayed silent, just enjoying each other. Her full skirt bunched around his legs, the silk swishing as they moved ever so lightly. Her scent, soft and sweet, filled his senses, and her heels clicked lightly against the floor when she stepped. The connection of their intense gaze held throughout the next few minutes, neither of them able to break away. If they had, they would have noticed both King Gabriel and others watching them with curious expressions. They would also have noticed Henry watching them with anger in his eyes before striding away from the ball.

## *ARIANNA*

ARIANNA HUFFED AS SHE MADE HER WAY DOWN THE NARROW passages. She paused for what must have been the twentieth time and readjusted her dress. It had been a stupid idea to wear it in the secret passages. The only way for her to maneuver was walking with her back against the wall, stepping side-to-side the entire way. Even though the secret passages were always clean and well lit, it didn't help matters any.

She'd thought about turning around and going back to the safety and comfort of her own room more than once. Each time she did, she also thought about the safety and comfort of Finn's arms and kept going.

Dancing with him had been almost as intense as their lovemaking was. The connection she felt when he was buried inside her was the same connection they'd made on the dance floor. It was like a drug, and she needed it.

She needed Finn.

When she finally saw Finn's door, she let out a sigh of relief. She'd left the ball as early as she'd dared, but it was still fairly late. She wondered if Finn would even still be waiting for her.

He was.

The second the door opened and she stepped inside, Finn was there barely a moment later sweeping her into his arms. His lips claimed hers while his hands shut the secret door and pushed her against it. Hot need filled her in an instant.

"Finn," she breathed as he kneeled down and his hands delved under the dress and through the layers underneath.

"I've spent hours waiting for you, wanting you. I thought I'd die from wanting you tonight, Princess," he said just before his head disappeared. Her hands plastered themselves on the wall behind her looking for purchase, while her panties were ripped away and Finn's mouth covered her folds below.

She cried as the first orgasm came in a searing flash, quicker than any had ever come before, even their previous lovemaking. Finn didn't stop, couldn't stop it seemed, and sent her crashing a second time all too soon.

She pawed at the dress, which was too hot, too fitted. She tore at her skirt, needing to feel the whole of Finn's body against hers.

His head eventually popped out from beneath her skirt. With his hair mussed and his eyes pools of dark moss green, he slowly stood.

Both of them were breathing heavily. Unspoken communication and need traveled between them for several long moments. Then they reached for each other at the same time.

Lips took and bruised where they went. They toppled backward, Finn taking the brunt of the fall, though his lips never stopped against hers. She tore at his shirt, sending buttons flying since he'd already removed his jacket, tie, and cummerbund. He undid the zipper on her dress, and a rush of air fell against her heated back.

They rolled and she found herself against the floor. He pulled down her dress, leaving only her lacy bra remaining. He stood over her, kicked off his shoes and socks, and then pulled off his pants and boxers in one swift move. His cock stood proud and erect against his stomach. She moaned and licked her lips at the sight of it.

"Take off your bra." His gruff voice sent goosebumps scattering along her skin as she did what he asked.

He kneeled over her, his cock in his hand, and placed it between her full breasts. The feeling of it heavy against her had her growing wetter by the second. He thrust between her breasts a few times, slow and steady, their eyes locked with each other. She wanted to taste it. She needed to taste him.

Her hands covered his firm ass and pushed him further up her body. When his cock was close enough, she took it in her hands and brought it to her mouth. She moaned as it slid inside. He shifted his hips, helping her along, and she couldn't get enough. He pulled out all too soon.

He moved back down her body and she spread her legs. His fingers teased her for mere moments, before he shifted away. Then, he pushed his cock inside her in one hard thrust. She sobbed at the wonderful feel of it.

He began thrusting, hard but controlled. She could tell he was holding himself back, so that she wouldn't be sore. Her heart tumbled a little more.

"Now, Princess. Now."

Her body did his bidding, and her back arched as the orgasm washed over her, wave after wave of it milking him dry. They both cried out at the force of it, at the force of their eyes locked on each other, at the primitive way they'd just taken each other.

Spent, Finn collapsed on top of her, then shifted positions so he was on the floor and Arianna was on top of him. He was still buried inside her, and she didn't want to let him go, not just yet.

"Did I hurt you?" he asked as he idly rubbed her back.

She shook her head as it nuzzled his chest. She had a sudden realization that she could nuzzle this chest for the rest of her life and it may not be enough.

"What's wrong?" he asked.

"Nothing," she said, her voice hoarser than expected. She cleared her throat.

"You just stiffened up on me. I can't fix it if I don't know what's wrong."

"Nothing's wrong."

Finn sighed. "All right. Do you want a bath? What can I do for you?"

"No bath." She paused, wondering if what she really wanted made her too needy. She asked anyway. "Would you mind just holding me?"

"For the rest of my life if I can."

She raised her head to face Finn's; his eyes were completely serious. "What did you just say?"

His hand cupped her face. "I said I'd hold you for the rest of my life if I can."

"That's crazy."

Now Finn stiffened. "It's how I feel. I guess you don't feel the same."

"It's not that. Finn, there's just so much up in the air right now. I can't commit to anything." Or anybody.

"I know, Princess." He brought her lips to his for a soft kiss and she fell pliant against him once more as the tension drained away. "I'm not pressuring you, but I want to be clear how I feel. These last few days have been some of the best of my life, and that's because of you."

"Because of the sex, you mean?" Her heart fell a little at the thought.

"No, though I'm not saying I don't enjoy that immensely with you. I feel that way because of you. I feel like someone really cares about me for the first time in my life. Am I wrong?"

"No. No, you're not wrong. I do care about you."

"Well, I sure as hell care about you."

"Really?"

"Really. I know you've had a tough time in the past, but I'm not that asshole you used to date. I'm just Finn. I know I don't deserve you, but I'll do everything in my power to make you happy."

"What are you saying?"

"I'm saying when all of this shit with my brother is done, I want to be with you, if you'll have me. I love you."

"Finn." She almost couldn't breathe. A memory of another man saying that flashed in her mind, but it wasn't the same. Older and wiser now, she could tell the difference between true feelings and manufactured ones. At least, she hoped she could.

Finn put a finger over her lips. "Don't say anything back, not just yet. Just think about it, all right?" She nodded. "Good. Let's get to bed."

They stood, Arianna gingerly removing him from her body; she would be sore in the morning but couldn't bring herself to mind.

Leaving their clothes in shambles, they walked to the suite's bedroom. As soon as they slipped into bed, they reached for each other, and heat bloomed fast and ripe once more. They spent all night making love, his hands claiming her again and again, her hands showing him what she wasn't quite ready to admit.

Afterwards, she slipped into an exhausted sleep, unable to even think about what the morning may bring.

# seventeen

## FINN

Finn woke to find an empty bed beside him. For a moment, he thought he might have dreamed making love to Arianna all night long. When he tried to move, however, and parts of his body ached as they'd never ached before, he knew it had been real.

He slipped out of bed and walked naked towards the front door of the suite. His tattered clothes were now draped over a chair and her dress was gone. She was gone.

Finn sighed as he made his way back to the bedroom, missing her already. Was it possible to feel so much?

In the bedroom, he kneeled down to an air vent. He carefully removed it, pulled out his 'in-case' backpack and removed his burner phone. He quickly messaged her, wishing her a good morning and asked if she'd made it back to her own room. He put everything back without waiting for her reply; it could wait until after his shower.

It was a good thing he waited.

As steam rose around him, suddenly the shower door ripped

open. Finn whirled around to find Henry there. He was furious, which wasn't unusual, but he gripped a newspaper in his hand.

"Your paper's getting wet," Finn said and finished washing the soap off his body.

"Get out of there. I need to speak with you."

"Clearly." Finn turned off the shower and stepped out, picking up a towel folded nearby for him.

"What is the meaning of this? Do you even care you're embarrassing me and your country?"

"What are you on about now?" he asked as he dried off.

"This." Henry shoved the newspaper in his damp face.

Finn wrapped the towel around his waist and then took what was a local Brazenbourg paper. Splashed across the front were pictures of him with a woman at a dance club.

"What the hell is this? These pictures are at least five years old. Jesus. That club doesn't even exist anymore."

"That's not what the papers are saying. They're saying you were with that woman two nights ago, along with two of her friends. There's a long list of women in there you've slept with in the last month and they claim the source to this is you."

"What?" Finn said with a disbelieving laugh. "Are you fucking kidding me with this? Are you telling me you believe this filth?"

"It doesn't matter what I believe. It's what the public believes."

Years of feeling unloved and unworthy welled inside him. "You're my damn brother. You should fucking believe me."

"What I should do is get rid of you, and that's what I plan on doing."

"What do you mean?" Finn asked, his voice deceptively mild.

"I finally have a reason to kick you and your bastard body out of my country."

It wasn't the first time Henry had taunted him with 'bastard' but it would be the last. "Brazenbourg is my home, too, you ass, no matter what you call me. Not only that, you can't banish me just because some newspaper slanders me and calls me a man whore."

"Oh, it's not just that, brother dear," Henry said with a grim smile. "The papers will also find out about your treasonous activities. That will be the headline this afternoon."

"What the fuck are you talking about?" Then he recalled the comments Arianna had heard Henry say about him, and realization dawned on him. "You're spreading these lies. You planted these stories."

"Well, you caught on quicker than I thought you would."

"Why?"

"Why? Because I hate you, that's why." Just as Finn had been holding back all these years, so, apparently, had Henry. Years of his dislike for Finn burst forth in a quick torrent of words. "I've put up with you for years since our parents died and I'm sick of it. Now, you dare threaten my marriage with Arianna and threaten my plans for Valleria? I won't stand for it, I tell you. I simply won't stand for it."

Plans for Valleria? What did that mean? "If Arianna wants to marry you, she'll marry you. It's that simple."

Henry pushed him and Finn staggered back, his damp feet skidding mildly on the tiled floor. "She even defended you, of all things, when I mentioned how completely useless you were to Brazenbourg. Then, I saw the two of you dancing last night; I saw the way you were looking at each other. She's mine, not yours."

A wave of possession fueled Finn's anger. "Arianna doesn't belong to you, you dickless bastard. You can't marry her against her will or the will of her father."

Henry laughed, clearly amused. "What I can and cannot do has nothing to do with Gabriel. I'll do whatever it takes and Arianna is my stepping stone to greatness."

Before Finn could respond, Henry spoke again. "You're not to enter my country ever again. You will leave Valleria today as well; I'll speak to Alex and ensure it happens. I don't care where you go or what you do. I don't care about you. You are, in fact, dead to me."

Henry's words left a bloodless slash across his heart. It was one thing to know your own brother cared so little for you, but it was another thing to hear him say it.

"If you come near me or Brazenbourg again, I will kill you. Goodbye, *brother*."

As Henry turned to leave, Finn spoke up. "Why do you hate me so much? What did I ever do to you?"

"You were born. You exist. You threaten to take what's mine."

"What are you talking about?"

"The crown! I am the ruler of Brazenbourg, not you."

"I know you are. You're the eldest son, for Christ's sake. How can I threaten your position?"

"You think I don't know that the people love you more than me? Well, after they read these articles, they won't give a shit about you, and that's just how I like it. No more will I have to hear whispers about my younger brother being a better leader than me. No more will I have to smile politely when people ask about you before they bother to ask about me. After your 'treason' comes out, no one will dare mention you to me ever again."

Holy fucking Christ. "Jesus, Henry. Did you ever care about me? We're the same flesh and blood. Doesn't that mean anything to you?"

"You have been a thorn in my side since you were born. So, no; the fact we are related, if we are related, means nothing. We're done. Do you understand me?"

Finn wondered how he could still be standing after such vitriol, how he was still managing to breathe with his world crumbling around him. "Yes, I understand. Goodbye, brother." Finn swallowed and blinked back the tears threatening to pool in his eyes.

Without another word, Henry strode out. When Finn heard him slam the suite's door, he collapsed to his knees. Wrenching sobs broke free, something that had not even happened when his parents had died. He had been too numb then. He wasn't numb now.

Arianna had opened his heart, and every feeling and crushing blow were felt acutely. He'd lost his brother and his country in one fell swoop. He had friends, but would they stand in a battle between him and the ruler of their country? He couldn't say.

As his sobs abated, he realized he still gripped the newspaper in his hand. As he let go, another thought came to him. If Henry thought Finn was a threat to Arianna, he would make sure she saw this.

Finn stood and began running at the same time, slightly slipping against the floor. He rushed to the air vent and pulled out his phone. Arianna hadn't messaged him yet, but he tried again anyway, letting her know that a false story about him had been planted in the paper, and pleaded with her not to believe it.

Next, he messaged Alex, asking him to meet him as soon as possible, and as discreetly as possible. Would Alex listen? Would he help him? He wasn't sure.

He just wasn't sure.

~

## ARIANNA

WHILE FINN HAD BEEN EXITING HIS SHOWER ABRUPTLY, Arianna had been exiting hers routinely. She had slipped away from Finn just as dawn had broken, not wanting either of them to be discovered. It had been difficult to leave him. Even in his sleep, he'd held tight to her when she'd tried to slip away, until she gave him a soft kiss and his hold loosened. It was as though he needed reassurance, even in his sleep, that she was still there. She liked being needed and wanted by Finn.

She sat down at her vanity and began to brush her long hair in steady, even strokes. She was so lost in thought, that she didn't hear the secret passage creak open in the outer foyer of her apartments. It was only when she caught the movement of someone in her mirror that she spun around on her stool and gasped.

When she saw who it was, she let out a sigh of relief. "Sarah,

Carolina, Cat—what are you doing here, besides scaring me half to death?"

Her sisters arranged themselves on her bed. "Why did you make your own bed?" Sarah asked as she laid across the bed on her stomach and rested her chin on her linked fingers. "Or has the maid already come?"

"I made it myself. I didn't really think about it, I just did it when I woke up," Arianna covered. She swung back around to face the mirror and continued brushing. "Now, why are you here?"

"Someone might think you don't like your sisters with that attitude," Carolina said from her perch against the headboard. "Rebecca and Grace wanted to come, too, but our brothers waylaid them."

Arianna put down her brush and faced her sisters again. "Sorry, I don't mean to be rude. I'm just exhausted. It was quite a party last night."

"Wasn't it?" Sarah said, a dreamy look in her eyes.

"How many times did you dance with that Italian businessman?" Cat teased Sarah.

"Only two or three times," Sarah said defensively.

"Uh-huh. And how many times did you dance with that Greek businessman?" Cat asked, a cheeky smile on her face.

"About the same," Sarah evaded. "What's it to you?"

Cat poked Sarah in the arm. "You, little sister, are boy crazy, and don't think Papa didn't notice."

"I'm not boy crazy," Sarah said as she sat up. "Boys are dumb. I'm *man* crazy." Everyone laughed. "I'm just having fun, not getting married. Didn't you find anyone interesting? You're the one with the clock ticking on her ring finger."

"Tell me about it," Cat grumbled. "I danced with a lot of men. I mean, they were all nice, but I didn't feel that spark, you know?" Arianna knew, but didn't say anything.

"How about you, Arianna?" Carolina asked. "You danced with those dishy princes from Brazenbourg. How were they?"

"Very nice," Arianna said and returned to brushing her hair.

"Mmm-hmm," Carolina said and crossed her arms over her chest with a smug smile.

"What does that mean?" Arianna asked.

"It means you like one of them. A tall one of them with dark brown hair and intense green eyes."

"What are you talking about?" As if she didn't know.

"We saw you when you danced with Prince Finn," Cat said in a sing-songy voice. "That wasn't a friendly dance."

"But we are friends." That much, at least, was true. "It would have been rude not to dance with him when we spent time together in Brazenbourg."

"I'm sure it would have," Cat said. "But the look on your face when you danced with Prince Henry versus Prince Finn was entirely different."

"If you're not keen on Prince Finn, can I have a go at him? He's so dreamy," Sarah said, with a far-off look in her eye. Why Arianna wanted to murder Sarah for encroaching on Finn was beyond her, but she managed to keep an even face.

"I think Prince Henry likes you, if that makes a difference," Carolina said as she adjusted one of her many necklaces. "He was mostly all smiles dancing with you, but then later he was nothing but dour and grumpy." Arianna wondered at that; had something happened? Finn hadn't mentioned anything last night. Was Henry upset at her for defending Finn?

"Why are we dissecting my love life?" Arianna said, avoiding their gaze.

"Ah-ha," Cat cried. "So you admit you have a love life."

God help her from nosy sisters. "Look, what's really going on here?" Arianna put down her brush and faced her sisters head on; she saw them exchange worried glances with each other. "Just spit it out."

"Prince Finn was in the news this morning." Carolina's soft words echoed through the room.

A hundred possibilities dashed through her mind, but worry

overtook them all. Was Finn in danger? She managed to keep her voice even. "Oh? For what?"

"For being, shall we say, promiscuous."

"What?" Arianna's eyes widened and her mouth dropped in surprise. "What are you talking about?"

After a nod from Cat, Carolina pulled out her phone and brought up the website for a newspaper from Brazenbourg. There, in crisp, vivid color, were pictures and a headline that couldn't be missed: *Prince Finn's Women*.

Her chest constricted and her eyes widened as she skimmed the article. Two nights ago? He was with some woman two nights ago? It was their one night apart, really, since they'd met. It could be true, couldn't it? But was it?

All of her fears and doubts bloomed to the surface again. Was she making another mistake? Had she misjudged another man who'd told her he loved her?

"What do you think?" Cat asked.

"Is it true?"

Her sisters glanced at each other. "Well, he does have a reputation, doesn't he?" Cat asked. "I mean, the article could be wrong. The press often blow things out of proportion, just like they did with Rebecca and Alex." A video of Alex and Rebecca had circulated just before they'd become an official couple; though the video had been innocent, the press had made it out to be much more.

Arianna simply kept staring at the photo of Finn dancing with another woman. She was beautiful, no denying it. She had small hips and a slim, toned body—things Arianna would never have. Maybe he didn't really love her, as he'd said last night. Maybe he just wanted sex, not forever, despite what he'd said. Maybe he was even in league with Henry, and this was all just part of his plan.

Pain slashed through her, hot and fast. She had begun to open her heart again, only to have it broken once more. Perhaps she was fooling herself where Finn was concerned. It wouldn't be the first time she had made a fool of herself, but it would be the last. Never again.

Arianna handed Carolina back her phone and returned to brushing her hair. "It's none of our business what Prince Finn does, is it? Did you need anything else? I need to get dressed."

Cat sighed and shifted off the bed. "No, we don't need anything else." She walked over to Arianna and leaned down to give her a hug from behind. They locked eyes in the mirror. All the siblings shared various facial features; with Arianna and Cat, it was the same slim nose and full lips, courtesy of their mother.

"Take care, Ari," Cat said and gave her a kiss on the head. "We know something's going on with you and Papa. You don't need to tell us if you don't want to, or if you can't, but we're here if you need us."

"Yes, we are," Carolina said as she joined the hug.

"Definitely," Sarah said as she also joined the hug.

Arianna smiled when she saw them all in the mirror, clinging to each other. Her heart may be breaking right now, but her family would see her through. She would be okay. She'd have a good cry after they all left, and then move forward with what she needed to do. There was no going back now.

As she said goodbye to the girls, she missed the message coming into her phone, as the soft notification pings were no match against the voices of four sisters. In fact, Arianna didn't even think about her phone until after she'd finished dressing, and by then it was already too late.

# eighteen

**FINN**

Finn had already finished packing by the time Alex arrived a few hours later through the same passage Arianna had used. She still hadn't messaged him back, and he was growing concerned. Did she believe the lies? He had to know.

"Finn," Alex said tersely. "Do you have any new information?"

"I didn't ask you to come here for that. I apologize if I made you believe otherwise."

"Are you sorry? Should I even believe you?"

So, Henry had gotten to Alex. Since Alex hadn't thrown him out of the palace, and was giving him time to explain himself, he may still have a chance. "You've seen the lies in the papers, then?"

"Lies? Are you saying that wasn't you in the photos?"

"It was me, that much is true, but it was me five years ago. That club closed down not long after that picture was taken. If you bothered to do any research before making accusations, you'd know what the truth was."

"I'm not talking about the papers this morning, though we'll get to that in a minute. I'm talking about the afternoon paper. Are you a traitor?"

"I am as much of a traitor as my brother is honest, which is to say, not at all. He planted both of those stories. I hadn't realized the other one had come out yet."

Alex's eyes narrowed. "Then how did you know about it?"

"My former brother."

"Former?"

"Yes. My brother came to me this morning, told me he'd planted the articles in the paper, and exiled me from Brazenbourg. He also went on to state that he would ensure I'd be exiled from Valleria, too. Is that why you're here? To kick me out?"

Alex ran a hand through his hair. "I was tempted, but I needed to confront you first. What the hell are you doing with my sister?"

Finn was startled by the abrupt change in topic. "What are you talking about?"

"Don't play dumb with me. Arianna wasn't in her room last night, and the secret hallway to your room smells of the perfume she usually wears."

Finn pushed his shoulders back. "She was with me last night, that's true. I told you when we met I wouldn't lie to you, and I won't."

Alex cursed. "I should pummel you for that."

"It takes two to tango, Alex. You should know that I'm in love with Arianna, and that I'll do everything in my power to keep her from marrying Henry."

Alex considered Finn for several moments. "Does she love you back?"

"I don't know," he said honestly. "Henry may have gotten to her today, hoping to sway her by the article this morning, about all the women I've supposedly been with. She's not returning my messages. I'd hoped to see her before I left."

"Left? I haven't exiled you, at least not yet."

"I have to go back to Brazenbourg. It's my home, and it's not safe. There are a few who will help me, and my contacts there may be able to help you. One of them hasn't checked in as we had arranged to, and I'm worried something may have happened to him."

"Are you helping Valleria because you want to get back at your brother? I won't have my country and my people caught in the middle of a revenge plot."

"Henry's not my brother anymore. I doubt he ever was. We're not like you and your brothers, Alex. There was never anything between us but Henry's ego."

Alex nodded. "I don't know if I can take you to see Arianna. She's called a meeting with both my father and me this afternoon. I have a feeling we're not going to like what she has to say."

Finn's gut clenched. "Do you think she'll agree to the marriage?"

"I think if she's seen that article, she's doubting you and herself right now. She'd think of it as her past repeating itself."

"I know. She told me about that asshole she used to date."

Alex's eyes widened. "Did she? She never mentions it unless she trusts the other person. She must trust you."

Finn sighed. "Or at least she did, until this morning."

Alex put a hand on Finn's shoulder. "I'll talk to her about it. Not for your sake, you understand, but for her own."

Finn nodded. "I just want to see her happy. I know I don't have anything to offer her, especially not now, but I don't want her to make a mistake she'll regret. She deserves better than that."

"Yes, she does," Alex murmured. "What's your plan from here?"

"Sneak into Brazenbourg, find my contact, and go from there."

"It won't be easy."

"My life has never been easy, so why start now?" Finn reached into his back pocket and took out an envelope, then handed it to Alex. "It's for Arianna. I understand if you don't want to be a go-between, but I'd appreciate you delivering it to her."

Alex tucked the note inside a pocket to the suit jacket he wore. "I'll pass it along, Finn. What do you think we should do about Henry?"

"I don't care about Henry. Just keep Arianna safe."

"You didn't even need to ask me for that one."

Finn nodded as he picked up his bags. "I'll be in touch. I may change my number as a security measure. If I do, look for the phrase 'church' in my first message."

"All right. Good luck to you," Alex said as he shook Finn's hand.

"And you," Finn said, and walked out. Each step farther from Arianna felt like a dagger to the heart, but he knew this was best. He had to fix this, and help Arianna. If he was very lucky, he would also find a way to help his people in Brazenbourg; they deserved a ruler who cared about them, not just the power he had over them.

## ARIANNA

ARIANNA SAT IN HER FATHER'S OFFICE AND LISTENED WHILE HE tried to talk her out of her scheme. Both Gabriel and Alex stood towering over her, unintentionally intimidating. She would not, however, be deterred.

"Our own spies are working on this, Ari," Alex said, his voice pleading. "We could know something as soon as this evening."

"You said the same thing yesterday and nothing happened. I've made up my mind; I'm marrying Henry."

Gabriel sighed. "Let's take a step back. If you want to marry Henry, you can wait until at least tomorrow to make a final decision or announcement."

"It's too late."

"What do you mean?" Gabriel's sharp voice cut through her resolve, but she held firm. "Have you gone off and eloped with him? It may not be legal if you have."

"No, of course not. I have told Henry that I'm accepting his proposal, and he's sending out a press release. It will hit the news soon, if it hasn't already."

Gabriel cursed, causing both Alex and Arianna to look at their father with wide eyes; Gabriel rarely cursed. "You defied me, Arianna. I'm disappointed in you."

The heat of shame flushed her cheeks. "I'm sorry. I did what I needed to do. Now we can stop this whole charade and move on with things. Henry said he'd give you what you need soon."

"But at what cost?" Gabriel muttered. "You're to stay in the palace, locked in your apartments until someone comes to get you."

Arianna slowly stood. "You're punishing me?"

"I'm protecting you."

"I'm not a child anymore. You can't just lock me away when I do something you disagree with."

"You will always be my child, Arianna. You locked yourself away for too many years, and now that you've finally opened yourself up again, you're running away."

"Running away? But I said I'm marrying Henry."

"But you should be considering marriage with someone else." Gabriel cupped his daughter's head, her wide caramel-colored eyes looking up at him. She'd always felt lost, he knew. Lost in a sea of siblings, unsure of her place. As a father, he supposed he had failed her; he should have made sure she knew how desperately she was loved by all of them. Well, he wouldn't fail her now.

Gabriel kissed the top of Arianna's head and she was pulled into the warmth of his arms. Tentatively, she hugged back. She heard his heart beating beneath her cheek, a sound so comforting she blinked back the hot tears welling in her eyes. After a few minutes, Gabriel kissed the top of her head again and pulled back.

"Think about what I said."

"I will, Papa." How could she think about anything but his words? Did he really think she should be considering marriage with Finn? How did he know?

"I'll come to you later. Go now. I must speak with Alex."

Alex reached out to her. "Wait."

She looked warily at him. "What?"

Alex pulled an envelope from his pocket. "It's from Finn," he whispered.

Finn? Alex had seen Finn this morning? Despite the fact she had made up her mind about Henry, her heart still wanted Finn. She wondered if he was okay.

"Take it, Ari. Don't throw it out. Just read it when you're ready. Please?"

Arianna took the envelope and nodded, then she turned and walked away without looking back. She had made her decision; there was no going back now. Had she looked back, she would have seen her father slump into his chair, and Alex put a comforting hand on his shoulder.

# *nineteen*

**FINN**

Finn spent the rest of the day traveling through Valleria and had remained tense the entire journey. He wasn't naïve enough to assume that Henry wouldn't have him followed; in fact, it had been easy to figure out exactly who it was. By the time Finn had transferred from Metz to the local bus system, he had managed to shake them off, hopefully for good.

Because he wasn't a wanted man in Valleria, it had been easy enough to take trains through the countryside and into neighboring France. From there he made it to the French-Brazenbourg border just as night fell. Knowing his name so close to the border would be easily recognizable, he chose instead to use one of his contacts and found lodging in a discreet chateau. From there, someone from Brazenbourg would help him cross the border.

The chateau boasted an extensive golf course, and he'd arranged to sleep in the course's clubhouse. The chateau itself was hosting a wedding this weekend, and it was best for Finn to stay away from the crowd. The wedding, however, had meant that food would be readily available and, having not eaten even breakfast that morning, Finn was running on fumes.

All of his thoughts centered on survival and Arianna. All through his journey, he had kept rereading the false articles about him, and wondered what Arianna thought about them. They'd only spent about a week together, but they'd come to mean so much to each other in that time, at least he thought they had. Did she have so little faith in them? In him?

Perhaps if he found out who was scheming against Valleria, then he would prove to her that he loved her. He hoped it would be enough, as he wasn't sure what else he could do. If she didn't want him, he knew there would be no one else.

He still hadn't received a reply from her. He just hoped his Princess was okay.

∾

## ARIANNA

After a restless day in her apartments, Arianna was ready for escape. Though her royal apartment boasted several rooms for her to wander in, including a full kitchen, she felt trapped and caged.

She could have ignored her father's edict. It would have been easy enough to escape the palace—and they both knew it—but her father's words had kept ringing in her ear all day: *I'm disappointed in you.*

She had dinner in her room alone, and had a scary feeling that this might be just what her married life would be like, though she refused to believe it. She and Henry might not care for each other, but they could grow to love each other. She would become a mother one day, and then that would change everything. It could work out, she assured herself. She would make sure it worked out.

She was about to give up waiting for her father and get ready for bed instead when the knock came at her door. When she answered it, she was startled by the person behind it.

"Henry. Whatever are you doing here?"

He pushed past her and entered. "Shouldn't a man see his fiancée?"

"I suppose, but it's not very proper, is it?"

Henry's lips contorted into a grim smile. "Proper? Oh, I think it's highly proper."

"Why don't we call Alex or my father as a chaperone?" There was a hard look in his eyes and she didn't want to be alone with him. She didn't feel safe.

"I don't think we need a chaperone." He glanced around the foyer. "I think you should show me around your apartments."

She wondered what he was up to, and how he'd found her apartment in the first place, but didn't ask. Later, she would wish she had. "All right, I'll give you a brief tour."

She took him around the living room, kitchen, offices, and other rooms before turning back towards the foyer.

"The bedrooms? Surely, you have one of those," Henry asked.

"Of course, but I don't think you need to see it."

"That's where you're wrong." He turned and walked farther down the hall, opening the doors to linen closets and guest rooms before finding her bedroom.

"Henry, I really must ask that you leave."

He ignored her, instead just wandering around and taking in the room. She had always been a fairly neat person, so thankfully there wasn't any mess or random undergarments lying about. He stopped in front of her dresser, and picked up the amethyst and emerald necklace she'd worn in Brazenbourg but not to the ball.

He turned to face her, his hands full of jewels. "I've just had dinner with your parents. I'll be glad once you come back to Brazenbourg for good and we won't need to see them again."

A cold, sick feeling bloomed in her stomach, and a little of her panic showed through. "What are you talking about? Just because I marry you doesn't mean I'll never see my parents again. We discussed this."

"I never agreed to that. You'll need to show your complete allegiance to Brazenbourg."

"Of course Brazenbourg will become my home, but I couldn't give up Valleria; the public wouldn't understand and it wouldn't be right."

"Right? Right? You don't have the first clue what's right." He walked over to her and placed something in her hand. When she looked down, she saw they were Finn's cufflinks; she had never returned them, but instead had placed them in her jewelry box, which sat atop the dresser. "These belong to my useless brother, don't they? Don't they?"

Arianna couldn't speak; she just shook her head, unable to believe she'd been found out.

"Have you slept with him? Have you?" He was moving even closer, forcing her to take a step back, then another, and another. She stopped only when she felt the bed behind her.

He pushed her down. "If you've slept with my brother, then you won't have any trouble sleeping with me right now. Although, I don't think we'll be doing much sleeping."

"Stop," she cried and quickly slid back, eventually stepping off the opposite side before his hands could get to her.

"I won't have a whore for a wife."

"I am *not* a whore." Her breath was coming in harsh gasps, fueled by adrenaline and anger. "Don't you dare call me that again."

"Are you pregnant? You'll have a formal test done before this wedding proceeds."

Pregnant? Her hands automatically went to her lower abdomen. Her mind did frantic sums and tried to remember if they'd ever been unprotected. She was on the pill; she'd remembered to take it every day, hadn't she?

"I can see by your face that it could be a possibility. Well, now with Finn gone, it looks like I'll be raising his bastard."

"What? What do you mean he's gone?"

"I've exiled him from Brazenbourg, and ensured that he would be exiled from Valleria. He'll never come near you again."

Despair filled her at the thought of never seeing him again. "What? He's your brother. How could you do that?" She couldn't believe his own brother would exile him.

"I take it you haven't seen the papers this afternoon?"

She hadn't wanted to look at any news since this morning; she hadn't even checked her phone. "No."

"If you had, you'd realize that he was a traitor to my country. Now, he's finally gone and hopefully dead."

*Dead?* An image of Finn, cold and lifeless, sprang to her mind and she cried out. "No."

"Oh, yes." Henry's grim smile sent chills through her.

"If I am pregnant, why would you even still want this marriage? I don't understand."

"I will claim the child as my own. No one is ever to know the truth."

"But why?"

"The car crash that killed our parents also injured me. Apparently, I cannot have children of my own. I always hated Finn but, after the accident, I knew he could become ruler because of my impotence. Brazenbourg is *mine*. No one else's."

What had she done? What had she agreed to? She'd trusted the wrong man, and betrayed the one she should have held close. History was once again repeating itself, but now there may be a child at risk because of her foolishness and rash behavior. *What had she done?*

Arianna let out another cry when Henry tore the delicate strands of the necklace apart with his bare hands, scattering the colorful jewels and gold across the room. "Valleria isn't your home anymore. It's Brazenbourg. It's time you accepted that."

He turned to leave, but then paused and faced her. "Oh, and Arianna?"

Arianna was frozen on the other side of the room, her eyes wary and her body stiff and defensive. "What?" she asked quietly.

"The next time I come to your bedroom, I want you naked and waiting for me." With that chilling demand, he walked out.

Only when Arianna heard the outer door close and silence ensue did she finally collapse onto the floor in tears. *What had she done?*

After her tears abated, her hand once again went to rest over her womb. There was a possibility she was pregnant, and with Finn's child. She imagined a young boy with his warm, green eyes, and suddenly hoped it was true. But what kind of life was she bringing a child into? She couldn't marry Henry, that was absolute, regardless of whether or not she carried Finn's child. Her child.

Their child.

She wondered what had become of Finn. Suddenly, the article this morning seemed too convenient, too over the top. Hadn't she seen and heard Finn's feelings for her firsthand? The pictures must be fake. Why hadn't she just asked him about the article instead of jumping to conclusions?

And a traitor? She *knew* how much he loved Brazenbourg; it was the same love her father and Alex, and all of them, really, held for Valleria. He would never betray his country. She spied his cufflinks fallen to the floor nearby, where she must have dropped them when Henry came after her.

*What had she done?*

She slumped farther onto the floor and her hand came in contact with two glittering jewels: one emerald and one amethyst. She rolled them around in her hand, feeling their smooth surface and remembering how the necklace had once felt as it laid against her skin. The first time Finn had seen her had been in this necklace.

And now Henry had destroyed it.

She had to speak to Alex; he might know where Finn was. First, however, she needed to speak with her mother. Mama always knew what to do.

Arianna used the secret passageways to travel from her

apartments to her mother's. Her father would still be in his office, she knew, but Mama always had too much to see to the day after a ball.

Arianna reached her mother's door several minutes later and knocked. "Mama? Are you there?"

Unlike the other secret doors, the one that led to the King and Queen's rooms could not be opened from inside the secret hallways unless it was the King or Queen themselves; only someone on the other side could open it, and so her mother did a few moments later.

"Arianna? Whatever are you doing here? Your father told you to stay in your rooms."

Arianna took barely a second to throw herself into her mother's arms. "Oh, Mama. I just don't know what to do."

"Oh, darling. Oh, my baby girl." Her Mama shut the secret door and then led Arianna to a living room. As they sat down on a long couch, Arianna tightened her hold on her mother's frame. Though her mother's waist had remained fairly slim, the rest of her body was curved and soft; perfect for a child needing comfort, no matter how old they were.

"Are you upset about your father?" Her mother stroked her hair with one hand and held her tight with the other.

Arianna shook her head. "I made a terrible mistake, Mama, and I don't know what to do."

"The engagement?"

Arianna nodded against her mother's bosom.

"This morning you thought it was the right thing to do. What changed?"

Arianna sat up. She took a deep breath and told her most of what happened during Henry's visit. Her mother's brown eyes darkened in anger with each word she spoke.

"Have you told your father?"

"It just happened and I came straight to you. Mama, there's something else. I think I could be pregnant."

Her mother gasped and her eyes widened. "Henry's?"

Arianna shook her head. "Finn's."

"Oh. Well, no wonder you don't want to marry Henry anymore."

"I'm not sure that I'm pregnant. Actually, Henry was the first one to suggest it." Accused her of it, more like.

"That doesn't give him the right to manhandle you."

"No, I know." She told her mother what Henry had said about raising Finn's child. "But I can't have my child grow up with a father like that. I just can't. Oh, Mama, what do I do?"

Her mother brushed back some of Arianna's hair, which was several shades darker than her own dark blond. She cupped her daughter's face, and caressed Arianna's cheek with her thumb. "Let's see if you're pregnant first. Then, we'll talk to your father."

"We need to talk to Alex, too." Arianna told her that Henry had exiled Finn. "I've got to find him, Mama."

"Where do you think he'd go?"

"Home to Brazenbourg, I'm sure of it. He loves the country and his people too much to abandon them to Henry's tyranny."

"Then we'll see what Alex can do. Come, I'm going to call the royal physician to check on you. It might be too early for a test to confirm, but we'll try it anyway."

"Oh, but he'll tell, won't he?"

"He's paid very well to be discreet, trust me."

The physician came quickly and, though the blood tests confirming the results would take time, several home pregnancy tests all confirmed what Arianna knew to be true: she was pregnant.

Even while the euphoria and shock of becoming a mother filled her, despair at never seeing Finn again did, too.

Her mother requested that her father and Alex both come straight to her as soon as possible; a demand like that was never ignored. Arianna was sitting, holding hands with her mother, when they arrived.

"Arianna, what are you doing here? You should be in your room." Her father's sharp voice caused the tension to grow and her heart to race. What would her father think of her?

"Sit down, Gabriel." With a pointed look from Genevieve, he sat down, as did Alex, whose face was etched with concern.

"I'm sorry I disobeyed you, Papa, but I needed help so I came to Mama."

"Help?" Gabriel's eyes narrowed. "Help with what?"

"It's all right. Go ahead and tell him. All of it." Her mother squeezed her hand in encouragement.

Arianna took a deep breath and told her father and Alex everything that happened during Henry's visit. When she got to the part about the bed, they both stood, eyes flaming with fury, and mouths in a hard line.

Her father's hand curled into a fist. "I'll kill the bastard with my bare hands."

"I'll help," Alex added.

Her father turned to her. "Why didn't you call for help? There are guards just outside your doors."

"I didn't think of it. I'm sorry, I know that's horrible, but I didn't. Not with what happened next."

She took another deep breath. "Henry asked me if I was pregnant with Finn's child. He said he'd raise the child as his own if I was."

Alex's eyes narrowed. "Why would he agree to that? He's just banned his only brother from the country. I can't see him wanting to raise the man's child."

"He's impotent. At least, that's what he told me. He was injured in the crash that killed his parents, he said. He knows this is the only chance to keep the royal bloodline going."

Alex cursed. "I knew we shouldn't have let him go."

The hair on the back of Arianna's neck tingled. "Go?"

"He left for Brazenbourg this morning. My guess is that he left just after visiting you."

"Finn." Arianna said the word aloud before she could restrain herself.

Gabriel's gaze softened on his daughter. "Do you love Finn?"

"Yes, I do," she admitted to both herself and them. "I do love him. Mama."

"I know, I know," her mother said as she pulled Arianna into her embrace. "It'll be all right."

The sight of his daughter crying tore Gabriel's heart in two. He sat down next to her and pulled her into his arms. As he stroked her hair, he remembered her crying as a young child with scraped knees or as a sister being teased by her older brothers. Now she was a woman, and what the hell was a father supposed to do when that happened, when all he could picture was the little girl she once was in his arms?

"Don't exhaust yourself," her mother said as she stroked Arianna's back. "It's not healthy."

"Why isn't it healthy?" Gabriel asked, though he already knew the answer.

"Because Arianna needs strength for our grandchild."

"Oh my God," Alex whispered. "Truly?"

Genevieve nodded. "We called the royal physician to examine her. He took some blood to confirm, but five home pregnancy tests say we should expect a bundle of joy."

Alex looked flummoxed. "But you've only known Finn for about a week. How is this possible?"

"That's more than enough time, my son," Gabriel said, as he continued to stroke his daughter's hair. "Trust me." He gave Genevieve a secret look; they knew only too well how quickly pregnancy could come when it wanted to.

"I'm sorry, Papa." Gabriel lifted Arianna's head and she faced him with teary eyes.

"Why would you be sorry for such a blessing?"

"I know it's not how you envisioned your first grandchild being born."

"I envisioned my grandchildren being born healthy to loving parents, and that's what you soon will be. Tell me: do you really love Finn?"

"Yes, Papa. I really do. I'm so sorry. I didn't mean to fall in love with him, honestly."

Her father laughed. "Of course not. Who does?"

"We need to find Finn," her mother said. "Arianna thinks he may be in Brazenbourg."

"He is," Alex replied. "Or he's well on his way there. He's sneaking across the border, from the French side."

"What does he plan to do?" Arianna asked, her voice hoarse from her tears.

"Confront Henry, I assume. He's also gone to check on his contacts regarding the information Henry supposedly has for us. In light of recent developments, however, my initial thoughts that he was just toying with us seem to ring true."

"I agree, my son," Gabriel said.

"What are you talking about?" Arianna asked.

Gabriel gave Alex a nod to speak freely. "We suspected, almost as soon as Henry's offer came, that something may be amiss. I admit, I was keen last month to at least meet with him, and hear what he had to say. I can say that not long after we did meet with him, I didn't trust him."

"You were right," Arianna sighed. *And she was wrong. Again.* Now, she had not only put her family's life in danger again, but now Finn's, the father of her child. *What had she done?* "We need to find him."

"We will," Alex said confidently. He strode over and took Arianna's hands, giving each one a kiss, before dropping a kiss to each of her tear-stained cheeks. "He'll contact me as soon as he knows something."

"Are you disappointed in me, Alex?"

"No, I'm not, and you shouldn't be disappointed in yourself, either. A positive attitude is best for a pregnant woman."

Arianna huffed a laugh. "An expert on pregnant women, are you?"

"I did live through Mama's seven other pregnancies, you forget."

"So did Cat."

"That's beside the point. I'm going to be an uncle, and Uncle Alex knows best." They all laughed.

Arianna pulled her hands away to brush away her lingering tears. "You're so full of it. I don't know how Rebecca puts up with you."

"Neither do I," he replied honestly. "Come on. Let's tell the rest of the family."

"Oh, Alex, Papa, Mama. I don't know about that."

"No one's judging you, my dear," Genevieve said softly. "Tell them, and let them make a fuss over you, all right? Then you can go to bed early. Tonight, you'll stay in here, in our apartments."

"Oh, Mama."

"No, I won't hear of anything different. Now that you'll be a mother, you'll understand the need to take care of your children, even when they're grown."

Arianna nodded. As they rose and left the room—Alex messaging the rest of her siblings to meet in the shared family living room—her hands once again went to her womb. She said a silent prayer for both Finn and their child.

*Please be safe, Finn. I love you, and I love our child.*

# *twenty*

## FINN

After a restless night's sleep, which had been filled with dreams of Arianna and nightmares of her slipping away from him, Finn woke early and met his contact at the edge of the golf course.

"George," Finn said and shook the man's hand. Had it only been several days ago since he was strolling by George's stand on Food Street with Arianna?

"Prince Finn," the bear of a man responded as he shook back. "I just want to say, right up front, that all of us vendors, and many other besides, don't believe the lies in the paper, not one word."

A small sense of relief filled him; at least not everyone was intent to believe Henry's fabrications. "Thank you, my friend."

They both climbed into his van and George began driving away. "I'm not the only friend you have; many have joined together to help you."

"I'm not trying to lead a revolution here."

"Neither are we; we only want to help, however we can."

"Can you get me over the border?"

"Yes. One of the border guards is a friend and has agreed to help us."

That didn't sit easy with Finn. "Are you sure you can trust him? Henry has spies everywhere."

"Trust me, Prince Finn. Henry does not have as many spies as he thinks. Let's go."

"How is the rest of the country faring with the news?"

"Split, I would say, though a majority of us don't believe a single word of those piece of shit articles."

"And the rest?"

"They either believe it, because they'll believe anything printed in a paper, or they're unsure of what to believe."

"This paper is usually quite reputable. I don't understand why they would print these lies."

"Word on the street is that Prince Henry forced their hand. My guess is blackmail, but that's unconfirmed."

But it was likely. Considering everything Henry had done to Finn, a little blackmail to get what he wanted would be nothing.

"Where am I taking you once we get across?" George asked.

"The capital."

"That's a dangerous place just now."

"I can't worry about that. I need to meet with some of my contacts."

"As you say, Prince Finn, but I'm going with you."

"George, you just said it's dangerous. You've got a family."

"That's true, but I've also got a country it's my duty to protect. Now hunker down in the back. We're almost to the border."

Finn hid underneath several piles of quilts and blankets. George's van had been filled to the brim with items in the back; if anyone tried to search, it would take them days to sort through it all.

His body stiff with tension and the need to remain still, he held his breath as they made their way through the border. These days, it was easy to cross from one European country into the next, but that didn't mean that Henry hadn't taken extra precautions in case Finn tried to go back.

After George chatted with the border guard for a few minutes, the van started moving again, and Finn breathed a long sigh of relief.

"You'll have to stay down until we get to the capital. I'm sorry, but I don't want to risk you being found."

Finn peeked through a blanket. "Thank you, George. Just let me know if trouble comes."

"Yes, sir," George said, and he sped off down the highway.

It was a few hours later when Finn came upon Jacob's café. Even at first glance, Finn knew something was wrong. Newspapers were scattered and ruffled near the entrance, the windows shuttered, and the café door was locked with no signs of light or life inside.

Finn and George returned to the alley where they'd parked the van and tried the back door; another bad sign: the door was unlocked. Jacob would never leave it unlocked.

As they entered the back office, Finn flipped on the lights. Then they both gasped.

Jacob lay unmoving on the floor, a small pool of dark blood beneath his head. His face was pale as light. Finn rushed to his side and took his pulse; it was faint but it was there. He was also barely breathing. While George called an ambulance, Finn tried to rouse him.

Finn slapped Jacob's cheeks. "Jacob! Jacob!"

After several long moments, Jacob groaned and shifted his head, then groaned even louder. George stepped down beside Jacob and gently probed his head and neck.

"Don't move, Jacob. It's Finn. Can you speak?"

"Barely," he whispered. "They got me."

"Who got you?"

"Didn't even see them coming. Just felt something bash my head in, and then nothing. I got too close."

"You'll be all right. We called for the ambulance."

"No cops."

"It's too late."

"Not too late for you." Jacob pulled Finn closer with what seemed like every last bit of strength. "You should take the dough in the freezer. Middle row, third from the front."

"All right, Jacob." There was no time to ask more questions; Jacob had closed his eyes and was fading fast. "My friend George is here. He's a butcher and a savant at cooking meat."

"Uh-huh," Jacob said, his grip slipping on Finn's shirt.

"Listen to me," Finn said with fierce determination, and Jacob's eyes fluttered open again. "You thought about stocking some cooked meats in your bakery, for the lunch crowd. You had a meeting with George. When the café door was locked, he tried the back and found you. Do you understand?"

Jacob nodded and his eyes closed again.

"How about you?" Finn asked George.

"I understand. I'll stay. Don't worry about your friend, though. Despite how bad he looks, he'll survive."

"How do you know?"

"I was a doctor in another life, but that's a story for a different day. Will you be okay on your own?"

"I'll have to be. I'll contact you if I need any help, but it's best to keep your distance from me now. I'm sorry. If we put it on record that you found him, they may come after you, and I never meant for that to happen."

George grinned smugly. "Let them try."

Finn nodded, then ran to the freezer. He grabbed the dough Jacob mentioned, and snuck out through the back door they had entered. He grabbed his backpack from the van—his other bags would just have to stay put—and used the alleys as a convenient place to hide.

He eventually found an abandoned warehouse and snuck inside.

He broke open the dough, letting frozen pieces scatter around the floor, and pulled out the papers hidden inside.

His eyes skimmed the papers, growing wider with each line of text. He felt himself getting weaker by the second as he read page after page, and his face paled to almost translucent white—almost as white as Jacob's had been. Holy fucking shit. Jacob had discovered everything: Henry's true motives and who had really betrayed Valleria, and it wasn't good.

With trembling fingers, Finn called Alex, who picked up on the first ring.

"Finn, how are you? Where are you?"

"I'm back in Brazenbourg, in the capital. I know, Alex. I know it all."

"Tell me."

"It's Henry."

"What about Henry?"

"He's your traitor."

"What? What the hell are you talking about?"

"Henry has been selling secrets to Gardar Rus and others. By the proof in my hands, Henry has been plotting against Valleria, France, and others for years. He's the one who arranged for Vlad to try to capture and torture your brother."

Alex cursed. "Why is he hell-bent on destroying us?"

"Based on these papers, he was trying to stage a power coup with Vlad, to take control of the various countries surrounding them. Even when Vlad failed last month, Henry kept going with his own plans."

There was stony silence for several seconds before Alex replied. "Damn it! If Henry hates us so much, why the hell is he engaged to Arianna?"

Finn collapsed against the dusty, moldy table he'd been using. "Engaged?" he croaked.

"Yes, sorry, I shouldn't have blurted it out like that. Arianna agreed to marry him yesterday morning."

"Fuck!"

"Wait. She also realized it was a bad idea and decided she'd made a mistake last night."

Hope bloomed in his chest, desperate to overcome the fear and despair that lay there, too. "She did?"

"Yes, and you're one of the main reasons for it."

"She doesn't hate me?"

Alex paused, as if considering something, then spoke again. "I'll let her tell you when this mess is over. It's not my place. Suffice it to say, I don't think she hates you."

"Thank God," Finn murmured and sagged in relief. "Can I speak to her?"

"No, and neither can I."

"What the hell does that mean?"

"She's gone. She left sometime in the night."

"Where did she go?"

"To find you."

"What? What the hell is she thinking?"

"She's thinking about you. Be on the lookout for her."

"Doesn't she have guards with her?"

"Just one, which isn't enough, in my opinion. She's traveling by plane straight to your capital."

"Why don't you stop her?"

"We're trying. She used a commercial flight so we can't just turn it around without arousing suspicion or the press. My brother, Marcello, is flying over to meet her, but he's still a few hours behind her. Until that happens, keep her safe. She's very fragile right now."

"What does that mean? Is she hurt?"

"In a manner of speaking. Look, you should know that Henry paid her a visit." Alex went on to describe what happened, but Finn got the impression he was leaving something out.

"Shit, he's such an asshole."

"On that, we agree. Why would he do it? Even if he married Arianna, there's no way he could ever be crowned king of Valleria."

"Maybe he planned to harm Arianna only, or perhaps he planned to kill us all; I just don't know." Realization dawned on Finn. "Maybe he planned an attack during a wedding?"

"Jesus. You think he'd kill all of us, and risk killing himself to rule Valleria? That's a long way around. Besides, he's already ruler of Brazenbourg."

"But it's not enough for him, it never has been. He'll only be the Prince of a small nation here; in Valleria, he'd be called 'King'. He always hated being called 'Prince', especially since I was called that, too."

"Your brother's mental state needs to be examined."

"Don't I know it?" Finn ran a hand over his face. "Look, I'm sending you a copy of these documents. Have your people take a look at them, and contact the International Police Force. I'll need their help." Finn scanned the documents with his phone and messaged them off to Alex.

"I've got the documents. What are you planning?"

"A confrontation. If I know my brother, he'll want to address the nation. Not just about the charges leveled against me, but about the future of Brazenbourg. I'll plan to confront him there as the whole country will be watching. It's my best chance."

"Hold on. Yes, I've just confirmed that he announced a speech tonight at seven local time. Can you sneak into the palace?"

"That shouldn't be a problem. Your brother is taking Arianna straight back to Valleria, isn't he? I don't want her near Henry." She shouldn't be near him, either; he wasn't safe.

"That's the plan. If you need his help, he can stay behind."

"Arianna is priority. Keep her safe. Let me know when you've got her."

"Will do. Take care, Finn."

"Same to you, Alex." *And take care, Arianna,* he prayed. *Stay safe.*

~

## *ARIANNA*

Arianna knew it was a crazy idea. However, since she'd had so many terrible ones recently, she figured one more probably couldn't make a difference. She hadn't planned to run away to Brazenbourg to meet Finn, but she'd had no other choice.

She loved him, and he needed help.

She'd lain awake for hours last night, thinking of him, praying she'd have a chance to beg his forgiveness for not believing in him. It was then that she'd remembered the letter from Finn that she'd received through Alex.

In it, he had declared his love for her, and his deepest hopes and dreams—dreams that included them together. Dreams she should have believed when he'd spoken them to her in the dark hours of the night. She had also finally checked her phone, and Finn's pleas to believe the articles were a fabrication clinched her decision. If only she had checked her phone earlier. If only. If only.

She rubbed her belly again, she couldn't seem to stop. She knew she needed protection, so she'd taken a guard with her. She knew he was reporting back to Marcello and the others, despite her orders not to. She couldn't blame him; his life was on the line now, too.

She needed to be with Finn. He was her future, she realized. Not just because of the baby, though it was certainly a consideration. She'd been such an idiot, though, she didn't know if he'd want to see her. She prayed he did.

Once the plane arrived in Brazenbourg, she'd expected some family member there waiting to take her back to Valleria. However, no one was there.

Her guard secured a car and they drove to the palace. She knew Henry would be alerted to her presence, and she would use that to gain entry. As far as he knew, she was still on board with the engagement.

He would learn that plans had changed, and that no one pushed her around.

She also had a feeling that Finn would try to come back here, and confront Henry. She didn't even want to think about what may happen if Finn lost. It wasn't an option, she thought as she absently rubbed her womb again. Losing him just wasn't an option.

# twenty-one

**FINN**

Finn managed to sneak into the palace using one of the service entrances. From there, he took advantage of the secret hallways, and made his way around the building.

A glance at his watch let him know that there wasn't much time left before Henry's national address. Alex had let him know that the International Police Force was on their way; they would wait until after Finn confronted Henry, but they would be in place and waiting when that happened. There was no telling how many allies Henry had in the palace, or how many may try to stop Finn.

He finally found the secret door leading to the throne room. Henry would complete his address from his office, just off of this room. After checking the peephole and confirming that no one was there, Finn exited and shut the door quietly behind him.

At the sound of footsteps, Finn quickly hid behind one of the thrones. His heart beat faster as adrenaline rushed through his system. Would he be found out? Was this the end?

But then the footsteps retreated, and he waited several seconds before checking the room. The coast was clear. Just as Finn was about to get up, he noticed some wires underneath the throne. As he took a closer look, he noticed it was a bomb, set to go off five minutes into his address.

Holy shit.

Finn immediately messaged Alex, who sent the warning to his contacts at the International Police Force. Finn tried to calculate how many people were working in the palace that night, how many people could be killed. He also wondered if Henry had arranged the bomb.

Since Finn knew nothing about diffusing bombs, he slowly stepped away. The bomb was under the throne meant for the ruling Princess of Brazenbourg, so Finn checked the other one; there was nothing there.

Fury, hot and vicious, speared through him at the thought of Arianna sitting here. His anger, however, would have to wait. Finn checked his watch again. One minute until the speech began.

Finn quietly opened the door to the offices. The rooms were full of people; he hoped he would blend in with them. Keeping his head down, he edged along the side by the wall, slowly making his way towards Henry. He wondered how many of the people here could be hurt by the bomb in the other room. Was that the only bomb? Were there more here lying in wait for them?

Finn positioned himself behind a tall television camera operator; Henry wouldn't see Finn until he was good and ready to reveal himself.

A man signaled a countdown to Henry. When he got to 'one', Henry cleared his throat and faced the camera.

"Good evening, citizens of Brazenbourg. I come to you tonight with both a full and heavy heart. I first want to address the joy in my upcoming marriage. Princess Arianna of Valleria is a beautiful, intelligent woman, and she will serve you well. I second want to address my shame in having such a traitorous brother."

Finn's hands fisted at his side. He checked his watch; there were only a few minutes left before the bomb went off. He had to evacuate.

Pretending he was a member of the crowd, he shouted, "Bomb! Everybody evacuate!"

The crowd gasped then began to disperse. "No, wait! I haven't finished my speech." Henry said as he stood and threw down his notes onto the desk.

"You'd rather everybody die listening to you?" Finn asked as he stepped into the light. Those remaining in the room gasped and Finn noted the cameraman kept the camera aimed at them both.

Henry's face distorted in rage. "You! You are no longer welcome in my country," Henry seethed.

"This is my country, my home. *You* are the traitor."

Henry grinned broadly. "No one believes you. You're finished. Guards!"

"They won't help you now, brother dear." The police entered the room and took hold of the guards. Finn held up the documents Jacob had given him, making sure the camera captured them. "Proof of your treachery. You have been conspiring against Valleria, France, and others in some twisted bid for power. You're finished. I'll make sure you're stripped of your crown and arrested on charges of treason."

Henry laughed, a full-bellied maniacal laugh that set Finn's teeth on edge. "You'll not stop me now. No one can stop me now." He continued laughing as Finn checked the time. Had the police diffused it? Were they safe?

From the corner of his eye, he saw her. His light, his love, standing there terrified. Her beautiful eyes were fixed on Finn and every protective instinct he had forced him to push Henry aside and go towards her. The police took hold of Henry while Finn ran across the room.

"You're too late," Henry laughed. "Too late! Now you'll both die and I'll never have to see either of you again."

"Finn, look out!" she yelled.

A blast shook the room—there was a bomb in Henry's office, too!

Finn pushed people out of the door and away from the blast,

when another explosion shook the room. Henry's laughter rang like a bell in the air after the blast.

"Arianna!"

"Finn!" She reached for him, but he was too late.

Another bomb detonated, this one between the two of them. The force threw Finn back in the air, and he landed on the floor. He saw the ceiling cave in, and it narrowly avoided destroying Henry's desk. Finn watched in horror as more falling debris took Henry and the police out with it. Henry's laughter suddenly stopped. *His brother. His one and only brother.*

His eyes welled with tears from the smoke, dust, and loss in the room, even while he frantically searched for Arianna. Another portion of the ceiling had caved in with the last blast and he couldn't see her.

"Ar-Arianna," he coughed. "Where are you?"

Ignoring the pain in his leg, he crawled on his hands and knees, death and destruction all around him. His palms were bloody and covered in soot by the time he reached the pile of debris nearby. He thought he saw a flash of blue, the color of the sweater she had been wearing, and he began to dig with his bare hands.

The air in the room was thick with smoke and he could barely breathe. Those alive around him, conducted their own search for survivors. He dug and dug until his fingers and nails were torn, and his chest was sore from the heaving breaths he was forced to take.

*Arianna. Arianna.*

Finally, he saw her hand, and dug even faster. He uncovered her face, bruised but alive. Her heart beat slow but true.

"Thank God," he cried. "Thank God. Please, Arianna. Please don't die." He continued to uncover her, revealing other bumps and bruises. He had to get her to the hospital. She had to live.

With strength born from sheer adrenaline, he picked her up and carried her away. A medic saw him and took her from him.

"Save her. Save her," he whispered before he fell to the ground. "Arianna," he breathed just before blackness took him.

~

## *ARIANNA*

ARIANNA SLOWLY BLINKED HER EYES OPEN, WHICH SQUINTED against the bright lights of the room. The sound of something beeping nearby seemed to grow louder as it filtered into her consciousness.

Her body woke just as slowly, but each ache and pain she felt made itself known. She groaned.

"She's awake," a familiar voice said nearby. "Arianna?"

Her hand was lifted and placed in someone else's; she knew that hand. "Mama?" she croaked.

"Yes," her mother sobbed and kissed her hand. "Oh, yes, my darling daughter. Just relax. Your father is bringing the doctor."

Doctor? Oh, no. The whole scene came rushing back at once, sending the beeping noises spiking as her heart beat faster.

"Relax. You're safe. The baby's safe."

*The baby's safe. Thank God, the baby's safe.* The beeping calmed down again. "Finn?" she whispered.

"He was hurt, too, but he'll be all right."

"Finn," she moaned.

"I know, my dear, sweet child. He'll be all right. Don't worry about him. Just focus on getting healthy for you and the baby."

"I hear our patient's awake," a woman said as she walked in and stood by Arianna. Her long white coat covered a gray silk shirt and fitted black skirt, and she stood on reasonable black heels. Her brown hair was pulled back in a ponytail, which swung from side-to-side as she examined Arianna and made notes in her chart.

After the exam was over, the doctor took a seat on Arianna's bed. "You're very weak, but very lucky. You'll have those bruises for a while yet, but with some strict bed rest for the next few weeks, you should be all right."

"The baby?"

"The baby seems to be doing just fine, but that's another reason I want you on bed rest. I'll give you some things to look out for; if any of them happen, call me."

"Can she be moved to Valleria?" Gabriel asked; he'd come back into the room after the exam had been completed, but Arianna hadn't noticed. "Papa."

"There, there, my child," he said as he took the opposite seat beside her and held her hand. "You're all right. The baby's all right. That's all that's important."

"To answer your question, King Gabriel," the doctor said, "I think it's best if she recuperates in Brazenbourg. I wouldn't want to risk anything happening during travel. We can try bed rest for a week and see how she feels after that, but I make no promises."

"Understood. Thank you, Doctor."

She smiled. "It was my pleasure. Just page me if you need anything, or let the nurses know."

After the doctor left, her mother took the doctor's place at Arianna's bedside. "Oh, Arianna, you frightened us all half to death."

"I know. I'm sorry. I'm so sorry. I never thought—"

"No one did, my child," her father said, interrupting her.

"How many?"

He knew what she was asking. "At least a dozen dead, mostly citizens of Brazenbourg, but some of the International Police Force lost their lives as well. The bombs managed to take out some supporting columns in the palace, so some of the upper floors were affected as well."

"Henry?"

Her father shook his head. Was it wrong to feel relief at his death? "Finn's really okay?"

"He is. Hurt, but he'll be okay. He saved your life."

"What?"

"It's true. The camera caught it all before it, too, was destroyed by the falling ceiling. He dug through the rubble until he found you, then carried you out to the paramedics."

"I don't remember any of it. I just remember him coming towards me, and then there was nothing." She'd dreamt of Finn calling her name, begging her, pleading her to live; had that been real, or just a dream?

Her father squeezed her hand. "Finn's a national hero."

"I don't know if he'll like that."

He chuckled. "No, I don't think he will, but the people love him. Now that they know the truth, they'll accept him as their new leader."

"Oh. I suppose Finn would be the ruling Prince now. I wonder how he feels about that."

"Why don't you ask him yourself?" a gruff voice came from the doorway.

Arianna gasped as she watched Finn being helped into the room by a nurse. He was wearing a robe over his hospital gown, which didn't hide the cuts and bruises on his face and hands. He was also walking with a distinct limp; why didn't he use a cane or a wheelchair?

Gabriel rose and went over to help Finn. "I'm glad you could join us."

"Thank you, Your Highness." Finn walked slowly towards the bed with their help, and sat down, letting out a sigh of exhaustion when he did.

"I thought we discussed this. Any man who saves my daughter can call me Gabriel."

"And you can call me Genevieve, and I don't want to hear another word about it."

"I'd listen to my wife; she's a force to be reckoned with."

Finn smiled, then winced at the pain it caused. "Of course. Gabriel, Genevieve."

Genevieve stood. "We're going to get some coffee and give the family a call. Why don't you two spend some time together?"

"Please stay. I didn't mean to chase you off."

"You didn't," Genevieve said with a smile and took her husband's hand as they walked out the door.

"They're subtle, aren't they?" Finn asked rhetorically before he turned back to look at Arianna. Just the power of his gaze had her heart jumping. As her heart monitor jumped, too, he smiled.

"I think you like me," he said as he cupped her face. Bandages covered his hands, but just the touch of his skin against hers had her sighing.

"I think I do, too. Oh, Finn, I'm so sorry, about everything. I should have trusted you. I should have—"

Finn put a bruised finger to her lips. "Shhh. None of that. You're okay. That's all that matters." Finn's smile turned to worry as he took in her bruises. "Oh, baby, what were you thinking coming here?"

"I was thinking about you." She laid a hand over his wrist. "I wanted to help you. I needed you, Finn."

Finn leaned forward and gently touched his forehead to hers. "I need you, too, Princess. But, please, for the love of God, don't do anything like that again. My heart stopped when I saw you there, with the bombs going off around us."

"I won't." After a pause, she said, "I'm sorry about Henry."

Finn sighed as he sat up again. "I'm sorry, too." She held his hand, letting death and grief have a few minutes.

"I don't understand why he set the bombs."

Finn shrugged. "We may never know. My guess is that he wanted to blame me for it, to prove once more that I was a traitor. The bombs were strategically placed for it. If he'd been sitting behind his desk when they went off, he'd likely still be alive."

"Oh, Finn. You can't blame yourself."

His hold tightened on her hand for a moment before he let go. "I know. That doesn't make it any easier, though."

"No, it doesn't. What happens now?"

"We try to move on, repair the palace, and find everyone who was allied with him. It might take us years to draw them all out."

"You're also the ruler of Brazenbourg now."

Finn nodded as he rubbed her legs through the blanket covering her. "I never expected it. Now, I'm not sure what to do."

"I could help you."

His hand stilled. "Do you really want to?"

"Yes. I want to help you, Finn."

He gave her a searching look before he spoke. "I love you, Arianna; that hasn't changed. But I'm not looking for a friend to help me out. I want someone to rule with me. I want that someone to be you."

"Finn."

"Rule with me. Be my partner, my best friend, and Brazenbourg's faithful Princess. And be the mother of our children." He put a hand over her abdomen, where their child lay nestled inside.

She gasped, avoiding his question for the moment. "You know?"

He nodded. "Your parents told me."

"I wanted to tell you. That's one of the reasons I came to Brazenbourg; I wanted to tell you in person." She lifted her hand to his cheek, and his hand covered hers against his face. "I wanted to see your face when I told you."

"Your parents said that the baby's okay. It wasn't hurt in the explosion."

"Thank God for that."

He kissed the palm of her hand and let it go. "Arianna, I know it wouldn't be easy being with me. You'd have to deal with the fallout from being engaged to my brother, to being with me and having our child. It's a lot to explain, and you'll probably have to explain it for a long time to come. Not to mention all the mess Henry left behind. I know I don't deserve you, but I think you could grow to love me, if you tried."

Tears welled in her eyes. "Oh, Finn. I do love you."

His breath caught. "You love me?"

"Oh, yes." Her hands delved into his hair and combed it back.

"Because of the baby?"

"Because of you. I don't just want you because you're the father of my child. I want you because you're you. You're kind, generous, and a wonderful leader, even if you don't know it."

"Does that mean you'll marry me?"

"Oh, yes, Finn. I'd be honored to be your wife."

"Arianna." He swept down and gave her a tender kiss; even when they wanted to devour each other, he still treated her with care and compassion. Finn said he didn't deserve her, but she thought it was she who didn't deserve him. She would spend the rest of her life proving she did.

His lips traveled from her mouth to kiss her nose, forehead, and cheeks, then down her neck and over her collarbone. He took a minute to rest his head against her chest, where her heart beat strong for him and their child.

She ran her hands through his hair and down his back. "We can have a quick wedding once I'm out."

"Certainly not. You will marry in a church with your head held high, and that's final."

"The White Church by the lake?"

Finn smiled, ignoring the pain this time. "Yes, if you don't mind."

"It sounds wonderful."

"It does at that." Finn reached into the pocket of his robe and pulled out a small velvet box. She gasped.

"You've already said yes, and a woman who marries me deserves a ring. She deserves a lot more than that, but I figure it's a good place to start."

He pulled out a beautiful ring in a halo setting. Set in the middle was an emerald of several carats, surrounded on all sides by a ring of diamonds, which extended onto the silver band. "It's beautiful."

"It was my mother's," Finn said gruffly as he slipped it on her finger. "I wish you could have met her and my father."

"So do I," Arianna said, marveling at the beautiful ring, when a thought occurred to her. "Uh-oh."

"What is it? Are you in pain?"

"No, no. It's just, I think you'll need to ask my father's permission before marrying me."

Finn smiled broadly. "I do, do I?"

"Yes. I mean, I don't think he'll refuse, but you never know."

"Stop worrying, Princess. I already asked him."

"You did? When?"

"When you wouldn't wake up." His smile dimmed as he brushed back a lock of her hair. "I told your father that I loved you and that I wanted to marry you as soon as you got healthy again. That's when he told me about the baby, and asked me if I was ready for that responsibility."

"What did you tell him?"

"I told him that I'd been dreaming of that possibility and that there was no way I was turning back from it, or from you. You're my dream, Princess, you and our babies."

"Babies? Plural?"

"You don't think I'm going to stop at just one, do you?" He leaned forward and kissed her, this time with a little heat that had parts of her waking up. They couldn't act on that heat now, but soon. Soon.

"I love you, Finn."

"I love you, Arianna." Finn slid down the bed and kissed her womb through the blanket. "I love you, too, little one."


THE END

###


Want more from this royal family? Get the next book featuring Playboy Prince Nate's love story!

Want a FREE Royals short story? Sign up for Marianne's newsletter (www.marianneknightly.com/newsletter) to get a steamy short story.

# *about the author*

Marianne Knightly is a pen name for the author of over thirty novels, novellas, and short stories of contemporary romance and romantic suspense. She is most well known for her Royals of Valleria series, a contemporary royal romance and suspense series set in her fictional country of Valleria®. Marianne lives in the Washington, D.C., metro area and loves to hear from readers all over the world!

To learn more about sales, future installments, and upcoming releases, please:

- Sign up for Marianne's newsletter: www.marianneknightly.com/newsletter
- Join the community on Discord and talk about books, get sneak peeks, and more: https://geni.us/MKNcommunity
- Become a member and get access to books before they publish, along with fun merch and more: https://geni.us/MKNmember
- Visit Marianne's Website: www.marianneknightly.com
- Follow Marianne on:

bookbub.com/authors/marianne-knightly

facebook.com/marianneknightly

goodreads.com/marianneknightly

instagram.com/marianneknightly

threads.net/@marianneknightly

tiktok.com/@marianneknightly

# *also by marianne knightly*

<u>Sign up for Marianne's newsletter</u> (www.marianneknightly.-com/newsletter) for exclusive news about sales and releases!

## **Royals of Valleria Series**

Meet the Royals of Valleria, a country as old as the fall of the Roman Empire. The reigning king and patriarch rules with his beloved queen. Nine children, now grown, ranging from the eldest twins to the youngest son, watch over the country they love and care for. Bound by honour, duty, and loyalty, follow their lives as they fall in love, face tragedies, and triumph against the evils facing them.

Book 1: Alexander & Rebecca

Book 2: Marcello & Grace

Book 3: Arianna & Finn

Book 4: Charlotte & Nate

Book 5: A Royal Holiday (Novella)

Book 6: Catharine & Edward

Book 7: Royally Ever After

Book 8: Lorenzo & Lily

Book 9: Sarah & Vittorio

Book 10: Permanently Princess (Novella)

Book 11: Ethan & Anda

Book 12: Crowned

Box Set: Books 1-3

Box Set: Books 4-6

Box Set: Books 7-9

## Royals of Valleria Short Stories

Story 1: **Delusional** (featuring Prince Alex & Rebecca)

Story 2: **Loved** (featuring Prince Alex & Rebecca)

Story 3: **Annoyed** (featuring Prince Alex & Rebecca)

Story 4: **Crush** (featuring Prince Alex & Rebecca)

Story 5: **Wish** (featuring Prince Alex & Rebecca)

Story 6: **Please** (featuring Prince Nate & Charlie)

Story 7: **Goddess** (featuring Prince Marcello & Grace)

Story 8: **Impatient** (featuring Princess Catharine & Edward)

Story 9: **Together** (featuring Princess Sarah & Prince Vittorio)

## Brazenbourg Royals Duet

Welcome to Brazenbourg, a small but mighty country nestled in the heart of Europe. Follow Prince Finn de Bara and his love, Arianna, former princess of Valleria, as they discover family secrets and battle for the future of Brazenbourg and their family.

Book 1: Bastard (*note: this book ends in a cliffhanger!*)

Book 2: Battle

Box Set (Full Duet, Books 1-2)

## Seaside Valleria Series

Welcome to Valleria, a country nestled along the Mediterranean. Whether it's the small towns or larger port cities, you're sure to find a friendly face—or more—along Valleria's seaside shores. Far from the politics of the palace, follow this group of friends as they find love, support each other, and perhaps even meet a royal or two at the local Masillian pub, the Seashell.

Book 1: Rush (Hector & Millie)

Book 2: Ripple (Persy & Sully)

Book 3: Raw (Frannie & Aiden)

Book 4: Ravage (Beth & Everett)

Book 5: Rise (Liz & Luke)

Box Set (Full Series, Books 1-5)

## The Italian Shipping Millionaires Series

Meet four sexy Italian men, brothers in all but blood and business partners. Follow their lives as they overcome past tragedies and pain, and open themselves up to love.

Book 1: Dante

Book 2: Adrian

Book 3: Giovanni

Book 4: Luc

Box Set: Books 1-4

Made in the USA
Middletown, DE
02 September 2024

60239604R00163